Lie for a Million

Don't miss any of Janet Dailey's bestsellers

The Calder Brand Series
Rivalries
Calder Brand
Calder Grit
A Calder at Heart

The New Americana Series
Paradise Peak
Sunrise Canyon
Refuge Cove
Letters from Peaceful Lane
Hart's Hollow Farm
Hope Creek
Blue Moon Haven
Lone Oaks Crossing

The Champions
Whirlwind
Whiplash
Quicksand

The Tylers of Texas
Texas Forever
Texas Free
Texas Fierce
Texas Tall
Texas Tough
Texas True
Bannon Brothers: Triumph
Bannon Brothers: Honor
Bannon Brothers: Trust
American Destiny
American Dreams
Masquerade
Tangled Vines
Heiress

JANET DAILEY

Lie for a Million

kensingtonbooks.com

KENSINGTON BOOKS are published by

Kensington Publishing Corp.
900 Third Avenue
New York, NY 10022

After the passing of Janet Dailey, the Dailey family worked with a close associate of Janet's to continue her literary legacy, using her notes, ideas, and favorite themes to complete her novels and create new ones, inspired by the American men and women she loved to portray.

All Kensington titles, imprints, and distributed lines are available at special quantity discounts for bulk purchases for sales promotion, premiums, fund-raising, educational, or institutional use.

Special book excerpts or customized printings can also be created to fit specific needs. For details, write or phone the office of the Kensington Special Sales Manager: Attn. Special Sales Department, Kensington Publishing Corp., 900 Third Avenue, New York, NY 10022. Phone: 1-800-221-2647.

KENSINGTON and the K with book logo Reg. US Pat. & TM Off.

Library of Congress Card Catalogue Number: 2024944015

ISBN: 978-1-4967-4481-4

First Kensington Hardcover Edition: February 2025

ISBN: 978-1-4967-4487-6 (ebook)

10 9 8 7 6 5 4 3 2 1

Printed in the United States of America

Chapter One

"I need help. I'm pregnant, Mrs. Culhane. The baby is Frank's."

The words replayed against the throbbing beat in Lila Culhane's head as she hung up the office phone and sank into the leather banker's chair that had been her late husband's.

Raking her blond hair back from her face, she muttered a string of unladylike swearwords. Wasn't it enough that Frank was dead—murdered in the stable with the unknown killer still at large? Wasn't it enough that Frank's grown children and ex-wife were scheming to evict her from the house and ranch that had been her home for eleven years—the home she had rightfully inherited?

Evidently it wasn't enough. Fate had just thrown Frank's pregnant mistress into the mess—a young woman Lila had learned about only one day before Frank was discovered dead from a massive injection of fentanyl.

What now?

She leaned back in the chair and closed her eyes. The house was quiet with the recent visitors gone. She could hear a trapped horsefly buzzing against the window. From the upstairs hallway came the sound of a vacuum cleaner as Mariah, the cook and housekeeper, went about her work.

Lila needed a drink. But this wasn't the time to dull her senses with alcohol. She needed a clear head to examine her options.

Crystal—that was the young woman's name. Against her better judgment, Lila had agreed to meet with her tomorrow at the Trail's End restaurant in nearby Willow Bend. It might have been smarter to have just hung up the phone and have nothing to do with her claim. But she needed to know, at least, whether Crystal was really carrying Frank's child or lying as a way to get money.

The manila envelope, holding the photos Lila had paid for, was taped to the underside of the center desk drawer. Not that there was a need for hiding it. Frank's infidelities were no longer a secret.

But that didn't mean she would share what she'd just learned—especially if Crystal was telling the truth.

Lila's hand shook slightly as she slid the photos out of the envelope and spread them on the desktop. Without a doubt, the handsome man in the motel room doorway was Frank. With his distinguished looks and air of wealth, he'd never had any trouble attracting women. Lila should have realized long ago that his cheating wouldn't stop with his second marriage. After all, he'd cheated on his first wife, Madeleine, with *her*.

As the wronged and angry wife, Lila knew she was a prime suspect in the ongoing investigation of Frank's murder. But right now, she had even more urgent concerns.

She'd studied the photos before. But now that she'd spoken with the mystery woman in Frank's arms, she saw the details with different eyes. Crystal had been photographed from behind. Her face didn't appear in any of the photos—just her long black hair and one of her hands, which rested on Frank's shoulder. The hand told a story of its own—the drugstore nails and the gaudy rings on three fingers. Lila knew good jewelry when she saw it. The rings were cheap fakes. Crystal was poor and undoubtedly after money. The only question was, how desperate was she?

Paying her to go away might be the simplest solution. Of course, Crystal would have to consent to an in vitro paternity test. If the baby didn't have Frank's DNA, that would be the end of the story. But if the young woman was telling the truth . . .

Lila dismissed the thought. She was inclined to believe that Crystal was lying. During her eleven-year marriage, Lila had tried everything to get pregnant. Since she'd given birth to a daughter at eighteen, she knew she wasn't infertile. And Frank had two children from his first marriage. After a time, when she'd failed to conceive, she'd begun to suspect he'd had a secret vasectomy. But the coroner who'd done his autopsy hadn't bothered to check. Now it was too late. His body lay in the Culhane family cemetery on a desolate hilltop, within sight of the house.

Nerves quivering, Lila put the photographs away, stood, and walked to the window. The ranch office gave her a view of the stable, the covered arena, and the paddocks beyond, where blooded American quarter horses grazed in the morning sunlight. Beyond the paddocks, in the larger pasture, Black Angus cattle fed on the drought-yellowed grass.

For the past eleven years, as Frank's wife and business partner, she had given her time, her energy, and her heart to this ranch and its program of breeding and training performance horses. It had become her world, her life. Now, with Frank's death, everything had been thrown into chaos.

With Frank's ex and her two adult children plotting to

take everything Lila had worked for, the one person she could count on had been Roper McKenna, her horse trainer and manager. But now, even his support was coming into question.

Lila was fighting battles from all sides; the last thing she needed was Frank's former mistress showing up pregnant.

Without conscious thought, she found herself leaving the house and heading down the cobblestone path to the stable, where Roper would be working the horses that were owned, boarded, and trained at the Culhane Ranch. Weeks ago, she would have taken him into her confidence and trusted him to understand. She might even have told him about Crystal.

But all that had changed after Roper qualified for Frank's place in the reining event of the year—the Run for a Million. Lila had known he'd be getting a lot of attention. Big horse breeders would be courting him, offering him money and prestige to train in their stables and compete on their horses.

She needed Roper. He'd worked for Frank before he'd worked for her. There was no one else she trusted to manage her horse operation. That was why she'd been prepared to offer him a partnership—the one thing he wouldn't get from anyone else.

But now she was holding back on the offer. Roper, who'd been her rock, was showing signs of dissatisfaction. The loyalty she'd felt from him was gone—if it had ever been real. Lila sensed that she was going to lose him, and she didn't know what to do.

In the covered arena, Roper had just put One in a Million through his paces—the pattern of rapid circles, dashes, and gallops ending in a spectacular sliding stop with a rollback. At the age of thirteen, the legendary stallion was still as sharp as he'd been a few weeks ago, when he'd won Roper a place as one of sixteen riders in the Run for a Million.

The big bay roan had the heart of a champion. But at his age, did he have the speed and stamina to win again?

The decision was Roper's to make—and he needed to make it soon.

Frank Culhane had qualified for the final event at the March Cactus Classic, riding Million Dollar Baby, a daughter of One in a Million. He'd also planned to ride the promising mare in the Run for a Million. But Frank's murder, followed by Baby's tragic death, had changed everything.

One in a Million had been Frank's horse, winning him more than a million dollars before being retired to stud at the age of ten. In the competition for Frank's place, it had been decided that Roper would show the aging stallion, but only as a tribute to his late owner. To everyone's astonishment, One in a Million had caught fire in the arena. His scores had put Roper in first place.

Roper walked the stallion to cool him down before turning him over to the grooms. The horse snorted softly, his hooves sinking into the thick layer of sand, loam, and sawdust that cushioned the arena floor. After his retirement at the age of ten, Frank had ordered that One in a Million be exercised and kept in good condition. With luck, the big bay roan could give the ranch another decade of stud fee earnings. But was he up for the stress of competing in the Run for a Million? Would he have even a prayer of winning?

The right horse could make all the difference, but reining events were a competition between riders. A rider could compete on any horse he or she chose. If thc rider was using a borrowed horse, the winnings would be divided between the rider and the horse's owner—typically a breeder, a rancher, or even a corporation.

If Roper were to compete on One in a Million, any prize money won would be split with Lila. But if Roper were to win on someone else's horse, Lila would be out of luck.

And that was Roper's dilemma.

Since his qualifying win, Roper had received numerous offers from owners who wanted him to ride their horses. Good offers. Great horses, strong and well trained, with sterling bloodlines. Some were already big money winners.

Time was running out. If his choice wasn't to be One in a Million, he needed time to try other horses and more time to work with the one he chose.

If he didn't choose the great roan stallion, he would be battling Lila all the way. He wanted to keep her happy—and keep his job. But more than anything, he wanted to win.

He could see Lila now, standing at the entrance to the arena. Tall, blond, and stunning in a white silk blouse and tailored slacks, she was built like the Vegas showgirl she'd been before her marriage. Roper's pulse skipped at the sight of her. He brought himself under control before he acknowledged her with a tip of his Stetson. She remained where she was, a ray of sunlight falling on her hair.

Lila was his employer, as Frank had been before her. To cross the line between them would be a mistake—especially now, while they were at odds over his choice of a horse. Still, sometimes, the urge to reach out and pull her into his arms was almost too compelling to resist. She was so fiercely proud of her own strength, yet so alone . . .

Roper ended the thought with a curse as he crossed the arena to the stable entrance, where a groom was waiting to take the stallion. After dismounting, he turned and walked back to where Lila waited for him. In her rigid posture and the stubborn jut of her chin, he read the signs of a coming showdown.

"Boss?" It was what Roper called her—Lila being too familiar and Mrs. Culhane too formal. Despite his misgivings, the word left his lips as a caress.

"It's time," she said. "I need to know what you're thinking."

Roper sighed and shook his head. "If you put One in a Million back in the arena, you know he'll give you everything he's got. But he's too old for this level of competition, Boss. He knows the routines and could probably do well in senior events. But he can't win against those younger horses."

"He did it once."

"I know he did. But his legs, his heart and lungs—they won't hold out forever. He could die out there or have to be put down. Even if he had a chance of winning, would it be worth the risk?"

Lila lowered her gaze.

"With luck and care, One in a Million could live another ten years," Roper said. "His stud fees and his colts could earn a lot more over time than he could ever win competing."

"We have other horses," Lila said.

"We do. They've got talent and good pedigrees, but they're still in training. They don't have the experience to win the Run for a Million. We were counting on Baby for that. She had it all."

"I could buy another horse."

"You could. I thought of that. But a trained horse with champion bloodlines would bankrupt the ranch. You'd have to find an investment group and buy in. There's no time for that now. As I see it, there's only one way to win."

"You mean for *you* to win." Her gaze hardened. "I know you've had some great offers, Roper. Are you going to take one?"

His jaw tightened. "I want to win. At least I want a fair chance."

"So you'd bring the horse here, board it in my stable, train it in my arena, and then, if you win—"

"I could arrange to go somewhere else."

"You'll have to if you're not working for me anymore." Lila let the threat hang, but Roper felt the sting of her words. The lady meant business.

"Let's not fight, Boss," he said. "I know where you stand, and I want to be fair. But I've got a lot of thinking to do. Can we talk again tomorrow?"

She exhaled, clearly impatient with him. "Fine. I've got a busy day planned tomorrow. I'll come and find you when I have a few minutes. But you'd better have something to tell me. I'm tired of being strung along."

Without giving him a chance to respond, she swung away from him and stalked out of the arena.

Roper cursed his indecision as he watched her go. Lila had relied on his support since Frank's death. He despised himself for letting her down, especially when she was dealing with other problems, including the fight to keep her property. He cared deeply for her. But a chance to win the Run for a Million was the dream of a lifetime. How could he throw it away by choosing an aging stud or an unprepared youngster from the ranch?

The conflict wasn't so much about the prize money as it was about loyalty. That issue was going to make his decision even more painful. Once it was in place, he feared that things would never be the same between him and Lila.

Could he live with that?

A groom was waiting with the next horse. Forcing himself to focus, Roper strode back across the arena, mounted up, and went to work.

In her haste, Lila had taken the wrong exit from the arena. She was still fuming over Roper's attitude when she found herself in the stable wing that led back to the house.

She was facing an empty box stall, still festooned with yellow crime scene tape. It was One in a Million's old stall, the place where Frank had been found dead from a massive injection of fentanyl in his neck.

The only witness to the crime had been the stallion. Removed to a different stall, One in a Million had been a bundle of nerves, trembling and snorting. Roper's skilled handling had finally calmed him. But the memory of his master's death would be imprinted on the big roan's brain for the rest of his life.

Frank's killer had yet to be found. Madeleine, Frank's ex, had confessed to hiring a mob hit on him—a hit that had never been carried out because Frank was already dead. Someone else, probably someone Frank had known and trusted, had injected him from behind. His daughter, Jasmine, had found his body the next morning, lying face down in the straw.

After Madeleine's confession, the FBI agent who'd stayed at the ranch had gone back to his office in Abilene. Tomorrow, he'd be returning to take up the investigation again. Maybe this time he would be able put Frank's murder to rest—a murder that had made the national tabloids.

Everyone in the Culhane family and on the ranch was under suspicion, including Lila herself. Now it appeared that there might be a new suspect—Crystal.

If Frank had been told about her alleged pregnancy, and

he'd refused to marry her, support her, or even believe her, that would have given Crystal motive to kill him.

Tomorrow Lila would be meeting Crystal at lunch. Would she be confronting a naïve young woman who'd been led astray? Or would she be facing a ruthless opportunist, capable of lying and murder?

CHAPTER TWO

From the window of his fourth-floor office, FBI Agent Sam Rafferty watched the setting sun cast shadows over the streets of downtown Abilene. It was time to leave for the day. But he needed to make sure his work was caught up before setting out for the Culhane Ranch in the morning.

The Frank Culhane murder case had become the albatross around his neck. When Madeleine Culhane had confessed to hiring a hitman, Sam had been sure he'd found Frank's killer. Even after Madeleine revealed that she had a terminal brain tumor, it made sense that she'd dispense with Frank so her children could fight Lila for the ranch.

The discovery that someone else had already killed Frank had rocked Sam's world. Something else had rocked his world even harder—falling in love with Frank and Madeleine's free-spirited daughter, Jasmine.

"So you're leaving tomorrow?" Nick Bellingham stood in the doorway of Sam's office. Nick, a white-haired man a few months from retirement, had been Sam's first boss at the Bureau back in Chicago. He had recommended Sam to replace him in the Abilene office, but only if Sam showed that he could perform the job.

"Yup." Sam turned away from the window. "It's back to square one for me."

"At least you know the people you'll be dealing with." Nick walked into the room. "Who's your money on? The widow? Or maybe the horse trainer?"

Sam shrugged. "It could be any of them, including Frank's lawyer son and the creepy neighbor with the game hunting ranch."

"You didn't mention the daughter—Jasmine, is that her name? She had her differences with Frank, too."

Sam shrugged again, trying to appear nonchalant. He'd broken the rules by sleeping with Jasmine—rules that could cost him his job. Nick didn't know about that, unless he'd guessed. "She won't be at the ranch this time," he said. "She's in Austin, looking after her sick mother."

"Well, you can't rule her out, either."

"True." Sam shuffled the papers on his desk, wishing his old friend and mentor would be on his way. "I've tried to leave things in good shape here," he said. "The reports are up-to-date and filed. I've no idea how long I'll be at the ranch, but I'll keep you posted."

"I know you will. And I know how badly you want to put this case to bed. I'll be rooting for you."

"How's the Divino investigation going?" Sam changed the subject. Louis Divino, a known racketeer, had moved his operation from Chicago to Texas. Nick had been trying to arrest him for years. But Divino was slippery, with sharp lawyers and hired goons to do his dirty work. It was no secret that he was a friend of Madeleine's and had helped her arrange the hit on Frank Culhane. But since the hit had never taken place, he was in the clear.

"Dead end," Nick said. "I was hoping to nail the bastard before my retirement, but it's looking like that job might fall to you."

"You're not retired yet, Nick."

"We'll see how it goes. Anyway, you'll have your hands full dealing with the Culhanes. Go on, now. Get some rest before you hit the road tomorrow."

"Thanks. At least I'll be driving a decent car this time." Sam picked up his briefcase and took the elevator down to the parking garage.

The black Chevy SUV he'd been driving belonged to the Bureau. His own car, an aging Toyota, had been left in Chicago. Sam had flown to Abilene for a job interview and been thrown onto the Culhane case the first day. He'd had no time off to return to Chicago and move his belongings out of the rented apartment where he'd lived since his divorce. Meanwhile, he was camping out in a dreary motel room.

After taking his cell phone out of his pocket, he checked for new messages. The only thing worth reading was a text from Lila Culhane confirming that his quarters in the guest bungalow would be ready for his arrival. He knew she wouldn't be pleased to welcome him back. But when the Bureau had made the request, she'd known better than to refuse.

The temptation to phone Jasmine at her mother's condo in Austin was almost eating him alive. He thrust the phone back into his pocket and started the vehicle. At times like this, Sam would have bargained his soul to hear her voice. But while he was back on the Culhane case, their relationship was taboo. For the sake of his job, they'd agreed to stay apart until the investigation was over. Even a phone call could be traced and checked.

The hell of it was, as long as the case remained unsolved, Jasmine couldn't be ruled out as a suspect. The fact that he loved her couldn't be allowed to matter. Sam's instincts, combined with the lack of evidence, told him she was as innocent as she claimed to be.

But what if he was wrong?

Before leaving the stable, Roper checked the stall gates to make sure every door was locked. A few weeks ago, he might have left the task to one of the grooms. But that was before a hired hand's negligence had let a wild animal into the stable. The huge hyena had escaped from the nearby game farm. After slipping through an open door, it had killed Million Dollar Baby, the ranch's prize mare.

Baby's tragic loss had set off a chain reaction of repercussions. The clash with Lila that morning had been only one of them. Now, with the Run for a Million just weeks away, Roper found himself at a crossroads.

Chet Barr, a leading quarter horse breeder, had offered Roper one of his best horses—a chestnut stallion named Fire Dance. Five years old, bred from a line of champions, the russet-coated horse had won several futurity events and was scoring well in big-time reining competition. Roper had seen him perform at the Cactus Classic and been impressed.

If asked, Barr would probably let him work with the stallion at his ranch near Amarillo. For Roper, there might even be a chance of a future job offer. But that would mean a permanent break with Lila. Was that what he wanted?

Barr was getting impatient for an answer. If Roper didn't accept the horse soon, it might be offered to someone else. There were other horses available, but Fire Dance had the look of a winner. Whether he had the heart was something Roper wouldn't know until he rode him in competition.

In the Run for a Million, with sixteen of the world's best horses and riders competing, anything could happen. But another event, the Shootout, which would take place a day earlier, was just as demanding and every bit as stressful. The Shootout was a qualifier. Out of more than fifty competitors, the five riders with the top scores would secure their place in next year's Run for a Million. Riders who didn't make the cut would have one more chance at the Cactus Classic in March, where the remaining eleven would qualify.

Even the riders in this year's big event would have to compete for a slot next year. Roper had already registered for the Shootout. Again, there was the question of which horse to use. But with so much hanging in the balance, including his job with Lila, he was too tired to make a decision tonight. He would get a good supper in his belly, sleep if he could, and start fresh in the morning. Maybe some answers would come to him.

The moon was rising by the time he crossed the employee lot to his aging Ford pickup and headed out the gate for home. Roper lived with his family on the small ranch they'd bought two years ago, when they moved from Colorado. Rich folks like the Culhanes looked down on them. But Roper's parents were honest and hardworking, and his younger half-siblings—three boys and a girl—were rodeo stars on the national stage. They'd even been featured on the cover of *Sports Illustrated*.

Roper had been a winning bronc rider until an injury had forced him to quit and become a trainer. Looking back, he reflected, the horse that broke his hip had done him a favor. He could only hope that Stetson, Rowdy, Chance, and Cheyenne would have the sense to move on before they got injured or washed up.

The four had been out on the circuit most of the week, but as Roper crossed the creek by the bridge, drove through the gate, and saw the motor home and horse trailer, his spirit lightened. He was always happy to have the young ones come home.

The mouthwatering smell of his mother's pot roast and fresh biscuits wafted through the open door of the simple clapboard house. There was a shabbiness about the place, but the need for corrals and a new stable had come before the vanity project of fixing up the house. Ever practical, his mother had insisted she didn't need new flooring, cabinets, or siding anytime soon.

The aging cattle dog mix came wagging out to greet Roper as he climbed down from the truck. After petting the dog, he washed his hands at the pump and went inside.

The rest of the family was in the kitchen. The three lanky, suntanned boys—Stetson, Rowdy, and Chance—were seated around the table. Kirby, their father, was in his wheelchair, sipping from the ever-present cup of whiskey-laced coffee that he drank to ease the pain of his back, crushed years ago by a massive bucking bull.

Twenty-year-old Cheyenne was filling the unmatched glasses with ice water. A petite brunette with sensual lips and fiery eyes, she was the media star among the four young rodeo champions. Roper was aware that she'd turned down modeling and movie offers to compete on the circuit with her brothers. How long that would last was anybody's guess.

Rachel, Roper's mother, paused to tuck a strand of graying hair behind her ear, then moved the platter of meat and vegetables from the counter to the table and took her seat at the far end. She'd been a beauty once, but years of ranch life, raising a family, and caring for a disabled husband had taken their toll. Now she was the steady rock of the McKenna family, her softness worn away and replaced by steel.

The family joined hands around the table and shared a brief blessing. Then they filled their plates and began eating. Rachel was the kind of cook who could turn the cheapest ingredients into a tasty meal. Even in hard times, they'd never wanted for good food.

Roper would have to move away if he were to leave the nearby Culhane stables and go to work for another ranch. That could prove a problem. His parents needed him when their four younger offspring were on the rodeo circuit. Of course, Kirby and Rachel could always hire some help. Between Roper's salary and the winnings of the young rodeo stars, they could easily afford it. But Rachel had always resisted. "I always believed folks should do for themselves," she was fond of saying. "Paying somebody for work you could do with your own hands is plain laziness and a waste of money."

"So how did the rodeo go, boys?" Kirby's gravelly voice broke through the low murmur of hungry people eating.

"Fine," Stetson said. "Rowdy won a buckle in bareback, and Chance was second in tie-down."

"Only second?" Kirby sipped from the coffee-stained porcelain cup. For a man whose system was steeped in alcohol, he was sharp. "And what about you, Stetson?"

"I took the bull riding with an 88, but I banged my shoulder on the dismount. It'll be sore for a while."

"Just rub some of your mother's liniment on it." Kirby's gaze shifted to Cheyenne. "And what about you, girl?"

"Jezebel went down on the third barrel. She's all right. That's what matters."

"And what about you? Were you hurt?"

"I'm fine, Dad." Cheyenne turned away from him to hide the darkening bruise on her cheek, but Kirby's sharp eyes missed nothing.

"Blast it, what happened?" Kirby demanded. "I told you not to cut so close to those barrels."

She shrugged. "I do it to win."

"Well, you can't do it forever. And if you don't stop, you could end up like me. Maybe you need to quit the rodeo and do something sensible, like beauty school."

"Leave her alone, Kirby," Rachel said. "Let her enjoy her supper in peace. She's got better ways to make a living than beauty school. If she took the modeling offer from that fancy magazine—"

"May I please be excused?" Without waiting for a reply, Cheyenne pushed back her chair, stood, and stalked out of the kitchen. Roper glimpsed tears as she rushed passed him.

As the screen door slammed, the boys exchanged glances. "She's been off her game all weekend," Chance said. "Maybe it's, you know, her time of the month."

"That's enough, Chance," Rachel snapped. "That's none of your business and not fit for the table. Not another word."

"Sorry, Mom." Chance speared another slice of pot roast.

Roper, who'd eaten all he wanted, stood and carried his plate to the sink. "I'll go out and make sure she's all right," he said.

"Fine." Kirby drizzled more whiskey into his cup. "Maybe you can talk some sense into the girl."

"Don't hold your breath, Dad," Rowdy said.

Ignoring the exchange, Roper opened the screen door and went outside. He'd expected to find Cheyenne huddled on the steps. When he didn't see her there, he crossed the yard. He found her perched on the corral fence, watching the horses that had been unloaded from the trailer.

Among them was Jezebel, the palomino mare she used for barrel racing.

Without a word, he joined her on the fence, slinging his leg over the top rail to settle beside her. Neither of them spoke at first, but the silence between them was comfortable.

"Is Jezebel all right?" he asked her.

"She seems all right. At least she's not limping, and she ate her oats earlier. What do you think?"

Roper took a few seconds to watch the mare. "She looks fine to me," he said. "It's you I'm concerned about. That's a nasty bruise on your cheek. Something tells me you've got more bruises that don't show."

She exhaled—a broken sigh, verging on a sob. "I don't want to do rodeo with the boys anymore," she said. "Stetson spent the night with a buckle bunny, and I think Rowdy is smoking weed, maybe more. Chance is headed the same way. Mom would have a fit if she knew. So much for having raised us by the Good Book."

"I take it you're not going to tell her."

"Heavens, no. That would only break her heart and make everything worse."

"So what are you going to do, Little Sis?" Roper asked.

Cheyenne watched the flight of a shooting star. A distant train whistle echoed through the darkness.

"That fall with Jezebel was a wake-up call," she said. "It was my fault, not hers. I'd lost focus and cut the turn too sharp. If she'd been injured, I would never have forgiven myself."

"You could've been hurt, too. Look at your dad. Look at me. Rodeo is dangerous business, even when you're not riding a bucker. And the lifestyle's tough, too. More cowboys die in road accidents than in the arena."

"It's not that," Cheyenne said. "I just feel burned out—

the culture, the people, even the sport. I want something different, Roper, and I think I know what it is."

Roper held his tongue, waiting for her to go on.

"You know that this year, the Run for a Million added a Cutting Horse Challenge," she said. "I'm not ready now, but with hard work I could aim for rookie status next year or even non-pro the year after."

"That's a tall order, Little Sis," Roper said. "Make sure you know what you're getting into."

"I was cutting cows on our Colorado ranch when I was ten years old. I know how to do it."

"But have you seen it in competition? It's intense," Roper said. "And being a rodeo champion won't buy you much. You can't just waltz into the big events. You have to work your way up. There are competitions every weekend. Winning takes time and experience.

"And no matter how good you might be," Roper continued, "in cutting, it's the horse that counts—a horse with the training, smarts, and cow sense to separate a cow out of the herd and keep it from running back, time after time. Believe me, those horses don't come cheap. You can't just use Jezebel."

"Don't patronize me, Roper. I know that. I've watched events on TV. And I know what good cutting horses cost."

"Can you afford one?"

"I think so. I've put half my winnings in the account for the ranch. But I've saved the rest."

"What about that modeling spread for *Vogue* magazine? How much were you offered?"

"A lot," Cheyenne said. "I turned them down, but they said to let them know if I changed my mind."

"You'd be smart to say yes. If you're serious about cutting, the money would buy you a better horse."

She gave him a tentative smile. "You know how I hate that sort of silliness," she said. "But all right, I'll grit my teeth and do it. When I have the money, I'll need your help choosing a horse. And I hope you can help me with training, too."

"Let's see how it goes," Roper said. "For now, I'll try to get you a behind-the-scenes pass to the cutting event at the Run for a Million. You can see the horses and get a picture of how they're trained and handled, maybe even meet some of the riders."

"You could do that? That would be amazing!"

"I said I'd try. Meanwhile, you work on getting the money for your horse."

Roper knew better than to make promises he couldn't keep. If he were to leave his job with Lila, he might not be available to help his sister. Cheyenne was a superb horsewoman, but she couldn't compete in cutting without rigorous training on her chosen horse. That included an enclosure where she could work with cows.

Two years ago, when she was eighteen and already doing rodeo, Frank Culhane had offered to train her in reining. He had taken her to the Cactus Classic in Scottsdale in the hope of rousing her interest. Cheyenne had turned him down flat.

Whether it was because she didn't care for the sport or that she'd felt uncomfortable with Frank, Roper didn't know. He had been in Colorado at the time, finalizing the sale of the family ranch there.

Now Frank was gone, and things were different at the Culhane Ranch. If Roper were to stay, Cheyenne might be able to do her training and keep her horse there.

If he were to stay.

He couldn't afford to wait any longer. He needed to decide on the horse, the arrangement with Chet Barr, and his relationship with Lila.

The choices he made tomorrow could be life-changing.

The sun was climbing toward midday when Lila drove her new white Porsche Carrera to Willow Bend. A hundred years ago, the town had been a prosperous center for the cattle business. Now, with most of the animals being trucked off to feed lots and the money going to big city banks, Willow Bend had shrunk to a quarter of its former size. These days, it served the surrounding ranches with a grocery store and ranch supply store, a gas station with a garage, a police and fire station, a small courthouse with an attached jail, a saloon, a school, and a decent restaurant.

The Blue Rose, a seedy, rundown motel on the outskirts of town, served visitors and the occasional tryst. Driving past it, Lila couldn't help wondering how many times Frank had bedded his young mistress there—and how many others there'd been.

Frank's son, Darrin, lived in Willow Bend with his pregnant wife, Simone. He practiced law out of his home office and managed the ranch's cattle operation, which his mother had been awarded in her divorce from Frank.

Since Frank's death, Darrin had declared war on Lila's right to inherit the Culhane mansion and stables. As she drove past his house—a large bungalow style, built by the founder of the town, Lila could imagine the red-headed weasel at his desk, working out the details of the lawsuit, to be set for court in the next few months.

Frank's will, made early in the marriage, had left the property to her *and* their future children. But since Lila had given him no children, and she wasn't a Culhane by blood, the lawyers were arguing that the will no longer applied and everything should go to his first family.

A nasty legal fight lay ahead. But Lila couldn't think about that now, not when she was about to meet the woman who claimed to be carrying Frank's child.

She parked at the curb in front of the Trail's End restaurant, behind a battered blue Hyundai Elantra with a mismatched door. If that was Crystal's car, she could be in desperate straits—or the car could be for show. Lila knew better than to assume anything about the woman she was about to meet.

Dressed simply, in khakis and a denim shirt, she slung her purse over her shoulder and climbed out of the Porsche. Willing herself to ignore her racing pulse, she walked into the restaurant. The busy lunch hour wouldn't start for another fifteen minutes. She hoped that would give her enough quiet time to find out what she needed to know. If Miss Crystal Carter turned out to be a fraud, this messy business would be finished.

The dining area was arranged with booths around the outside and tables in the center. Lila scanned the booths. Spotting Crystal took no more than a few seconds. She was seated in the corner, sipping a soda. She looked up as Lila entered the room, then lowered her gaze. She was young and pretty, just the way Frank had always liked his girls.

Close up, she was even prettier, with doe eyes and a cloud of dark curls. Her makeup was heavy, the red lips, blue eyeshadow, and false eyelashes too dramatic for Lila's taste, but she did have good skin. The woman's left hand, splayed on the table, exhibited the same fake nails and rings that Lila had seen in the photo as it rested on Frank's shoulder.

"May I sit down, Miss Carter?" Lila asked in a formal

voice. The last thing she wanted was to appear sympathetic.

"Sure." She was wearing a black tee that outlined her swollen breasts.

Lila slid into the booth and ordered a Coke with lemon from a passing server. "Just a few questions for now," she said, skipping the usual pleasantries. "How far along are you?"

"I took one of those drugstore tests last week," she said. "I'm already getting morning sickness, so I figure about three months. Once I start to show I'll probably have to quit my job. That's when I'm really going to need help."

"And what's your job?" Lila asked.

"I'm a hostess at the Jackalope Saloon down the street. That's where I met Frank."

"And you're sure your baby is his?" Lila forced each word.

"Oh, absolutely. Whatever you might think, I'm not a tramp. I loved Frank. He was . . . the only one."

"Did Frank know about the baby?"

She shook her head. "I was going to tell him, but . . . you know." Her voice broke in a muffled sob. "Now I don't know what to do."

Was she grief-stricken or just acting? Lila took a deep breath. "Now comes the big question. Are you willing to submit to a paternity test?"

A startled look flashed across her face. "Can they do that—even before the baby's born?"

"It's done all the time these days." Lila squeezed the lemon slice into the Coke that the server had left. Sipping the drink, she studied Crystal's reaction. After a moment, she took a business card out of her purse. "Here's the number and address of a doctor in Abilene. He's agreed to take the sample and set up the test. I will pay, of course, and furnish a sample of Frank's DNA. He'll phone me with the results. If it's a match, then we'll talk. If not, we're done. Give him a call. All right?"

Crystal looked confused. "But won't it hurt the baby? And what about me? I'll have to miss work to drive to Abilene. I know the baby is Frank's. Can't you just take my word for it?"

Holding back a storm of rage, contempt, and fear, Lila laid a $10 bill on the table for the drinks, slid out of the booth, and stood. Given free rein, she would have grabbed Crystal by the shoulders and shaken some sense into her. Instead, she kept her icy demeanor.

"Miss Carter, until you take that paternity test, this conversation is finished. If the baby is Frank's, I'll contact you. Otherwise, you and I will have nothing more to say to each other. Do you understand?"

Crystal's chin quivered slightly. "Do you need my phone number?"

"I already have it." Fighting her emotions, Lila turned away from the table, left the restaurant, and drove away in her car.

She had hoped to get some answers from Crystal. But she'd only come away with more questions. Was the young woman as naïve as she'd appeared to be? Had she loved Frank or simply seized on a rare opportunity? Was he really, as she'd claimed, the only one?

For now, all Lila could do was wait for the results of the paternity test.

By the time Crystal finished her Coke, the lunchtime customers were arriving. For a moment she was tempted to pocket the money Lila Culhane had left for the drinks. But someone could be watching, and she didn't need that kind of trouble.

She left the restaurant and then climbed into the beat-up blue Hyundai parked at the curb. Earlier, she'd glimpsed the white Porsche through the window. Lila, that cold bitch, had everything. The lady was a real ice queen—probably that way in bed, too. But in the end, Frank had found a woman who could give him the love he needed.

When she turned the spare key she'd found, the Hyundai's engine coughed to life. The car, which needed a valve job and a muffler, wasn't hers. Judd, her ex-boyfriend, wouldn't need it until he got out of jail—if he got out. Dealing crack could get him months, even years, behind bars.

By the time he got out, she wouldn't need his crappy car anymore. She would be sitting on a pile of money—unless her baby turned out to be not Frank's but Judd's.

She shifted down and pulled away from the curb, her sweating hands locked on the wheel. Why hadn't she been aware that the paternity test could be done so soon? She'd hoped for more time to get help from Frank's family, maybe a new car and a decent place to live. The reckoning wasn't supposed to come until the baby was born. By then, even if the DNA wasn't a match to Frank's, she would have gained something.

But that time window had closed. Lila wanted proof now. Unless the test proved that Crystal was carrying a Culhane, Frank's widow wouldn't even talk to her.

If Frank was the father, that would put Crystal in a strong bargaining position. Lila would want that baby, or at least want to see it well cared for. With luck, she'd be willing to pay.

But if the kid was Judd's, that would be the end of her hopes. Crystal didn't want Judd's baby. She didn't want to have it or raise it. She would have a decision to make.

What were the odds? She hadn't slept with Judd after

she'd hooked up with Frank. But the last time had been close enough for the count. Her periods had never been regular. And she'd never bothered with birth control. Too expensive and too much bother.

There was one thing she needed to do. She had never made a clean break with Judd. Now that Frank was gone, Judd could be expecting her to come back to him. She needed to see him one last time, to make him understand that they were through.

She touched the pocket where she'd put the doctor's card. The stakes were high—all or nothing. But the sooner she knew the truth about her baby, the sooner she could move forward with some kind of plan.

She would call the doctor tomorrow.

CHAPTER THREE

Darrin Culhane was checking out a porn site on his desktop computer when he heard the front door open. He closed the screen with a click of the mouse. His wife had returned from shopping.

Moments later, Simone walked into his office and collapsed in the client chair. She looked damp and exhausted, strings of blond hair clinging around her pretty face. Her pregnancy was already beginning to show. The limp yellow sundress she wore was splitting a seam at the waist. Or maybe she was just gaining weight. Darrin hoped not. He couldn't abide heavy women.

"Did you find what you needed?" he asked her.

She sighed. "The pharmacy didn't have my antacid pills. I had to settle for Tums. But there was a sale on chocolate fudge ice cream, so I bought two half gallons. I put them in the freezer. Heavens, it's hot out there!" She fanned herself with a ranching magazine she'd found on the desk. "Oh, I saw Lila's car parked in front of the restaurant. There's no mistaking that white Porsche. I can't believe she could get a brand-new one so soon after her old one was wrecked."

"It's called good insurance." Darrin glanced away, avoiding her gaze. He'd had a hand in the wreckage of his stepmother's last car. That damned FBI agent had almost nailed him for it. But his mother had used her confession as a bargaining chip to keep her son out of prison.

Then Madeleine had turned out to be not only innocent but dying from a brain tumor. He should have guessed something was wrong from the erratic way she'd been acting. At least when she passed she would leave him with a pile of money. But as long as Lila possessed the house and stables, the money would never be enough.

Especially not for Simone.

"What were you doing while I was out?" she asked.

"I was going over the notes from my mother's attorneys. I'll be conferencing with them next week to update the case against Lila." The paperwork had come up on Darrin's monitor screen when he clicked out of the porn site.

"Do we have a court date yet?" she asked.

"Not yet. But that's not up to us. It's up to the court."

"Well, can't you do something?" she demanded. "Talk to the judge. He was a friend of your father's. Surely he can do you a favor."

"That isn't how the system works. There are rules—"

"So bend the rules. You said we would raise our children in that house. You promised me you'd fight to get it for us."

"I'm trying, Simone. I really am."

Darrin *had* tried. But his plan to sabotage Lila's car and make her death look like an accident had failed and almost gotten him arrested. He'd kept the story from his wife for her own protection as well as his. But at times like this, he was tempted to tell her the truth.

"Well, you're not trying hard enough." Simone was on her feet now. "I want to be in that house by the time the baby comes. If we can't get a court date, then we'll have to go after Lila. I know she's sleeping with that no-account horse trainer of hers. If we could catch them at it and threaten to expose her—"

"Do you really think she'd give up the house and stables to protect her reputation? You don't know Lila. She'd laugh in your face."

Simone's breath made a huffing sound. "Well, then, we'll have to dig a little deeper, won't we? That FBI man is coming back to take up the murder case again. If we could prove that Lila and her lover conspired to kill your father, they'd be behind bars and the house would be ours. We wouldn't have to wait for the court." She tugged her sundress down over the slight bulge of her belly. "We're going to need help. What about Mariah? She knows everything that goes on in that house. Would she spy on Lila if we asked her to?"

Darrin weighed her words. When it came to proving Lila's guilt, his wife was like a dog with a bone in its teeth. Most of her suggestions were impractical. This time, however, she might have come up with something.

"That's not a bad idea," he said. "Mariah might help us as a favor, especially if we offered to reward her. But she'd be even more willing if my mother asked her. Mother's bought Mariah's loyalty over the years. Mariah would do anything for her."

"So go ahead and call her. Do it now. We don't know how much longer she'll be alive, do we?" Simone flounced to the door, where she turned back to face him. "I'm going to get some ice cream before I watch my game show. Do you want some?"

Darrin shook his head. The pressures he was dealing with had triggered a gnawing pain in his gut. Maybe he was getting an ulcer. Ice cream might help. But what he really wanted was a shot of bourbon.

"I mean it, Darrin," Simone said. "Call your mother

now. For all we know, we could be planning her funeral tomorrow."

And counting our inheritance.

She didn't say it, but he knew what she was thinking. He was thinking the same thing. When Madeleine passed on, the ranch's cattle operation, her condo, and her stock investments would be left to her two children. Even after splitting everything with Jasmine, his inheritance would make him comfortably wealthy. But only with the house and stables could he and Simone become *the Culhanes*, with all the power and prestige the name implied. He knew what had to happen. But why couldn't Simone let him handle things his way, like a man? The pressure was getting to him.

"Well, don't just sit there." She walked back to the desk and hovered over him. "I'm waiting. Go ahead and call her."

Something snapped in Darrin. He rose partway out of his chair. "Leave me alone!" he snarled. "I don't need you to tell me what to do. I can think for myself!"

"Fine. Then stop fiddling around and start thinking! I'm tired of—"

Simone's words ended in a gasp as his hand came up and slapped the side of her face, hard enough to send her reeling backward.

With a cry, she righted herself and ran from the room.

Lila had seen the black Chevy SUV pull up to the guest bungalow on the far side of the house. That would be Agent Sam Rafferty, returning for a second try at solving Frank's murder. Sooner or later he would want to talk with her. That would be the time to tell him about Crystal, her pregnancy, and her possible motive for killing Frank.

But it could wait until tomorrow. This evening, she was still overwrought from the meeting with Frank's pregnant mistress. And she had yet to confront Roper about his promised decision.

A light had come on in the bungalow. Sam would be settling in. The well-stocked kitchenette had snacks and sodas as well as supplies for the coffeemaker. She would have Mariah send someone out with a meal for him.

Lila wasn't happy to have the FBI back in her life. If only Madeleine had been found guilty, things would be settled by now and she could move on to fight other battles. But she'd had little choice but to let Sam come back to the ranch. And she still needed to know who'd murdered her husband. Maybe when she did, she'd finally be able to mourn.

At least Sam was soft-spoken and respectful, not like some lawmen Lila had known. But the man was not to be underestimated. His sharp instincts missed nothing. She would need to weigh every word she spoke to him.

After passing through the house, she walked out the back door. Cloaked in evening shadows, the patio was a peaceful refuge. A cool breeze stirred the potted palms and rippled the surface of the pool. Lila sank onto the chaise, leaned back, and released the breath that felt as if she'd been holding it in since morning. The day had been hellish, and it wasn't over. She still had to deal with Roper.

The stable was dark except for the security lights, but Roper's pickup truck was still in the parking lot. She would take a moment to rest her tired eyes before she went to look for him.

And then what? What if he wanted to leave? How would she manage without the man who had become her rock? And how would she deal with the truth—that he hadn't cared enough to stay?

Crickets were chirping in the long grass beyond the fence. Eyes closed, Lila let the soothing sound flow through her. She took deep breaths, willing her tense body to relax.

But her thoughts were still jumping like frenzied rabbits from worry to worry. *Crystal . . . the lawsuit . . . the FBI . . . the horses . . . and Roper. Roper most of all.*

"Boss?" His deep voice jolted her to awareness. She opened her eyes to find him standing over her. "Are you all right?" he asked.

Lila sat up, swung her legs off the chaise, and stood. "Are you saying that I'm still your boss?"

A corner of his mouth twitched in a half smile. "For now, at least. Walk with me."

His hand brushed the small of her back, guiding her through the patio gate and down toward the pastures, their way lit by the rising moon. The stars were emerging from the dark blanket of the sky. Windmill blades creaked softly, pumping water for the sprinklers that kept the horse paddocks green even in this dry summer.

They walked in silence, Lila on edge, waiting for Roper to speak. From the game farm that bordered the ranch property came the sound of gunshots from a heavy caliber weapon. Their neighbor, Charlie Grishman, collected old, sick, and unwanted exotic animals and charged big money for clients to hunt them on his ranch. Some poor, helpless beast, most likely a former pet or show performer, was dying out there in the darkness.

Lila shuddered. The memory was still raw. The hyena that had killed Million Dollar Baby had also killed a young cowboy. The monster, now dead, had almost surely escaped from Charlie's compound during a raid by an animal rights group. But Charlie had disavowed any responsibility.

"That evil little man! Every time I hear that gunfire, I feel sick," she said. "I'd give anything to shut him down. I tried to get Frank to do it, but he didn't care. As long as Charlie kept his menagerie off our property, Frank was fine with him as a neighbor."

"For what it's worth, I'm with you, Boss," Roper said. "You could take him to court, but if he has a business license, what he does on his own land is perfectly legal."

They were making polite conversation, putting off the things that needed to be said. Lila had had enough. She was tired of waiting.

At the fence, she turned to face him, her impatience boiling over. "You said you were with me, Roper. But are you really, or do you plan to leave? Stop dragging your feet and tell me what you've decided."

She glared up at him, braced for bad news.

All day, Roper had been racked by conflict—wanting to be free, to make his own choices, to win if he could. But there were people who needed him—his parents, his sister, and Lila. If he were to leave, she'd be hard put to replace him with a man she could trust. But didn't he owe something to himself? Didn't he have the right to seize his dream, no matter who he had to leave behind?

He'd imagined telling her he was leaving. His mind had even rehearsed what he was going to say. But now, as her coppery eyes blazed into his, searing her brand on his soul, Roper faced the truth. A different man might walk away. But he wasn't that man.

"Damn it, Roper." Her voice quivered with impatience. "Talk to me—now!"

The dam Roper had built against his emotions trembled and burst, releasing a flood of forbidden yearnings.

Jerking her close, he kissed her, not gently but hungrily. His arms crushed her against him, his mouth bruised her lips. The taste of her, the scent and feel of her, roused his senses to a frenzy. His body burned with the urge to take her. But somehow, he found the wit to mutter, "You'd better stop me now, Lila, or it'll be too late."

* * *

"*No.*" Lila caught fire in his arms, murmuring the words between kisses. "Don't stop . . . don't you dare stop."

She pushed against the hard ridge that pressed her belly, needing him, needing the release he could give her. There was a world of rules and reasons why they shouldn't be doing this. Right now, none of them mattered.

A small shed, built to shelter the sprinkler controls, stood next to the fence. Roper pulled her into it. The space inside the walls was barely enough to hide them from view, but it was all they had. Driven by a blazing urgency, she unfastened his belt and yanked down the zipper to open his jeans. Her hand found and clasped him. He was rock hard and ready. Wanting him was like wanting air to breathe.

Her slacks and panties dropped around her ankles. She shook one foot loose from its sandal, freeing her legs to wrap his hips. He lifted her against him, using her weight to lower her onto his jutting shaft. She moaned, her head falling back as he filled the hollowness inside her. Her legs pulled him deeper, meeting each thrust. This was what she'd denied herself for as long as she'd known him. And if she burned in hell for it, she wouldn't be sorry.

Stars swam in her head as the dizzying sensations mounted to a shattering climax. With a cry and a whimper, she spiraled back to earth.

That was when he withdrew, turned away, and finished on his own. Her disappointment was tempered with gratitude. He had protected her the one way he could. That was Roper, keeping his presence of mind even as she lost hers.

Still quivering, she sagged against him, resting her head on his chest. He stroked her hair before he spoke. "Get your clothes on, Boss. It's time we had our talk."

Lila went rigid. Had he planned this? Was what had just happened his way of saying goodbye?

Without a word, she pulled on her clothes, tucked her shirt in her slacks, and found her missing sandal. For one wild, reckless moment, she'd almost imagined herself in love with Roper. Now she was prepared to hate him.

They stepped outside, the moon so bright that its light was almost harsh. Lila stumbled into a shallow ditch. He steadied her with a hand on her elbow. "My truck," he said, nodding toward the employee lot.

Fighting angry tears, she let him usher her across the asphalt to where his pickup was parked. He unlocked the passenger door and helped her into the seat, then went around to the driver's side.

"Spare me the suspense," she said as he settled beside her. "Just tell me."

"I'm not going to tell you, Lila," he said. "I'm going to ask you."

She gazed ahead, through the windshield, waiting.

"Hear me out," he said, speaking to her profile. "When I've had my say, you can give me a yes or no. All I'm asking is that you listen."

"Go ahead."

He turned toward her in the seat. "You know I want to win the Run for a Million. And you know how I feel about using a thirteen-year-old stallion."

"Yes. We've been through all that before."

"Chet Barr is willing to lend me Fire Dance. In the morning, I plan to call Chet and tell him I want to use the horse—but I want to train with him here."

"Here?" Lila's pulse raced. So Roper might not be leaving after all. But he already knew how she felt about donating stable space, food, care, and arena time to someone else's horse—especially if she had no stake in a win.

Was that why he'd made love to her? To soften her up for a favor? Lila seethed as the lingering pleasure faded. She didn't want to believe Roper was taking advantage of her. But that was how it appeared. It was time to get tough.

"I want to be fair with you, Boss," he said. "If you let me train here, I'll still be able to do my regular work. I'll pay you a boarding fee for the horse and extra for his arena time, so you shouldn't be out anything for his keep. Does that sound all right?"

She gave him a stern look. "Maybe. But only if you don't win. You say you want to be fair with me. Fine. If you finish in the money, I want a cut of your share."

Roper gave a low whistle. "You drive a hard bargain, lady."

"I'm not a lady, I'm your boss," Lila said. "If you win, I'll take twenty-five percent of your prize."

Lila could see him doing the math in his head. If he were to win the Run for a Million, his share would be $500,000. One-quarter of that amount would be $125,000. It was a lot of money. But if she'd been a man and had demanded that much, Roper wouldn't have been surprised.

"Another thing," she said. "That little tangle back in the sprinkler shed—as far as you're concerned, it never happened. And it's never going to happen again. You can take it, or you can leave it and pack your gear. Let me know your final decision in the morning, after you've talked to Chet Barr. Maybe he'll give you a better deal."

With those words, Lila opened the door of the truck, slipped to the ground, and closed it behind her. As she strode toward the house, she forced herself not to look back. Her hands had begun to shake.

Maybe she'd pushed him too far. What would she do if Roper left rather than give in to her demands?

But she already knew the answer to that question. She would grow up. Frank was gone, and she was on her own. She couldn't depend on a man, not even Roper, to rescue her and take charge—especially now, with so many things at stake.

Roper was her employee, not her partner and not her lover. If he thought he could manipulate her, the man had a lot to learn. She had asked for no more than she deserved. He would play by her rules or go his own way—and if he did, fine. She would carry on without him.

As she neared the back door, thoughts of those stolen moments in the shed swept over her—his mouth plundering hers, her legs wrapping his hips. She forced the memory from her mind. When she faced Roper again, she would pretend that nothing had happened between them. She could only hope that he would do the same.

Otherwise, how could they go on working together? Maybe it would be better for them both if he left.

The kitchen lights were on, but there was no sign of Mariah, which was odd. Never mind, Lila had other concerns. She turned the lights off, then went upstairs to her room.

Roper drove out through the employee gate and turned onto the main road. Tires spat gravel as he headed for home, driving a little too fast. All he wanted was to get someplace where he could sort out his churning thoughts.

A jackrabbit bounded through his headlights. He swerved onto the shoulder and slammed on the brakes, barely missing the animal. The truck screeched to a stop inches from the edge of a steep-sided bar ditch.

With the rabbit flashing off into the dark, Roper switched off the engine and sank back into the seat. As his racing pulse began to slow, the encounter with Lila unspooled in his memory. He had never planned to make love to her. But at the end of a frustrating day, his restraint had snapped.

He wanted to stay. He liked being close to the family that needed him. He especially liked being in charge and the pay that came with the job—better than he could expect at a new ranch. Even Lila's demand for a cut of his winnings was hardly a concern. Sixteen of the best riders in the world would be competing in the Run for a Million. Roper had tried to convince himself that he could win. But even on a top horse, the truth was he'd be doing well to make a respectable showing.

The trouble was with Lila. After what had happened tonight, how could they go back to their former relationship, which had worked as long as they hadn't crossed forbidden lines? How could they work together now that those lines no longer existed?

Roper started the truck, then pulled back onto the road. In the distance, he could see the lights of the McKenna ranch. His younger siblings would be home for a few more days. Then they'd be back on the rodeo circuit. Would Cheyenne be going with them? That remained to be seen.

He drove over the creek bridge and through the gate, looking forward to his mother's cooking and the sight of the four young faces around the table. Instead, he pulled up to the house to find Rachel, Stetson, Chance, and Cheyenne waiting for him on the porch. One look at their faces was enough to tell Roper something was wrong.

Kirby, in his wheelchair, was visible in the doorway. The dog crouched at his feet. There was no sign of Rowdy.

Dread tightened its grip as Roper climbed out of the truck. Cheyenne flew down the steps to meet him.

"We've been waiting for you, Roper." Her eyes glistened with unshed tears. "Rowdy's in jail. He was arrested in town for cocaine possession. Mom is fit to be tied."

Roper released a breath. He'd feared some kind of awful accident. At least his brother was unhurt. But the boy could be in serious trouble.

Roper glanced up at his mother. Rachel stood ramrod straight between her sons. Her expression could have been chiseled in stone. She'd prided herself on raising her children by the Good Book. Rowdy's arrest would be a bitter pill for her to swallow.

Beside her, Stetson stirred uneasily. Chance's gaze was fixed on his boots. The two had probably been chastised for not keeping their brother in line. But something told Roper they weren't surprised. If Cheyenne knew about Rowdy's drug use, the others surely did, too.

Roper knew they'd been waiting for him to get home. As the firstborn, it would be up to him to handle the situation.

"Say the word, and I'll go," he told his mother. "If Rowdy's bail has been set, my credit card should be enough to cover it and get him out of jail. If not, at least he'll know we're here for him."

Rachel was dry-eyed, her expression still frozen. "Fine. Get him if he's ready," she said. "But don't be too easy on the boy, Roper. Folks around here might not give us the time of day because we're not rich. But I've always been able to hold my head up because I've raised a God-fearing family. When word of this gets around, they'll click their tongues, look down their prissy noses, and call us trash. Rowdy has disgraced the family name, and I want to make sure he knows it."

Tired as he was, Roper climbed back into the truck and headed for Willow Bend. His young brother deserved to have a strip taken out of his hide. But Roper, who'd battled alcoholism in his younger years, knew what a powerful enemy addiction could be. Rowdy was going to need support just as much as punishment.

At least one thing was settled. Roper couldn't desert his family at a time like this. Tomorrow he would accept Lila's terms, arrange for the stallion's transfer to the Culhane Ranch, and try to make the best of a touchy situation.

A low, white stucco building housed the county offices, the police station, the court, and the jail. Roper parked in the visitor lot and accessed the jail by the rear entrance. The facility was small and showing signs of long use. Its open-barred cells were partly visible through a door that opened off the waiting area.

When Roper gave his brother's name to the uniformed woman behind the counter, she nodded. "You can see him, Mr. McKenna, but there'll be a short wait. We only allow one visitor at a time back to the cells. There are two people ahead of you."

"Is there any chance I can pay his bail and take him home tonight?" Roper asked.

"I'm afraid not. His bail hearing will be held tomorrow morning. Then, depending on the judge, you can make the arrangements. Please sign the registry, then have a seat. You'll be called when it's your turn."

Worn Naugahyde chairs in neon colors were arranged around the small waiting area. After a brief security pat down, Roper chose one at random and sat down. The next person ahead of him—a young woman leafing through a tattered copy of *People* magazine, was seated on the opposite side of the room. She was extraordinarily pretty and petite, with doll-like features and a cloud of dark hair. She was dressed in a black motorcycle jacket, tight-fitting jeans, and high-heeled black boots.

Roper tried to avoid looking directly at her, but he couldn't help noticing the hands that held the magazine—the long crimson nails, probably fake, and the glittering rings that adorned her fingers.

Something stirred in a shadowed recess of his memory. He could have sworn that he'd never laid eyes on the girl before. But the sense of recognition was as unmistakable as it was mysterious.

He might have opened a conversation with her, maybe asked if they'd met somewhere before, but that would sound like a pickup line. The girl was attractive but not his type, and he wasn't looking for company.

As if she'd felt his curious gaze, she looked up from the magazine and gave him a melting smile, which made her face appear even prettier. The situation had become awkward. Should he speak? Maybe smile back?

Roper was saved from a response by the previous visitor to the cells—a thin bespectacled stranger who had the look and demeanor of a lawyer. He passed through the waiting area and out through the exit without a word or glance in either direction.

"Miss Carter." The female officer at the desk spoke. "You're next. You may go in now."

The girl put down the magazine, stood, and took a moment to fluff her hair, as if she wanted to make an impression. Maybe she had a boyfriend in there. But he knew that was none of his business. As she strutted down the hall in her high-heeled boots, he settled back to wait his turn.

Chapter Four

There were just two men in the cells. One was a lanky young cowboy, sitting on his bunk with his face buried in his hands. The other man was Judd Proctor.

Judd was fit and husky with craggy features, shoulder-length sandy hair, and unsettling, golden eyes, like a hawk's. By now, he'd been in jail for more than two weeks. His hair hung in greasy tangles, and there was a gravy stain on his rumpled orange jumpsuit. Crystal understood that the jail required prisoners to shower, but she could smell his sweat as soon as she stepped through the doorway.

Once upon a time, she'd thought Judd was sexy. She'd ridden behind him on his Harley, clinging to his muscular body and feeling like a queen. But then Frank Culhane had shown her a different kind of life and a different kind of love. After his tragic death, she'd never looked back. She'd moved on, and she was determined to keep moving.

She wasn't proud of the things she'd done with Judd—especially the drugs she'd tried. She'd never become addicted, and she'd quit after hooking up with Frank. But she couldn't help worrying that they might have affected her baby.

As Crystal approached the cell, still keeping her distance, he rose, shuffled forward, and leaned against the bars. The young man in the next cell paid them no attention.

"It's about time you came to see me, baby," Judd said. "I've been wondering what you've been up to since your rich boyfriend kicked the bucket."

"I'm working, mostly, and looking for a job in a classier place. I don't have to stay in this shithouse town forever. Was that your lawyer who just left?"

"Yeah. My trial's set for next week. He thinks he might get me off. It was entrapment, he says. That means I was set up. I could walk out of court a free man."

"That's great." Actually, it wasn't great. Crystal would have preferred him out of the way and unable to interfere with her plans.

His powerful hands gripped the bars, as if he wanted to bend them apart and reach out to her. "I've been missing you too long, baby," he said. "You hurt me bad, taking up with that rich old bastard. I'm not sorry he's dead. But when I get out, we can forget him and pick up where we left off. I can't wait to get you in the sack again, girl. I've been thinking about the things I want to do to you. It'll be like before, only better."

Crystal stifled a groan. Things were going from bad to worse. She had to finish this. She fought the wave of nausea that swept over her. She shouldn't have bolted down that chili dog after her shift. If Judd figured out she was pregnant, he could ruin everything.

"Oh, baby." His unearthly golden eyes welled with tears. "It's driving me crazy, being locked up like this. The only thing keeping me sane is knowing you're out there, waiting for me."

Crystal summoned her courage, braced for his reaction,

and forced herself to speak. "That's enough, Judd. I wish you well, but I'm not waiting for you. I came here for one reason tonight—to say goodbye."

"What the hell—"

"You heard me. I deserve better than a greasy drug dealer who lives over a garage and can't even get a decent job. I deserve better than a life of waiting for you to get out of jail. We're done, Judd. This time for good."

Turning her back on him, she walked away. But the sound of his voice, swearing and yelling, followed her out of the cell area and down the hall.

"You little bitch! Who's banging you now? Have you found yourself some other old prick with money? Well, you can go straight to hell! Hear me, bitch? Go to hell!"

Wanting to get away, Crystal raced down the hall, through the reception area, and out the door to her car—Judd's car, she remembered as she started the Hyundai's engine. With luck, she wouldn't need the old junker for long. If things worked out, she'd be able to buy any car she wanted.

Maybe even a Porsche like Lila Culhane's, but red, or maybe black . . .

As the shouted curses died away, Roper exchanged glances with the woman at the counter. She shrugged. "You get used to that sort of thing in here," she said. "You can see your brother now, Mr. McKenna. Ten-minute limit on your visit. You'll hear a bell when time's up."

Roper walked back down the hall. Rowdy, still in his jeans and plaid shirt, was huddled on the edge of his bunk. When Roper spoke his name, he raised a tear-ravaged face. Roper was torn between hugging his brother and wanting to shake some sense into the young fool. With iron bars between them, he could do neither.

"I'm sorry, Roper," he muttered. "How's Mom? I know she'll want to kill me."

"Mom's disappointed. We all are. We thought you'd been taught better. What happened, Rowdy?"

Rowdy sighed. "A guy at Jackalope's gave me a sample. He said he'd sell me more if I wanted. I took it out to my car to try it. The cop was right there, like he'd been waiting for me. I think I was set up."

"Have you used cocaine before?" Roper asked.

"No. Never. Honest."

"I'm not sure I believe you, brother. If you'd never used it, why did you take it, and how did you know what to do with it? I'll ask you again, Rowdy. Have you ever used cocaine?"

"Maybe . . . once or twice."

"Sure. How about marijuana?"

"Heck, everybody does that."

"Everybody? You mean like your brothers? Your sister?"

"Not Cheyenne. Maybe the boys. But I don't know for sure." He wiped his nose on his sleeve. "Hang it, Roper, I just want to go home! When are you going to stop grilling me and get me out of here?"

"Not until after your bail hearing tomorrow. And only then if the judge lets you go. Either way, I'll be there for you."

The warning bell rang, signaling an end to the visit.

"Don't go, Roper," Rowdy begged.

"Get some rest. I'll see you before your hearing." Roper forced himself to turn away and leave. Damn fool kid. He deserved to spend a night in jail. Maybe it would bring him to his senses. Meanwhile Roper had to call Chet Barr in the morning, get the stable ready for Fire Dance's arrival, and put things right with Lila. After what had happened between them tonight, things would never be the same between them. They would have to find new ways to get along.

And if that didn't work? If he couldn't keep his hands off her—or even keep from thinking about it?

Forcing the thought from his mind, Roper started the truck and headed out of town.

"Hey, kid, are you okay?"

The raspy voice startled Rowdy. He looked around. The rough-looking man in the next cell was watching him with his unsettling yellow eyes. "Sorry, kid, I didn't mean to scare you," he said.

"That's all right. I'm fine," Rowdy said. The man looked like someone his mother would have warned him about, but he seemed friendly enough. And any conversation was better than the silence of this place.

"I'm sorry about your girlfriend," Rowdy said.

"Yeah, that sucks." The man moved closer to the bars that separated the two of them. "When I get out of here, that bitch is going to pay. She'll be sorry for trying to dump me."

Something in his tone sent a chill up Rowdy's spine. He decided to change the subject. "I heard you say that your lawyer is going to get you off. How is that supposed to happen?"

Rowdy's newfound friend raked his greasy hair back from his face. "You know what entrapment is?"

"Not really. I just heard the word. Mainly from you."

"Entrapment means I was set up. A guy I didn't know made a buy. His partner arrested me. They were both cops. They're not allowed to trick me like that. If my lawyer can prove entrapment, I'm free as a bird."

He aimed a stream of spittle at the toilet in the corner of the cell, making a direct hit. "I heard what you said to your brother. If you really got set up, and you could prove it, you could claim entrapment, too."

"Do I need a lawyer? Yours, maybe?"

"Good lawyers cost money. You'll have a public defender tomorrow. They're mostly crap, but you can get a better one later. Just plead not guilty tomorrow and take it from there."

"Thanks for the advice," Rowdy said.

"You're a sharp boy. I could use somebody like you in my business. If you want to make good money, come see me after you're out. Just ask for Judd at Jackalope's."

"Thank you kindly, Judd," Rowdy said. "I make pretty good money riding broncs in the rodeo, but I'll keep you in mind."

"Do that, kid," Judd said as the overhead lights dimmed. "For now, I'm going to get some shut-eye."

He stretched out on his bunk and turned to face the wall.

Rowdy lay gazing up at the ceiling. He could hear the opening and closing of doors, muffled voices, and the sound of footfalls as the night shift came on. The place smelled of urine, bleach, and stale food. He hated it. But he wasn't as stupid as he'd made himself sound to Judd. He just wanted to learn enough to get out of here. He was too young, and too smart, to have his life ruined by one crappy arrest.

Sam woke with a start. The bungalow was quiet except for the whine of a mosquito in the dark bedroom. He was a sound sleeper, especially when he was tired. But just now, something had awakened him.

There it was again—this time he recognized the sound of his cell phone. Rolling onto his side, he grabbed it off the nightstand. The display window read *Unknown Caller.*

"Hullo," he muttered, taking the call.

"Sam, it's me."

His pulse leaped. Relief battled worry as he found his voice. "Jasmine—are you all right?"

"Yes, I'm fine, Sam. I bought a burner phone. I didn't want to risk getting you in trouble."

Hearing her voice made him feel like a lovestruck teenager. And even a burner phone, linked to his number, wouldn't be entirely safe. But she wouldn't be calling without a good reason. "What is it?" he asked. "Is something wrong? Your mother, is she—"

"No, mostly she seems about the same. But she says the headaches are getting worse, and I've noticed her stumbling sometimes, as if she can't keep her balance. She won't use a cane."

"Have you talked with her doctor?" Sam asked.

"Mother hasn't seen a doctor since we got here, or even called one on the phone. She says as long as the tumor's incurable, there's no point. She doesn't want to die throwing up and losing her hair. She just wants to live her life and let the end come when it comes." Her voice broke slightly.

"Knowing your mother, I'm not surprised," Sam said. Madeleine Culhane was a force of nature. Even when he'd had to arrest her for murder, Sam had admired her strength. He'd even liked her. And she'd made it clear that she'd liked him—especially as a match for her restless daughter.

"Does your brother know she's stopped treatment?" he asked.

"Mother wants to tell him herself. Darrin has a way of jumping in where he's not wanted. I expect she'll wait until things get worse. I've been helping her arrange her affairs. No surprises so far."

"I'm sorry," Sam said. "I wish there was something I could do to help."

"Where are you, Sam? Are you back at the ranch?"

"I got in last night. I'll start questioning people again in the morning. For the record, I'm glad it wasn't your mother who had your father killed."

She sighed. "So am I. Not that it would have made much difference. But it'll make the memories easier when she's gone."

"I love you, Jasmine. I wish you were here right now."

"So do I. But I'm needed here. I'd ask you about the case, but I know you're not allowed to talk about it."

"Will you let me know how it goes with your mother? You know that I won't share this with anybody. And be careful how you use that burner. Don't call me unless it's urgent."

"Don't worry, I won't. Get some rest now. I love you, too, Sam."

They ended the call. Sam lay back in the bed and tried to sleep. But he was wide awake now. A glance at the bedside clock told him it was 4:15 in the morning. Resigning himself to an early start, he dressed, made a cup of coffee, and took it onto the broad front porch. As he settled into a chair, he remembered sitting out there with Jasmine, their talks, and the lovemaking that had sometimes followed.

There was no way she would have murdered her father—unless there was something about their relationship she'd kept secret. He would trust Jasmine with his life, but it was his job to think like a cop. Everybody was a suspect, even the woman he loved.

Restless, Sam set his coffee cup on the porch and wandered down toward the paddocks. The first light of dawn cast the eastern hills into soft silhouette. In the grassy pastures, awakening birds trilled their calls on the morning air. The windmill creaked faintly in the breeze. Soon the ranch hands would be arriving to start their day. For now, except for the line of stock trailers, the employee lot was empty. Even the house was quiet.

But not everyone was asleep. Distant lights, barely visible, were moving on Charlie Grishman's game ranch. Looking beyond the fields, Sam could make out what appeared to be a huge truck pulling up to the animal compound. Was it some kind of delivery, made at an hour when it might not be noticed?

Charlie, a former math teacher, had turned a patch of worthless scrub land into a moneymaking operation. It was a deplorable business—unwanted animals kept under wretched conditions, then turned loose to be shot by would-be game hunters. Sam detested the little man. But Charlie was legally licensed. Policing him was not Sam's job.

Still, Charlie was on Sam's list of murder suspects. He lived alone and had no supporting alibi. It would have been easy enough for him to ambush Frank in the stable and plunge the deadly syringe into his neck. The only thing missing was a motive. Charlie was sitting pretty, piling money in the bank. Why should he risk it all by murdering his neighbor?

Sam planned to visit him in the next few days. But his first interview would be with the person who'd moved closer to the top of his list—Frank's glamorous widow.

Charlie paid the driver and watched the large enclosed delivery truck roll out of the gate. As the red taillights faded, he turned around to admire his prize.

Molly, a fifty-year-old Asian elephant, stood in the special enclosure Charlie had built with thick timbers and chain-link fencing. Her trunk was moving, exploring her new surroundings, maybe looking for food. Her massive weight shifted from side to side. A rumbling sound rose from her throat.

Owned by the proprietor of a bankrupt kiddy zoo, she'd spent most of her long life giving rides to children and their parents. Destined for a sanctuary, she'd ended up here when Charlie had offered the owner $5,000. Offers to hunt her were already coming in from Charlie's clients.

But Molly was far from an ideal game animal. Like most females of the Asian species, she had no tusks. The taxidermist had promised to add fakes for a more impressive trophy. But nothing could be done while Molly was alive.

Worse, Molly was as docile as a milk cow. She could be ridden, petted, and led without any resistance. Over the next couple of weeks, that would have to change, along with her name. It would be up to Charlie and his helpers to destroy her trust and turn her into a beast that would be a challenge and a thrill for any hunter to shoot.

He would start after breakfast. For now, he would give her some water and hay and post a guard to keep an eye on her. Then he would go back inside, check the offers in his email, and celebrate with a glass of Scotch.

When Sam saw Lila having her morning coffee on the patio, he took it as an invitation to join her. She looked up as he came through the wrought iron gate. The outdoor table was set with a linen cloth and an extra place. A single pink rose in a glass vase stood next to a carafe of coffee and a plate of buttered toast.

"Good morning, Agent Rafferty." She was flushed and rumpled, her eyes in shadow, as if she'd had a sleepless night. "I was expecting you," she said, forcing politeness. "Please have a seat. Would you like some coffee? As I recall, you drink it black."

"Thank you." He pulled out the chair across from her and sat down. The coffee would be his second cup, but that was all right. "And thank you for your hospitality," he said. "I know you aren't overjoyed to have me back."

"True. But if this is what it takes to find Frank's killer, I wish you a productive stay." She filled his cup from the carafe. "How is Madeleine? Have you heard?"

"I assume she's the same." His reply skirted the edge of truth.

"Would it shock you if I were to say that I wish she'd been guilty—especially since she actually meant to kill Frank?"

"Nothing shocks me anymore," Sam said. "All I want to do is find the truth."

She poured more coffee into her cup. ""Speaking of the truth, there's been a new development. And if this doesn't shock you, nothing will."

"I'm all ears."

"I know the identity of Frank's secret girlfriend—the woman in the photos. I've even met her. Her name is Crystal Carter. She's pregnant—and she claims the baby is Frank's."

Sam listened as Lila told him the whole story. How Crystal had called her pleading for help, how they'd met at the restaurant, and how Lila had insisted on a paternity test before talking with the young woman again.

"I arranged payment for the test, and I'll be waiting to hear from the doctor," she said. "He'll take Crystal's blood sample. Frank's DNA was collected at the crime scene. The doctor can get a copy of the results. When he has both, he'll send them to the lab. The analysis shouldn't take long."

"They can do that?" Sam asked. "Don't they have to get a sample from the baby's amniotic fluid?"

"No, this new way is safer. As I understand it, they can separate the baby's DNA from the mother's blood and match it against the alleged father's. It can't give legal proof that a man is the father, but if there's no match, it *can* prove that he isn't. That's the way I understand it."

"I'll take your word for that." Sam's coffee had cooled. He put the cup aside. "Did Frank know about the baby?"

"She planned to tell him before he was killed. At least that's what she claimed. But she could be lying. I've been thinking, what if she'd told him about the baby and demanded that he marry her, or at least give her money? He could have refused. That would have given her motive to kill him and take her story to me."

Lila's hands crumpled her linen napkin. "When I couldn't get pregnant, I began to suspect that Frank had had a secret vasectomy. I'll never know if that was true, but if it was, he'd have known at once that the baby wasn't his."

"Have you checked his medical records?"

"Yes. There's nothing. But for whatever reason, he could've had the operation done off the books—somewhere like Mexico."

"I'll need to talk to Miss Carter," Sam said. "Can you tell me how to find her?"

"She said she was working afternoons at Jackalope Saloon in Willow Bend. You've seen her from the back in the photo. She's petite, brunette, and pretty. You'd recognize her hands—the nails, the rings. I can give you her phone number, too."

"Thanks." Sam reorganized his mental list, with Crystal at the top. He would talk to her today if he could track her down. "What about the paternity test?" he asked. "When will you know the results?"

"That will depend on when Crystal goes in for the test and how long the results take. The doctor promised to rush the lab work for me. Of course, if I never hear, that will be my answer."

"What will you do if she's telling the truth? Have you thought about that?" Sam asked.

"I don't know. It will depend on what she wants. To paraphrase my grandma, I'll cross that bridge when I come to it."

Lila passed Sam a sheet of notepaper with a phone number written on it. Sam had pocketed it and was standing up to leave when he saw Roper's battered Ford pickup pull into the employee lot. Lila's gaze followed his as Roper climbed out and, without a glance in their direction, strode toward the stable.

Sam glanced at Lila. Her lips were parted, her hands twisting her napkin. The signs were subtle, but Sam sensed a new conflict between her and Roper.

"I heard that Roper will be taking Frank's place in the Run for a Million," he said. "Will he be riding that big roan stallion?"

"No," Lila said. "He thinks One in a Million is too old, and none of our other horses are ready for the competition. He plans on borrowing another horse from a breeder."

"And the breeder will get half the prize if he wins. Where does that leave you?"

"We're still negotiating." She didn't look pleased. "I'm asking for a cut of his share if he wins. But I don't know what the fuss is about. Roper will be competing against the best riders in the world. Even on a great horse, there's no way he's going to win. We're going to war over nothing."

Going to war. Sam had been right about the conflict between them. But was it just about horses and money? Sam's success as a lawman had hinged, in part, on his ability to read people. Something deeper was going on here. But he would leave it for now, at least until he'd gotten

Roper's side of the story. Taking his leave of Lila, he followed the cobblestone path to the stable.

Roper was high on Sam's suspect list. His parents had backed up his alibi, but they could be lying to protect him. And his motive was undeniable. Frank's death had bought him a chance at the Run for a Million. Now, if Sam's hunch was right, it might have bought him something more.

The stable hands were arriving, their vehicles pulling into the parking lot. Roper had disappeared into the stable. Following the sound, Sam found him sweeping out an empty box stall. A cart piled with clean straw stood outside the sliding gate.

Roper looked up as Sam stepped into sight. "So you're back on the job, are you?" he said.

"I'm afraid so. Maybe this time I'll catch the real killer. Can I give you a hand with anything?"

"Thanks for the offer, but I'll pass." Roper put the broom aside and began forking straw to cover the floor mat in the stall.

"Is this for the new horse?" Sam asked.

"Not really new, just borrowed for the competition. Fire Dance should be arriving late today. I guess Lila told you he was coming."

"She mentioned he might be. That was all."

"What else did she mention?"

"That the two of you were still negotiating."

Roper forked a heap of straw and flung it, almost angrily, into the far corner of the stall. "The negotiations are over. You can tell Lila that she won. She'll be getting everything she asked for."

"You might want to tell her yourself."

"That'll have to wait," Roper said. "I've got a lot going on here, and I'm due in Willow Bend by eight this morning."

Was this something new? Sam remained silent, waiting for Roper to volunteer more.

Roper raked the straw to make a thick, even layer. "All right. Since you're bound to hear about it sooner or later, I need to be in court for my fool brother's bail hearing. Cocaine possession. First arrest. For now, he'll have a public defender who won't give a damn about him. I figure he'll need somebody there to make sure he's all right."

"What about the rest of your family?"

"They're keeping their distance. My mother's angry at him for disgracing the family. My stepdad can't get there alone. And the youngsters don't want to show up and call attention to what's happened—Rowdy's arrest would make juicy back page reading in the tabloids."

"So it falls on you to play the big brother," Sam said. "I'm sorry, Roper. Family problems are the worst."

"You sound like someone who knows. What about your family? I've never asked you."

"One ex-wife, no kids. My brother died young in a car accident and my parents are long gone, so there's just me. I don't know what I can do to help your situation, but if you need anything—within the limits of my job, of course—feel free to ask."

"Of course. Thanks anyway."

Sam felt the chill in his words. The last time he was here, he and Roper had formed a cautious friendship. But everyone at the ranch was a murder suspect, and this man was among the most likely. Roper would surely be aware of that.

Roper finished with the stall and spent a few minutes directing his workers. Then he went out to his truck.

As Sam watched him drive away, he reflected on what he'd seen and heard. When Roper had talked about Lila and their so-called negotiations, Sam could sense the frustration he was barely holding back. There was something going on between the two of them. But unless it concerned

Frank's murder, it was none of his business. For now, all he could do was watch and wait.

It was too early yet to catch Crystal at work. He would drive to Willow Bend after lunch and hope to find her. If she was telling the truth about her pregnancy—or even if she was lying—her situation could cast his case in a whole new light.

Chapter Five

Roper had posted his brother's $500 bail and followed Rowdy's truck home, where his mother waited to lay on the shame. Against the advice of his public defender, Rowdy had elected to plead not guilty. His trial had yet to be scheduled. Meanwhile, since Rowdy couldn't leave the county to compete in the rodeos, he'd be put to work on the ranch, finishing the stable and building more fences. He'd whined and complained about that, but Roper couldn't be bothered to listen. His brother had some hard lessons to learn.

After seeing Rowdy safe with the family, Roper turned the truck around and headed back to the Culhane Ranch. By now it was midmorning. He'd spent a couple of precious hours handling Rowdy's situation. Now it was time to deal with his own.

Lila was his first priority. With Fire Dance already on the road and due sometime that afternoon, he needed to square things with his boss.

His beautiful boss.

As he drove, the memory swept over him—Lila's legs wrapping his hips, her eager body, her little cries as he brought her to climax.

With a curse, Roper forced the images from his mind. But his body remembered—the feel of her skin on his, the fragrance of her hair, her seeking mouth, and the warm moistness that had welcomed him home . . .

As he turned the truck into the employee lot, he could see her standing on the patio. Was she waiting for him? Did she know that he'd already arranged for Fire Dance's delivery?

Braced for the confrontation that had to come, Roper left his truck and strode across the lot and up the path to the patio gate. She held her ground, waiting for him to come to her. Only as he opened the gate and stepped through did she speak.

"Sam told me you'd sent for the horse." Her voice carried a distinct chill.

"Did he also tell you that I'd accepted your terms?" Roper faced her, taking stock of her stubbornly set chin and the flash of temper in her coppery eyes.

"He did. At least you could have told me yourself."

"There wasn't a good time—I was dealing with a family problem. I called Chet Barr last night because I needed to let him know my decision. By then it was too late to bother you."

"And today? What's your excuse?"

After a morning that had tried his patience, Roper's temper broke through. The woman might be his boss, but he wasn't accountable to her for every minute of his life. "My kid brother was in jail for cocaine possession. I was there to post bail and make sure he went straight home. And if you're expecting an apology—"

"Of course not." Her expression softened. "I'm sorry about your brother, Roper. I hope he'll be all right. But you could have called."

"It wasn't the most pressing thing on my mind. The horse will be here this afternoon, and I'll have my hands full. I've agreed to your terms—all expenses for Fire Dance and twenty-five percent of my prize if we win. If you want to draw up an agreement, I'll sign it."

"That won't be necessary. I'll hold you to your word."

"Thanks. I mean it, Boss." Roper hadn't meant for the informal name to sound like a caress, but it had. He and Lila would have a lot of tension to work through, especially after Fire Dance's arrival. But at least they'd made it this far.

"We'll talk later," he said, turning away. "I'll be working if you need me."

"I'll keep that in mind."

Her words followed Roper as he strode away. He'd do well to remind himself that she was in charge. But in the weeks ahead, he'd be walking a tightrope between the need to meet her expectations and his burning desire to win.

Sitting on the bed in her rented room at the Blue Rose, Crystal keyed the doctor's number on her phone, then quickly cancelled the call. Her hands trembled as she put down the phone.

She wasn't ready for the test. She was too scared. What if the baby turned out to be Judd's? All her hopes, all her plans for a better life would be gone—and she would be faced with the prospect of an unwanted pregnancy.

Lighting a cigarette, she took a long, languid drag. Smoking was bad for the baby, but she needed something to calm her nerves.

If only she could find out about the baby's father before going to Lila's doctor for the test. As things stood, Lila would get the test results first. Then she would make the follow-up call to Crystal. Crystal would be at her mercy—the bitch could even lie to her if she chose not to deal with Frank's baby and its mother.

Of course, Crystal could go to another doctor first. But

because she had no insurance, the test would cost more than she could afford.

After tamping out the cigarette in an empty plastic soda cup, she did a search on her phone. She found several labs in Abilene that advertised walk-in DNA testing. But the price was still too high.

Then she remembered something. Last year, a cocktail waitress named Monique had a paternity test done on her unborn baby. Single and uninsured, she could not have paid for a regular test. She had to know somebody or know of a place to get it done cheap.

Monique was still working the night shift at the saloon. With luck, she'd be there tonight, willing and able to give Crystal the information she needed.

It felt good to have a plan in mind. Still thinking about the test, Crystal swung off the bed, walked into the bathroom, and started her makeup ritual. Besides her own blood, the test would require a DNA sample from the possible father. She had nothing from Frank, but that was all right. Judd had left plenty of DNA in his car—beer cans, cigarette butts, soiled napkins, tissues, and more. Surely she could find something that would work. If Judd's sample came up negative for a match, that would mean the baby was Frank's. Simple.

So why did she feel so nervous?

Dressed in her hostess outfit of tight jeans, a fitted black tee, and high-heeled boots, she checked the time on her phone. She was already late for her afternoon shift at Jackalope's. Picking up her purse and keys, she strode outside to the junk heap that passed as a car.

Sam was waiting when the saloon opened. Taking a booth, he ordered a Michelob and settled back into the shadows. A few customers wandered in to sit at the bar, where an elderly bartender was setting up drinks. Country music blared over speakers mounted above the bar. So far, there was no sign of the hostess Sam had come to meet. He sipped his beer and waited.

Moments later, she arrived, rushing in through the back entrance. Her high-heeled boots clicked across the wooden floor. Sam recognized her at once from the photos he'd seen and from Lila's description. Despite her overdone makeup, she was even prettier than he'd expected. Sam could understand how a man such as Frank—past his prime and fighting to hold on to his youthful virility—might become infatuated with her. But was this beautiful young woman an innocent victim or a predator, capable of extortion and possibly murder?

Now, while the place was quiet, would be the best time to question her. Sam slid out of the booth. Displaying his badge, he walked over to where she stood. "Miss Carter, I'm Agent Rafferty, FBI," he said, letting the music cover his voice. "I need to ask you a few questions."

Her eyes widened like a startled animal's. "Am I in some kind of trouble?" she asked.

"No. I just need to verify some information. Can you sit with me for a few minutes?"

She glanced around the room. "Just for a few minutes," she said. "I'm on the clock."

"Understood. I won't keep you long." He motioned her toward a seat in the booth.

Crystal faced the FBI agent across the table. He was a good-looking man with movie star features and the bluest eyes she'd ever seen. But something in his unsmiling manner set off alarms in her head. Maybe Judd had said something to get her in trouble.

"What's this about?" she asked him.

"I'm investigating the murder of Frank Culhane," he said. "I understand you knew him."

The dread inside her chilled and darkened. So this wasn't about Judd. It was worse. "But didn't you find the man's killer?" she asked. "That's what I heard."

He shook his head, his expression unreadable. "It turned out we were mistaken. I asked you a question, Miss Carter."

Crystal sighed. "All right, yes, I knew Frank," she said. "He came in here sometimes. He seemed lonely. We were friends."

"Anything else? According to Lila Culhane, you were more than friends. In fact, you told her that you were pregnant with Frank's baby. Is there any truth to that?"

Crystal's gaze dropped to the table. "We were in love," she said. "He wanted to marry me. He would have if she hadn't—I mean, if he hadn't been killed."

The blue eyes narrowed. "I caught what you almost said. Were you about to tell me that Lila killed her husband?"

"Who else would have done it? Frank was going to leave her. He'd promised me he would." Crystal could imagine how naïve she must sound. All to the good.

"Did Frank know about the baby?"

"I never got the chance to tell him. Lila's insisting that I take a paternity test before she'll even talk to me. I'm making the arrangements. But I really shouldn't have to bother with that. I know my baby is Frank's. There was nobody else. Why can't she just believe me?"

"I'll ask you straight out. Where were you the night—or morning—when Frank was killed?"

"Sleeping in my room at the Blue Rose. I was alone."

"And you were there all night?"

"Yes. I didn't see Frank. He'd told me he was busy." She glanced around, looking for any excuse to get away. Three cowboys, sweating and dusty from a morning on the range, had just walked in through the front door. Crystal slid out of the booth. "It's back to work for me. I hope you've heard enough, Agent."

"For now." His face revealed nothing as he passed a card across the table. "Call this number if you have anything more to tell me. Don't be surprised if I pay you another visit."

"That's fine." She tucked the card into her pocket. "I have nothing to hide. And everybody's welcome at Jackalope's."

Forcing a playful smile, she sashayed over to meet her customers. Inside, she was shaking. Clearly, the agent had tried to catch her in a lie. How much did he know that he wasn't telling her? Did he actually suspect her of murder?

Only one thing was certain. She couldn't trust the handsome FBI agent. He was clearly out to trap her any way he could.

Smiling and chatting, she showed the cowboys to a table. When she turned around again, Rafferty was gone.

While he was in town, Sam decided to pay a call on Darrin and Simone. He hadn't talked with them since before Madeleine's arrest. Sam was aware that Jasmine's brother was up to his neck in schemes to get rid of Lila, including his part in causing her car accident. Technically, with charges dropped against his mother, Darrin was subject to arrest. But Sam and Nick had agreed to let him run for now and watch where he led them.

As he mounted the steps to the historic bungalow-style house, Sam remembered coming here the first time with Jasmine as his guide. They'd arrived to hear a violent argument through the front door. Had anything changed? Sam was about to find out.

As he raised his hand to ring the doorbell, he heard voices from the far side of the door. After a moment of listening, he realized he was hearing a TV talk show. Sam rang the bell.

After a short delay, the door opened a few inches. Simone peered up at him. "Oh, it's you," she said. "What are you doing here? Haven't we told you everything we know?"

"I'm sure you've heard that your mother-in-law wasn't responsible for Frank's death," Sam said. "I'm back on the case, and I need to talk to both of you again. Is Darrin here?"

"He's in court this afternoon."

The narrow opening of the door remained. She seemed almost frightened.

"If you're uncomfortable being alone, I can come back when Darrin's here," Sam said. "Is there a good time?"

She hesitated. Then the door opened wider. "No, it's all right," she said, stepping back, giving Sam room to enter. "You can come in. I was just watching TV. I can turn it off. Would you like some ice cream?" Sam detected a note of desperation in her voice.

"It's tempting," Sam said, "but I'll pass, thanks. I don't plan to be here long."

Only as she bent to pick up the remote from the coffee table did he notice the blaze of florid color down the left side of her face—the early stages of a nasty bruise. Sam had seen marks likes that before. Simone had been slapped—hard.

Switching off the television, she turned away, trying to hide the evidence; when it became clear that he'd already noticed it, she faked a laugh. "Don't I look a fright? I got up in the night and stumbled into the doorframe. I've tried putting ice on it, but . . ." She shrugged. "I'll just have to wait until it goes away—and watch my step. Being pregnant has made me so clumsy."

"My sympathies. I've taken some clumsy steps myself." Sam sensed that she wouldn't want him to voice the truth. "Are you all right?"

"Yes, I'm as right as rain. Have a seat on the sofa, Agent. You're sure you wouldn't want some ice cream? It's chocolate, the best."

"You've talked me into it. But only if you'll have some with me." He was doing his best to put her at ease.

"Certainly. But only a little bit for me. Darrin says I'm getting fat."

"Not too much for me, either. I gained ten pounds on my last visit to the ranch." Sam took a seat and watched her walk into the kitchen. Her sundress was tight through the bodice, the waist hitched up to ride above the slight bulge of her belly. But that was as it should be. She was pregnant. What kind of husband would slap his pregnant wife and taunt her about putting on weight? The last modicum of respect Sam might have felt toward Darrin was slipping away fast.

But he was a federal agent, here to solve a crime, he reminded himself. It was his job to view every suspect without prejudice and without emotion. That included Darrin, Simone, and even Jasmine.

Simone returned with two small bowls of chocolate ice cream. She handed one to Sam and sat down on the far end of the sofa, turning to face him. Sam spooned a taste and nodded. "Not bad," he said.

"It's my favorite brand, and it was on sale." Simone took a spoonful, swirling it in her mouth before setting the bowl on the table and fixing her gaze on Sam. "Agent, I invited you in for a reason. I've suspected all along that

Lila was having an affair with her horse trainer, but I had no proof. Now I do."

"Go on." Sam had sensed the tension between Lila and Roper, but this was new.

"We have a witness who saw them—not exactly doing it, but that had to be what was happening."

"Who was the witness?" Sam demanded.

"It was Mariah. Darrin's mother asked her to keep an eye on them, and she did. They were in that little shed that houses the sprinkler controls. Mariah saw them go in and come out."

Sam tried to picture the shed. Not much room in there. But room enough, he supposed.

"So you were in touch with Darrin's mother?"

"Darrin called her," Simone said. "She agreed to phone Mariah. Mariah would do anything for her."

"How is Madeleine doing? Did she say? Did Darrin talk to Jasmine?"

Simone shook her head. "I guess not. But we were talking about Lila and her affair. Now that we have proof—"

"But proof of what?" Sam's ice cream was melting. He set the bowl on the coffee table. "There's still no proof Lila was having an affair while she was married to Frank. And even if she did, I can't arrest people for sleeping together. I'm looking for evidence in a murder case."

"But what about motive, means, and opportunity? They had it all."

"True. And I appreciate your efforts to help the case. But what I need is proof that will hold up in court. I'm still looking for that." Sam stood up to leave. "You have my card. Call me if there's anything more you need to tell me."

"I'll let Darrin know you came by," she said, reaching for the remote. "Is there anything I should tell him?"

"That's up to you. Don't get up, Simone. I'll see myself out. Thank you for your hospitality and your time."

He left her and drove away, lost in thought. Darrin was capable of violence. Did that mean he was also capable of murder? As for Simone, she'd shown herself to be ambitious, even scheming. But she and her unborn baby were vulnerable. It wasn't Sam's place to interfere in a marriage without cause. He could only offer her a lifeline in case the situation became dangerous. Maybe tonight he would risk a call to Jasmine. She was in the best position to understand her brother. She might have some insights to offer.

But what was he thinking? Hadn't he just told Jasmine not to communicate with him except in an emergency?

He was nearing the ranch when a red Corvette roared around him on the two-lane paved highway and sped on ahead. Sam swore as he recognized the car and its driver. It was Charlie Grishman.

The Corvette had been Jasmine's, a prized gift from her father. When Charlie had found evidence that she'd been with the animal rights group who'd raided his property, set a fire, and freed many of the animals, the Corvette had bought Charlie's silence and kept Jasmine out of jail.

Now the little rat was wasting no opportunity to flaunt the beautiful car. Sam watched as he made a hard left turn, ground the gears, and sped up the graveled side road to his ranch. The way he was abusing that car, it would serve him right if he crashed it.

Tomorrow, Sam resolved, he would pay a call on the man. He'd been to Charlie's place before. He wasn't looking forward to the noise and foul odors of the place, the wretched pens and cages, and the frustration of not being able to change the situation. At least Jasmine had tried. She couldn't help it if the protest, meant to attract attention, had spiraled out of control.

Charlie was still on Sam's list of suspects. But so far, he'd been unable to come up with a motive. Maybe he needed to take a closer look.

Could Frank have done anything to make an enemy of Charlie? True, he'd kept Charlie from pursuing Jasmine—probably threatened him with bodily harm if he came near her. But that hardly seemed like a reason for murder.

But what if there was another connection—a hidden connection—like blackmail? Charlie was certainly capable of that. It was how he'd gotten his hands on Jasmine's Corvette.

Maybe he'd discovered a secret from Frank's past and was extorting money from him. But no—Sam dismissed the idea. Why would Charlie kill off his cash cow? And it didn't make sense that Frank would be blackmailing Charlie either.

It could be something else, then. Or maybe nothing. Sam would keep his eyes and ears open tomorrow when he paid a call on Charlie and his menagerie.

His thoughts shifted as he drove in through the ranch gate. Roper's truck was back in the lot, along with a luxury-class truck and horse trailer, parked outside the stable. Sam could see the Barr Stables logo on the trailer's side. Roper's horse for the million-dollar reining event had arrived.

Fire Dance snorted, yanked at his halter, and tried to bolt as Roper led him down the trailer ramp and into the stable. Chet Barr had warned him that the stallion could be skittish at first, especially in a new place, so Roper was prepared for some hijinks. Still, it was a relief to get the nervous horse safely in the stall.

Speaking softly and avoiding any sudden moves, Roper backed out of the stall and closed the gate behind him.

He'd hoped to be in the arena before day's end. But the stallion needed time to calm down.

Looking over the gate, Roper studied the horse he'd chosen to carry him in the Run for a Million. The stallion was magnificent, from the flare of his nostrils to the muscles of his powerful haunches. His coat was the color of a newly minted penny, his large eyes alert and intelligent. But the most striking thing about Fire Dance was the energy that quivered in every muscle, every movement. If that energy could be focused on his performance in the arena, he would be unstoppable. If not, the jumpy, suspicious horse could be a disaster.

"Hello, boy," Roper murmured. "You and I have got a lot of work to do and not much time to get it done. For starters, we'll be learning to trust each other."

Hayden Barr, Chet's son who'd delivered the stallion, had come up behind Roper. "Fire Dance is a great horse," he said. "But he's got a mind of his own. I competed on him in the last Cactus Classic. We didn't make the cut—let's just say we had a disagreement that cost us points. He's got the potential to win it all, but you have to show him who's boss."

"I can see that already," Roper said. "I hope I can handle him."

"Dad wouldn't have offered you the horse if he didn't believe you could." Hayden was in his early twenties, tall and lean, and he moved with the easy grace of a natural rider. With dark hair curling low over his collar, arresting hazel eyes, and a lopsided smile, Hayden bore no resemblance to his stocky, blond father.

"So, are you registered for the Shootout?" Roper asked him.

"Not this year," Hayden said. "I've got a prime cutting horse, and I'll be going for the Cutting Horse Challenge.

The competition is killer, but I'll never make it if I don't take a chance. I'm in this to win."

"Aren't we all? But good luck with that. I'll be cheering for you." Roper signed the paperwork that Hayden had brought—two copies, specifying the terms and limits of the stallion's use, liability for damages, and any financial arrangements involved.

"We'll be picking up the stallion in Vegas after the event. Let us know if there's a problem."

"Will do. Tell your dad I'll be doing my best to win that million for both of us."

After Hayden left, Roper turned his full attention back to Fire Dance. Staying outside the stall for now, he studied the horse over the gate. The stallion eyed him, clearly sizing him up. He snorted, his ears twitching and shifting.

Roper's success as a rider and trainer depended on his bonding with the horse, allowing him to use and receive silent body signals. The key to that bond was trust—and winning Fire Dance's trust could be a challenge.

The stallion knew the routines and could do them perfectly, at dazzling speed. Roper had seen him compete. But without that vital connection between horse and rider, there'd be no chance of winning.

"What a beautiful horse." Lila had come up behind him. She spoke softly to avoid startling the stallion. "He looks spectacular. When are you going to ride him?"

"I was hoping to start today. But he needs time to settle in. I'll try him in the morning—first thing, before the workday starts. I'm aware that I agreed to keep up with my regular schedule. That means I'll be training with him early mornings and late evenings."

"I take it you won't be getting much sleep." A smile played around her lips, stirring the memory of her kisses. For a fleeting moment, Roper dared hope she might give him more time. But this was Lila. She would hold him to his promise.

"Sleep is the least of my concerns," he said. "In fact, I plan to spend the night here, with Fire Dance. I want him to know that, even in a strange place, I'll be here to keep him safe."

"In that case, I'll have some supper sent out," Lila said. "I want you and the stallion to do well, even though you won't be riding for the Culhane Stables."

"You should, since you'll be getting a hundred twenty-five thousand dollars in prize money if we win."

"Yes, there is that," she said, and turned to go.

Too late, as she walked away, Roper realized he'd rebuffed a sincere effort to make peace. But it was too late to apologize. And now, from far down the row of box stalls came a shrill and angry call.

One in a Million had caught the scent of a rival stallion. He was screaming his challenge.

CHAPTER SIX

Crystal had stayed past the end of her shift to wait for Monique. The wait paid off. Monique, who'd married the father of her baby, was willing to share the phone number of the friend who'd done her in vitro paternity test.

"Tony works in a real lab," Monique explained. "He's just an assistant and not cleared to do the test, but he knows how. For five hundred dollars cash, he'll meet you and take your samples. Then he'll go into the lab after closing time and run the test. You should get a call from him in a day or two. The results won't hold up in court, but if you're just curious—"

"That'll be fine, thanks." Crystal was relieved that Monique hadn't asked for details about her situation.

She called the cell number from her car and was lucky enough to reach Tony on the first try. She listened as he told her what to do, where to go, and what time to be there.

She would have to drive to Abilene to meet him, deliver the cash and samples, and get her blood drawn. That could be managed. As for the payment, Judd had drug money stashed in his room above the garage. Crystal still had the key he'd given her. She could help herself to the five hundred, with enough extra for the trip. It was only fair that Judd contribute to something that could be his fault.

As she started the car, she could feel the excitement pulsing through her veins. She was taking charge of her future. With luck, what she learned over the next few days would set a course for the life she'd dreamed of.

And if the baby turned out to be Judd's?

That would be bad news.

Roper had passed a sleepless night in the stable. He'd spent most of the time talking to Fire Dance, brushing him, and even singing to him, getting the stallion accustomed to his scent and the sound of his voice.

One in a Million had needed attention as well. The older stallion was accustomed to sharing the stable and paddock with other males—his own offspring and other colts he'd known from their weanling days. And he got along fine with other stallions at show events. But this was different. It was as if, in Fire Dance, the big roan sensed a threat to his territory and his place as number one horse in the stable. His deeply buried ancestral genes were urging him to defend what was his.

Roper had spent time trying to calm him in the night. He'd never known a well-bred and well-trained horse to behave this way. Maybe witnessing Frank's murder had traumatized the big roan in ways that even a horse expert couldn't understand.

For now, the two stallions would need to be kept apart. Later this morning, after the grooms arrived, One in a Million could be turned loose in the paddock to run off his nervous energy. Roper hoped that, with time, One in a Million would calm down and come to accept his perceived rival.

At first light, Roper found the saddle, bridle, blanket,

and leg wrappings that had been delivered with Fire Dance. The young chestnut stallion was still edgy, but wearing the familiar tack seemed to remind him that it was time to go to work. He followed meekly as Roper led him through the stable and out into the arena, talking to him all the way.

"It's all right, boy. You'll do your job, I'll do mine. We're going to become a team, and we're going to win that million-dollar prize . . ."

As he put a boot in the stirrup to mount, Roper found himself wondering whether he believed his own words. Had he made the right decision choosing this horse? He thought about the times he'd ridden One in a Million in practice and in their single stunning competition—their wordless connection, as if the big roan could read his mind. Roper had known from the beginning that the great horse would give all that was asked of him, and more.

Even as he settled into the saddle, Roper could hear the muffled challenge calls from the far side of the stable. He closed his ears to the sound. One in a Million had been a true legend with the heart of a champion. But he was too old, too slow, and too fragile to compete for the year's biggest prize in reining.

Roper felt Fire Dance's body tighten beneath him as he nudged the stallion to a walk. But as the warm-up progressed, the horse began to relax. As Roper nudged him faster, he fell into the rhythm of an easy trot. His smooth gait was like the feel of driving a pricey new car.

As they eased into a routine of turns, gallops, and sliding stops, taking it slow at first, Roper's doubts began to lift. Fire Dance was an impressive horse. With trust and communication, they could become a winning team—even *the* winning team.

Someone was watching from the open side of the arena, standing in a shaft of morning sunlight. Roper's pulse quickened as he realized it was Lila.

He hadn't expected her to show up. But it meant something that she'd cared enough to come. Now that she was here, he wanted to show her what Fire Dance could do. With a tightening of his knees, he urged the stallion to a lope. The horse responded to his touch, swift and sure, changing directions on cue. Confidence growing, Roper urged him to the gallop that would end in a sliding stop.

With his attention focused on the horse, Roper was barely aware that the grooms had arrived and started their work in the stable. Only as Fire Dance had completed the slide and was taking the backward steps that would end the pattern did Roper hear the frantic shouts and the sound of running feet.

In the next instant, One in a Million exploded out of the stable and into the arena. With a scream of fury, he headed straight for Fire Dance.

Startled, Fire Dance reared. Still in the saddle, Roper fought to pull the younger stallion back, away from the attack. Freeing a boot from the stirrup, he tried to distract the big roan with a kick to the shoulder. But One in a Million was relentless, rearing, flailing his hooves, flashing his teeth as he tried to bite his rival. Fire Dance screamed as a flying hoof struck his hindquarters. Roper reined him back, but One in a Million kept coming, determined to do some damage.

Suddenly someone was there, leaping in from the side to seize One in a Million's halter. Roper's heart lurched as he realized it was Lila. She gripped the halter with both hands, trying to pull the big roan down, but against his strength, her slight weight was no more than a feather. She was pulled off her feet and swung like a rag doll against the stallion's side.

"*No!*" Roper cried out as she lost her hold and fell to the arena floor, landed hard, and lay still.

The grooms—three strong young men—were running in

from the stable. Two of them flanked One in a Million and seized the stallion's halter from either side. Wrestling him under control, they maneuvered him back to a safe distance. He stood between them, eyes rolling, sides heaving. The third man grabbed Fire Dance's reins, freeing Roper to fling himself out of the saddle and race to where Lila lay.

Sick with worry, he dropped to his knees next to her. She lay curled on her side. Her eyes were closed. The slight rise and fall of her ribs, beneath her cream silk blouse, told him she was still breathing, but that didn't mean she was all right. She could be badly injured, even dying. Lord help him, what if he'd lost her?

Not daring to move her for fear of injuries, he gave her shoulder a gentle squeeze. "Lila," he murmured. "Can you hear me?"

A whimper rose from her throat. Her eyelids fluttered and opened. She blinked, her expression confused. "What . . . happened?" She mouthed the words.

"You got tossed," he said. "Can you move?"

Cautiously, she straightened one leg, then the other. Her hands stirred, opened, and closed. So far so good. Watching her, Roper realized he was sweating with relief. "Take it slow. Don't try to sit up yet," he said. "You've had a nasty fall. You could be in shock, maybe even have a concussion or internal injuries."

"The horses . . . ," she said, finding her voice.

"Yes. The horses. They're all right." He remembered then that the grooms were there, holding the horses and waiting for his orders.

"Take One in a Million to the paddock and turn him loose," he said. "Make sure he has water. And have somebody keep an eye on him." Roper didn't have to ask how the horse had escaped his stall. One of the stable hands had likely opened the gate for cleaning, expecting no trouble. The stallion had bolted.

"Take Fire Dance back to his stall," he told the other groom. "Rub him down, check him for any injuries, and make him comfortable. If he's hard to handle, close the gate and leave him. I'll be there as soon as I can."

"You can go now, Roper." Lila was sitting up. "Just get me on my feet. I'll be fine."

Looking at her, thinking how close he might have come to losing this precious woman, Roper felt his relief turn to anger. As the grooms and horses vanished into the stable, that anger boiled over.

"Damn it, Boss, you could've been trampled to death. You're lucky to be alive! What in hell's name were you thinking?"

Lila's head went up. The jut of her chin showed her stubborn pride. "Don't lecture me, Roper. What if One in a Million had torn into Mr. Barr's valuable horse and injured him, maybe even killed him? Somebody had to stop what was happening."

"But you didn't help. All you did was get yourself slammed around and damn near killed. I could deal with an injured horse if I had to. But, blast it, I don't know if I could deal with losing you!"

Her eyes met his. He saw the flash of vulnerability before she looked away, and he knew he'd said too much. She had to know that he had feelings for her. They'd even made love—a mistake they'd both be wise to regret. But this was the wrong time, and he'd be a fool to hope that the time would ever be right.

He'd made a mistake, bringing the stallion here to train. Roper knew that now. He should have said goodbye to Lila and left for good. But now it was too late to change things. Against his better judgment, he'd fallen in love with her.

Standing, he held out his hand. "Do you feel okay to get up?" he asked her.

"I told you, I'm fine. Nothing broken."

"We'll see about that. Take it slow." Clasping the free hand she offered, he began to ease her up. "Tell me if something doesn't feel right. After a fall like that—"

"I said I was fine." She put her weight on her feet. "See? Go take care of the horses. I can—" She swayed against him. "Sorry, just a little dizzy, and my shoulder hurts. I think it might be . . ."

He caught her, supporting her against his side. "No arguments, Boss. I'm taking you to the house. Mariah can drive you to the clinic and get you checked over. And if you ever do anything that stupid again, so help me—"

"Stop fussing like an old biddy hen, Roper. You've got bigger problems on your hands. All right, if you insist, I'll ask Mariah to drive me to the clinic. Just get me into the house."

Drinking his morning coffee on the front porch of the bungalow, Sam watched the unfolding drama—first, Roper supporting Lila across the patio and into the house; then, minutes later, the black Escalade, Frank's former vehicle, roaring down the driveway with Mariah at the wheel and Lila in the passenger seat. As the Escalade cleared the front gate, Roper was seen racing back down the path to the stable.

Sam was curious. But barging in, demanding fast answers to his questions, would get him nowhere. Until he knew more about what had happened, and whether it had a bearing on his investigation, he could learn more by watching and listening.

But the questions were already swarming like hornets in his mind. Had Lila's evident injury been an accident or another attempt on her life? And did Roper's clear concern for Lila back up Simone's claim that the two were lovers?

That would give added weight to the theory that Roper was the killer. Motive, means, and opportunity—the horse trainer had all three in spades.

And what about Mariah? If the housekeeper was still taking orders from Madeleine, other motives could be at work. Would Mariah obey an order to kill? Would Lila be safe with her?

When Sam had returned to the Frank Culhane murder scene, he'd expected a rehash of things he'd already learned. But he couldn't have been more wrong. Being here again was like starting over—new facts, new relationships, even new people.

Sam had decided to skip breakfast this morning. He was planning a visit to Charlie Grishman's place, and the thought of that foul-smelling compound and those wretched animals killed any appetite for food. Last night, the distant boom of rifle fire had awakened him from sleep. Charlie was still in business, and evidently, business was thriving.

Twenty minutes later, wearing his badge and Glock, Sam was driving the road to Charlie's game ranch. It was a shame he couldn't prove Charlie guilty of Frank's murder. It would give him a world of satisfaction to see the vile man hauled off to jail while the animal welfare people cleaned up the mess he'd left behind.

The main entrance to Charlie's property was closed with a locked bar across the driveway. Beyond the gate, parked in front of the rambling frame house with its wide verandah, was the red Corvette Charlie had extorted from Jasmine.

Leaving the SUV, Sam ducked under the bar and walked up the driveway. The high-walled animal compound—chain-link mesh interwoven with plastic strips to hide the view—rose on the far side of a graveled lot, which held several trucks, four-wheelers, and assorted equipment for hoisting and hauling. Two ravens perched on a power line, as if waiting to share a meal.

The morning breeze carried the stench of rotting meat, musty hay, and animal dung. Sam, who'd been here before, had been braced for the odors. But what shocked him was the sound that rose from behind the wall—something between a trumpet blast and an anguished scream. He'd heard that sound only in movies. But he knew at once the kind of animal that had made it. The realization sickened him.

The front door of the house opened. Charlie strolled out onto the verandah. A cocky little man, dressed in rumpled khakis, he gave Sam a mocking grin.

"I heard you were back, Mr. FBI man," he said. "I heard your girlfriend's gone, too, the little bitch. Can't say I'm sorry about that. Come sit down and ask me whatever's on your mind. I've got nothing to hide."

Sam stood at the foot of the steps. "Charlie, please tell me that the animal I just heard isn't what I think it is."

Charlie's self-satisfied grin widened. "What you heard is going to make me big money," he said. "Come on, I'll show it to you."

Sam followed Charlie across the equipment lot to the high-walled animal compound. With every step, he fought the impulse to grab the man by the scruff of the neck and punch him black, blue, and bloody—not only for the way he made his living but because of the way he'd treated Jasmine.

Before inheriting the land he owned, he'd been her high school algebra teacher. He'd been obsessed with her ever since that time, calling her and even sending her flowers. For now, he seemed satisfied with possessing her car. But for how long would that be enough?

Had he wanted her enough to get her protective father out of the way? Sam couldn't rule out that question.

The gate to the compound was ajar. At this hour, Charlie's hired workers would be feeding and watering the captives—hay and chopped weeds for the grazers and a goat or feral pig carcass, and maybe some roadkill, for the big carnivores. Charlie wasn't particular about their diets. The only aim of feeding them was to keep them alive until they could be hunted and killed.

The elephant was standing inside a small enclosure fashioned of heavy timbers—a tired old female with the saddest eyes Sam had ever seen. She was making low whimpering sounds as she swayed, shifting her weight from side to side in a rocking motion, as if to comfort herself. Sam was horror-struck even before he noticed the chains around her ankles, wound so tightly that the metal links were biting into her flesh.

"I paid five thousand dollars for her, and the bids are up past twenty thousand," Charlie said. "Not a bad profit margin, eh?"

Sam fought the urge to grab the evil little man and shake the life out of him. "Charlie, I can't believe anybody would pay to shoot that pathetic creature," he said.

"Maybe not the creature you see," Charlie said. "But give us a little more time to toughen her up. Once she's mad enough to charge, shooting her will give any hunter his money's worth."

"So you're tormenting her to make her mean?"

As if in answer to his question, one of Charlie's hired men strolled in through the gate carrying what looked like a long-handled spear with a hook. The burly fellow was moving toward the elephant pen.

Sam could guess what was about to happen. He would have stopped it if he could have, but stepping in would only make matters worse for the poor creature. Jasmine had tried to shut Charlie down. But her near arrest, when she'd joined that animal rights demonstration, hadn't worked either. It had only created chaos.

"Seen enough?" Charlie asked.

"More than enough." Sam turned back toward the gate.

"In case you're wondering, I run a legal business." Charlie joined him, walking at his side. "I pay my taxes like a good citizen, and I have a notarized bill of sale for the elephant. She's my property, to do with as I please."

They passed through the gate. From behind them, the sound of anguished trumpeting filled Sam's ears.

There had to be something he could do—at least he had to try. He would make some calls when he left here.

"Does the elephant have a name?" he asked.

"My animals don't have names. They're just property, like those fancy Angus steers on the Culhane spread. And their deaths won't be any more cruel than getting herded down the chute of a slaughterhouse."

They had reached the foot of the porch. Charlie climbed up to the second step, putting his face on a level with Sam's. "Some bleeding hearts, like Jasmine and maybe you, look down on me because of what I do. But I'm a successful businessman. Nine years ago, I took this worthless piece of scrub land and built it into an enterprise that brings in five times as much as I made teaching those miserable teenage brats. I've got money in the bank and more in stocks and real estate. I've earned the right to be treated with respect. So now I'm inviting you, man-to-man, to come up on the porch and have a drink with me."

Sam almost declined. After seeing the conditions behind that wall, he didn't feel inclined to share a drink with the man. And he knew for a fact that Charlie hated him because of Jasmine. Far-fetched as it seemed, he could be walking into some kind of trap.

But as a lawman, he had a job to do. That job included

interviewing any and all suspects in a murder investigation. With a reluctant nod, he followed Charlie up the steps.

"What's your pleasure?" Charlie asked, motioning him to a safari-style canvas chair. "I've got some good Scotch."

"It's too early in my day for alcohol," Sam said, sitting. "But if you've got a cold Coke, I'll take that."

"Suit yourself." Charlie disappeared through the front door and came back with a chilled red-and-white can. For himself, he'd poured a few fingers of Scotch in a glass. "So Madeleine didn't have Frank killed after all." He settled in a nearby chair, sipping his drink. "If you're wondering how I know, Willow Bend is a small town. I have my sources. And just to save you time, I'll tell you straight out. No, I *still* did not kill Frank Culhane."

"Noted." Sam popped the tab on his Coke can. "So let's start with this. How would you describe your relationship with Frank?"

Charlie shrugged. "Live and let live. We weren't friends, but neither of us wanted trouble—especially if it interfered with business. I would never have killed him. He wasn't worth killing."

"And Jasmine? I know you wanted her attention."

Charlie's pale eyes flashed pure hatred. Was it for Frank, who'd protected his daughter? Was it for Sam, who'd claimed the woman Charlie desired? Or was it for Jasmine, who'd rejected and humiliated him for years?

"That wasn't a killing matter," Charlie said. "Jasmine thought she was too good for me. Killing her father wouldn't have changed that. Neither would killing you. At least I got the Corvette—and you can have the woman. Her little caper with those animal rights jackasses cured me of my lovesickness once and for all."

Charlie emptied his glass and set it down. "Here's a little secret," he said. "I told you my animals didn't have names. But that elephant's become an exception. I've given her a new name. Do you want to know what it is?" He leaned toward Sam, his breath reeking of bad hygiene and whiskey. "I call her Jasmine," he said.

Only as he was driving away, after a few more routine questions, did Sam allow himself to shudder. Was Charlie Grishman mentally ill or just plain evil? Was he dangerous or just a big talker? Something had to be done about him and those poor animals.

After returning to the ranch, Sam wasted an hour making phone calls. The three animal protection groups he called dealt only with domestic pets. The state fish and game department didn't regulate the hunting of exotic animals on private land. He had slightly better luck with the Department of Agriculture, which oversaw conditions in zoos, among other things. Yes, Charlie's game ranch had been reported for animal abuse. The place was on their list, but an inspection had yet to be scheduled.

"We're backlogged for at least three months," the woman on the phone told him. "I'm sorry, we do all we can, but we're understaffed and underfunded."

Sam identified himself as an FBI agent. "Could you tell me who submitted the report on Mr. Grishman?" he asked.

"I'll check." There was a silent pause. "Yes, here it is. The report was submitted by Ms. Jasmine Culhane."

Sam ended the call with a sigh. Now he understood how easily Jasmine had fallen in league with the group that had raided Charlie's ranch. He shared her frustration.

But there was one thing he'd learned from his futile phone calls. If there was a way to shut down Charlie's dirty business, it wouldn't be through government regulators. And, as Jasmine's misadventure had proved, it wouldn't be through violent demonstrations either. The only way to stop Charlie's business and get his animals removed would be to remove Charlie.

He'd come here to solve a murder, Sam reminded himself. But Charlie was a legitimate suspect. Maybe Charlie wasn't the murderer he was seeking, but if he could link Charlie to any criminal activity—say, drugs, contraband, or even human trafficking—reporting the man to the proper authorities could be enough to get him arrested or at least cause him to lose his business license. That would make it easier to call in a rescue team for the animals.

Thanks to Nick's help, Sam was set up with warrants to inspect the bank records of the Culhanes, the McKennas, and Charlie. He could bring most of them up on his FBI-linked laptop. He would also spend time at the public records office in Willow Bend checking land boundaries, water rights, and ownership histories for any disputes that might have arisen. He might have done this when he was here earlier, but Madeleine's confession had made the search unnecessary, or so he'd believed. This time everything was different. Now he would inspect every line of data. The process would be tedious but necessary when searching for evidence in a murder case. He would also look for anything that might incriminate Charlie Grishman. Maybe Charlie was being blackmailed by Frank. Or maybe Charlie was hiding other secrets.

Sam suppressed the urge to call Jasmine on her burner phone. Even if it was a business call, she would have her own concerns and responsibilities. It would be selfish to burden her with his. And he certainly wouldn't tell her about the elephant and the name Charlie had given the poor creature.

He would be going over Jasmine's bank records along with the others. Not that he expected to find any surprises.

If Jasmine had killed her father, which was unlikely, it wouldn't have been over money.

And there was no way that Frank's murder would have been an impulsive act. To get the fentanyl and the syringe, and to lure Frank to the right place, would have taken cold, careful planning. *Cold* and *careful* were words that would never apply to Jasmine.

But what if he was wrong? What if he didn't know Jasmine at all?

Chapter Seven

The sun had peaked in the blazing Austin sky when a tissue-wrapped bouquet of red roses arrived at the door of the condo. Jasmine accepted the flowers, tipped the delivery boy, and carried them into the kitchen to be trimmed and arranged in a crystal vase.

She didn't waste time looking for a card. Jasmine knew she wouldn't find one.

She carried the finished arrangement into the living room—an elegantly appointed space with French doors that opened onto a balcony with a view of Lake Travis. Her mother looked up from the bestseller she was reading. Dressed in a flowing Indian caftan, with her abundant curls dyed to their original fiery hue and clipped into a twist, Madeleine Culhane hardly resembled a woman on the verge of death. But this was one of her good days.

"Thank you, dear," she said, glancing at the flowers. "Put them there, on the coffee table, where we can enjoy the fragrance."

Jasmine set the vase on the glass-topped table, next to an antique Limoges ashtray. To her daughter's dismay, Madeleine continued to smoke, arguing that, with time so short, a few cigarettes would make no difference.

Jasmine eyed the bouquet. "They're from *him*, aren't they?"

Madeleine smiled. She was a stunning woman in a powerful, almost masculine way. So far, her terminal glioblastoma had done nothing to detract from her looks. "Of course, they're from him, dear, just like all the others. Louis knows how much I love flowers."

Jasmine still found it hard to accept that her mother was in a romantic relationship with Louis Divino, the notorious crime boss. They'd supposedly met after Divino had moved his operation from Chicago to Texas. Over time, their friendship had deepened into something more. And that was all Jasmine cared to know.

She'd made it clear to her mother that she disapproved of the man—especially since he'd helped Madeleine arrange the failed hit on Frank. Jasmine had done her best to forgive her mother's behavior, which was irrational and had likely been caused by the tumor in her head. But for Louis Divino, there could be no such forgiveness.

"Is he coming by today?" Jasmine asked her mother.

"Yes, a little later. He'll be bringing lunch, some takeout from my favorite Chinese restaurant. There'll be plenty of food, dear. You're welcome to join us at the table."

"Thanks, but I'll just raid the fridge. Carmela always leaves us something on her day off." Jasmine had been about to go back to her room but changed her mind. She'd been meaning to have a serious talk with her mother. She'd put it off long enough.

Sinking onto an ottoman to face the couch, she fixed her mother with a stern look. "We need to talk," she said.

"My goodness. This sounds serious." Madeleine dog-eared her place in the book and laid it on the coffee table next to the roses. "You look as if you're about to tell me you're pregnant—which I wouldn't mind a bit, as long as the father is that gorgeous, blue-eyed FBI man. Is everything all right? I overheard you talking to him on your phone."

Jasmine sighed. "No, I'm not pregnant. And you know that Sam and I are keeping our distance until the investigation is over. This is about you."

"If you're ordering me back to those bloodsucking doctors, you can forget it."

"No, it's not that." Why did her mother have to make everything so difficult? She'd even refused to give Jasmine the names and numbers of the doctors she'd seen.

"So it's about Louis, isn't it? I already know what you're going to say to me, dear. The man is a gangster. He's had people murdered. The FBI has been after him for years. If he's arrested, I could be implicated, too, or get my poor little heart broken." Madeleine paused to take a cigarette from a silver case, light it, and exhale a curl of smoke. "Sweetheart, in its own way, having a terminal condition can be very liberating. I can do anything I want—eat what I want, smoke and drink all I want, and love the man I choose—all without consequences. It's a free pass. And if you don't approve, that's too bad."

"And what about the consequences you leave behind for your family?"

Madeleine shrugged. "That's not my problem."

"What about the fight to get the ranch back? You were so determined—"

"It'll be your fight. Yours and Darrin's. My lawyers will be at your disposal. You'll have enough money to pay them. Just make sure they earn every cent. That's as much as I can do for you."

Madeleine stubbed out her cigarette in the ashtray, picked up her book, and opened it to the page she'd marked. Taking her silence as dismissal, Jasmine walked back to her room, sat down at her computer, and took up the job search she'd started earlier.

Tired of waiting by the phone for the acting and modeling gigs that no longer came her way, Jasmine had resolved to start a new career path. But after weeks of googling, searching, and submitting résumés, to jobs that turned out to be mostly scams, she was becoming discouraged. The positions listed with decent salaries required skills and experience she lacked. Even menial jobs such as cleaning and dishwashing required some kind of job history, as well as references.

It wasn't as if she needed the money. Her future inheritance from her mother would leave her well-off. But she was tired of being a useless toy. She wanted to be independent, to make her own way in the world.

Because she'd done a number of TV commercials, Jasmine had decided to look into sales jobs. At least she knew how to look pretty, smile nicely, and convince her audience that the product she was pushing was something they shouldn't live without. That should be worth something. But that still left her with a wide range of choices.

She was googling the requirements for a Texas real estate license when she heard the doorbell chime. Her mother was probably resting. With a sigh, Jasmine rose from her seat at the desk and hurried out of the room to open the front door.

Louis Divino stepped across the threshold and closed the door behind him. If Jasmine had been producing a movie, she would have cast him as the character he played in real life. Dressed in a black silk shirt and immaculately tailored summer trousers, his thick iron gray hair pomaded and groomed, his skin deeply tanned, with a prominent mole on his cheek, he look every inch the handsome, aging Mafia don.

Jasmine hated him.

"Jasmine, would you mind?" He handed her the large white plastic bag he carried, weighted with cartons of Chinese food. While he strolled into the living room to greet Madeleine, Jasmine carried the bag to the dining room table, unpacked the cartons, and laid out two plates along with utensils, cloth napkins, two wineglasses, and a half-empty wine bottle from the fridge. From the living room came the sound of Divino and her mother talking in low voices. Jasmine didn't have to ask whether they were lovers. Sometimes he took her out. Hours later he would bring her home, disheveled, flushed, and giggling like a schoolgirl.

Jasmine had never told Sam about Divino's visits. It would only worry him. And if Sam were to act on his worries, it could put him in danger. Besides, much as Jasmine disliked the mobster, didn't her mother deserve some happiness at the end of her life?

They came into the dining room together, Madeleine leaning slightly on Divino's arm. He held out her chair and helped her sit. Then he looked around at Jasmine, who stood at the entrance to the hallway.

"Only two places set?" he asked. "You know you're welcome to join us, Jasmine."

"Thanks, but I've got work to do on my computer," Jasmine said. "Enjoy your lunch."

She turned and walked into the hallway. Divino's invitation had been no more than a gesture. Sharing a meal with the couple would have been awkward for everyone involved.

Returning to her room, she took up the computer search she'd been doing when Divino arrived. But now she'd lost focus. She found nothing that fired her enthusiasm.

In spite of the door she'd closed, the faint tinkle of china and flatware and the low murmur of conversation drifted to her ears. Her throat felt dry and scratchy. She should have grabbed a cold soda from the fridge before retiring to her room. But she could still get one. Walking in and out of the kitchen shouldn't create much of a disturbance.

Leaving her room, she stepped out into the hallway, took a few steps toward the kitchen—and stopped, galvanized by the conversation at the table, which she could now hear clearly. She wouldn't have chosen to eavesdrop. But she couldn't walk away from what she was hearing.

"I won't rest easy till I get that damned fed off my tail." Divino's voice was a low growl, not meant to be overheard. "Nick Bellingham's been after me since our time in Chicago. He's determined to take me down before his retirement."

"But he's got nothing on you," Madeleine said. "Isn't that what you told me?"

"Yes. But the bastard hasn't given up. He came by my office to see me yesterday. He's like a bloodhound, barking up the same old tree. He asked me again about the hit on your ex. It appears he's out to prove that I was lying to him, and the hit was real."

Jasmine's heart crept into her throat. If Divino's hit man had really killed her father, her mother would be implicated. Madeleine could be arrested and charged again.

"But you gave me my money back," Madeleine protested. "Did Agent Bellingham ever talk to your hit man?"

"No, and he won't. I made sure of that." Divino's chuckle was humorless. "For God's sake, don't give me that look, Madeleine. I put him on a plane with a one-way ticket to the Bahamas. Bellingham doesn't even know his real name."

"But the FBI already knows that we arranged the hit. They just don't know why. I let them think it was about my children's inheritance—get rid of Frank, plant evidence to blame Lila, and the ranch would be theirs. The feds will never know that Frank had found out about the drug money laundering. He would have turned us both in and taken over my share of the estate."

Jasmine stood in the hallway, frozen in shock. Drug money laundering? What was her mother talking about? And it almost sounded as if the hit man she and Divino hired had killed Frank after all.

"So far, the feds can't prove a thing," Divino said. "But Nick Bellingham's making me nervous—him and that new man, Rafferty. If they dig deep enough—"

"Don't you dare touch Sam Rafferty. I've chosen him to be the father of my blue-eyed grandchildren."

"I'll keep that in mind," Divino said. "But if it comes down to him or me—"

"Let's talk about something else," Madeleine said. "All this doom and gloom is threatening to spoil my appetite. How about refilling my glass with more of that good pinot noir?"

As the conversation faded, Jasmine slipped back down the hall to her room. With the door closed behind her, she leaned against it, shaking. She needed to warn Sam about what she'd overheard. But what if that warning drew him into danger? Divino was capable of killing anyone he believed to be a threat. That included Sam's boss, Nick Bellingham—and maybe Sam. He was also capable of lying about the failed hit on Jasmine's father.

There was more at stake here. If Jasmine were to share what she'd heard, she'd be putting her mother in danger of arrest and worse. Louis Divino appeared to love Madeleine, but if he suspected she might use what she knew to bargain for immunity, he was capable of silencing her.

And if he were to discover how much Jasmine knew about him, Madeline wouldn't be the only one silenced.

The burner phone she'd bought lay on the desk, next to

her laptop. She stared at it, torn by the urge to call Sam and tell him everything.

But that wasn't going to happen. There was no step she could take without endangering someone she loved—or herself. All she could do was wait.

Roper was working a buckskin mare in the arena when the black Escalade, with Mariah at the wheel, rolled through the front gate and pulled up to the front porch. Pausing the horse, he watched Lila climb out of the passenger side and mount the steps. She was walking on her own, but her left arm was in a sling. Probably a dislocated shoulder that had been set. Relief swept over him as she vanished into the house. She'd been lucky. The battling stallions could have killed her with a blow.

He checked the impulse to hand off the mare and go rushing after Lila. That would be presumptuous. Even questioning Mariah would be out of line. He would be smart to focus on his job and wait for Lila to come out to him.

Sunset was streaking the sky by the time Roper finished with the lineup of horses he was training. There'd been no sign of Lila. Was she all right? Had some trouble kept her away from the arena? Or had she simply decided to see less of him?

Roper cursed himself for caring. She was his boss, that was the only certainty. Despite what had happened between them, he had no business mooning over her like a lovestruck teenager.

One in a Million was settled in his stall after a day outdoors. Roper made sure the big roan was comfortable. Then he found Fire Dance, cross-tied and saddled him, wrapped his legs, and led him into the arena. The hired help had left for the day. Roper was alone with the horse he'd chosen to carry him to the million-dollar prize.

The chestnut stallion quivered and snorted, probably recognizing the place where he'd been attacked that morning. Roper spent a few moments stroking him and murmuring soft words of comfort.

"It's all right, boy. You're safe. You'll be fine."

He swung into the saddle and felt the tension in the horse's body. Fire Dance was well trained, but he'd lost trust in the man on his back. Roper understood. The young stallion had been doing his job, behaving as he'd been taught, when the attack struck out of nowhere. And his rider hadn't kept it from happening. Now, in the same place with the same rider, how could he not be scared?

Fire Dance had no visible injuries, but he was probably sore. Lila had talked about installing a water therapy feature in the new training facility she wanted to build. That would have been helpful now. But it was a long way from happening.

Roper started the stallion at an easy walk, testing his gait for any sign of pain. Little by little he eased the horse into the performance routine, taking it slow. Physically, Fire Dance seemed fine. But he was clearly nervous, hesitating with each move, as if he expected his angry rival to come charging into the arena again. Bringing back the spooked horse's confidence was going to take time—or a miracle.

By the time Roper had finished working the stallion, rubbed him down, and put him away, it was dark outside. Looking toward the house, he could see the light on in Lila's room. It was time to go home.

Tired and hungry after the long day, he drove through the gate and parked at the house. The horse trailer and other road vehicles were missing, gone off to another rodeo. The summer season was known as Cowboy Christmas because of so many chances to win prize money. Stetson and

Chance, at least, would be back on the circuit. Cheyenne had said she wanted to quit, but her horse, Jezebel, was gone from the corral, so she may have changed her mind. The terms of Rowdy's bail wouldn't allow him to travel, so he'd be missing out. Roper could only hope his brother was behaving himself.

The dog crossed the porch to greet Roper as he mounted the steps. He scratched the shaggy ears. Through the screen door he could smell beef stew, warming over from last night.

The kitchen table was set with four places. Kirby sat in his usual spot, sipping from his stained coffee cup. Rachel stood by the stove, stirring the stew. Tonight Roper noticed a weariness about her, the sagging shoulders, the mouth pressed into a thin line. There was no sign of Rowdy.

"Your brother's somewhere outside, Roper," she said. "Go and fetch him. We'll be eating in a few minutes."

Roper walked back outside. He hadn't seen Rowdy when he drove into the yard, but he found him by the paddock, leaning on the fence.

"Suppertime, brother," Roper said. "Mom sent me to fetch you."

Rowdy didn't answer or even look around. Not a good sign.

"Are you all right?" Roper asked, remembering his mother's sour expression.

"I'm fine. Just not hungry."

Rowdy was always hungry. Roper could have made a joke about it. Instead he chose to wait, giving his brother a chance to open up.

After a long moment, Rowdy exhaled. "Mom looked through my truck," he said. "She found a bag of weed under the floor mat. You were lucky not to be there, Roper. You didn't have to hear what she said to me."

"You had weed?" Roper shook his head. "I'm trying not to judge, but maybe you deserved what she said to you."

"Did I deserve to be told that I was going to hell? That I'd shamed her in front of her church and her friends? That she wished she'd never given birth to me?"

"Knowing Mom, I imagine she was as angry with herself as she was with you. She raised you to be a good man, and now she thinks she failed. But she still loves you. And it's not too late to show her who you really are."

"Damn it, Roper, you always try to see the good in people. It's time you realized that some of us are nothing but shit."

"Stop beating yourself up. Come on. You need to eat." Roper took his brother's arm and led him away from the fence. Rowdy kept on talking as they walked back to the house.

"I don't have to put up with this. I've got money in the bank, and I'm old enough to be on my own. To hell with this so-called perfect family. I don't need them to make it in rodeo. I can do it by myself."

"What about that drug charge?"

"I'm not stupid. I got the name and number of the lawyer from that guy, Judd, in the other cell. I've already called him. He thinks he can get me off. Once that's cleared away, I'll be gone."

They washed their hands at the pump and mounted the porch, both of them silent now. Roper had looked at his family as the one constant in his life. But Cheyenne already wanted to be on her own. And now Rowdy was threatening to leave. How long before Stetson wanted his own life, leaving young Chance to finish growing up and be gone, as well?

Change happened. That was the way of things. But when it came, it wasn't always easy to accept.

* * *

Last night, Crystal had driven all the way to Abilene and met Tony at a truck stop on the edge of town. On her way there, she'd almost had a change of heart. What if she'd been set up to be beaten, robbed, and maybe raped? Or what if she was about to be infected with some awful disease from a contaminated needle?

But the man who had come out to her car and introduced himself as Tony had looked like a nerdy student—young, slightly overweight, with thick glasses and a buzz cut. He'd put on fresh gloves and opened a sealed needle to collect blood from a vein in her arm. The procedure had been quick and skillfully done.

Afterward, he'd covered the needle site with a wad of clean cotton and a superhero bandage. She'd given him the money and a plastic shopping bag stuffed with everything she could find that might have Judd's DNA on it.

"I'll do my best to make something work," he said. "But no promises. I usually ask for a cheek swab, but . . ." He shrugged. "I understand the problem. When I have something, I'll call you."

It went without saying that even if he couldn't do the test, the money would be nonrefundable.

For the next twenty-four hours, Crystal's mood had swung wildly between anticipation and dread. All day she'd waited for her phone to ring. What if the baby turned out to be Judd's? Her first plan had been to get rid of it. But she found herself softening toward the speck of life growing inside her. She could always keep the baby, maybe get Judd to marry her. But the two of them would make horrible parents—not unlike Crystal's own parents had been.

Lying awake in her bed now, she remembered growing up—the drinking, the screaming fights, the days with no food in the house. Her mother had made it clear that they'd married because of *her*. She'd never wanted a baby, especially a girl. Neither had her father. Crystal had run away at sixteen and never returned home. She'd found jobs cleaning motel rooms, washing dishes, and waiting tables. She was pretty enough to attract men, but most of them had only wanted one thing from her. Crystal had wanted more—security, respect, and love. For a time, she'd held out for those things.

But then she'd fallen for Judd, a dashing road warrior who'd offered her a world of thrills. She'd stayed with him, adapting to his rough lifestyle. But over time, he'd come to remind her of her father—self-indulgent, controlling, and violent.

She'd been looking for a way out when Frank Culhane had walked into her life. Frank, who was everything Judd wasn't. For the first time, she'd experienced what it was like to be with a successful man who truly cared for her. She knew he was married, but when they were together, she could tell that he loved her.

If only he'd lived to learn about the baby. He would have divorced his wife and married her, she was sure of it.

Turning in the bed, she watched the moon's reflection through the tattered blinds on her window. She had one last chance to better her life—but only if the test gave her the right answer. If she were religious, she might pray for that answer. But she didn't believe in miracles. God wasn't going to change an unborn baby's DNA—especially not for her.

Incredibly, she heard her phone ring.

Groping for it on the nightstand, Crystal knocked the phone on the floor. She scrambled after it on her hands and knees, finally seizing it on the third ring.

"Hello?" she gasped.

"Ms. Carter, this is Tony." The voice sounded distant.

She could barely hear it over the pounding of her heart. "I have your test result. I couldn't be a hundred percent sure because of the poor sample you gave me. But the match appears to be negative."

"*Negative?*" Crystal sagged against the side of the bed. "You mean the man isn't my baby's father?"

"That's right, as far as I could tell. Have a nice night, and don't call me again. Our business is done."

The call ended, leaving Crystal sprawled on the cold linoleum floor, nauseated with relief.

Negative.

It was as if she'd won the lottery. Her baby wasn't Judd's. She was carrying Frank Culhane's child.

CHAPTER EIGHT

Lila stood on the front porch saying goodbye to her daughter. Gemma, a nursing student at TCU in Fort Worth, gripped the handle of her wheeled carry-on bag. Her rental car waited at the foot of the steps.

"I can stay longer, if you need me, Mama." Gemma resembled her grandmother—tall, slim, and practical-looking, with short light-brown hair and hazel eyes. Lila's love for her twenty-year-old daughter was fiercely protective. If she kept her child at a distance, it was only to shield her from the craziness at the ranch.

"You really didn't need to come at all," Lila said. "I can't believe Mariah called you when I hurt my shoulder. I'd have been fine."

"I know. But I would have worried about you—especially after that awful accident with your car. This ranch has become a dangerous place. Be careful. I've only got one mother."

"And I've only got one daughter." Lila pulled her close for a quick hug. "Be safe, now. And call me."

"I will. And you do the same."

Lila watch the blue Toyota disappear down the road.

Saying goodbye was always hard. But there was nothing for Gemma here on the ranch. She was better off building a separate, useful life for herself.

Lila had become pregnant as an eighteen-year-old college student. The father—a charming, irresponsible boy—wouldn't have cared even if she'd told him. She'd quit school, had her baby, and left the little girl with her grandmother while she'd found work as a dancer in a Vegas casino show to support them.

When nine-year-old Gemma had needed a life-saving heart operation, Lila had paid for it the only way she could: by finding a rich husband. Frank had been married to Madeleine at the time, but even that hadn't stopped her. Not only had she wed the handsome, wealthy rancher, she had fallen in love with him.

She'd done her best to be a good wife. But now, or so it seemed, it was time to pay the piper.

She reached across her body and massaged her left shoulder. Four days had passed since she'd been flung to the arena floor by the frenzied stallion. The sling was gone, but the joint was still sore from the dislocation. Healing would take time.

Roper's truck had been in the parking lot since first light. He'd been working early and late with Fire Dance. But she hadn't spoken with him since he'd helped her into the house and turned her over to Mariah. Gemma had arrived that night, making it hard for Lila to get away. But now, she'd been cooped up in the house long enough. With Gemma on her way back to Fort Worth, it was time for a visit to the arena.

She went back inside the house and cut through to the patio. She had just started down the path to the stables when her cell phone rang. Lila was tempted to ignore the call or send it to voice mail. But then she saw the identity of the caller. It was the doctor who'd agreed to do the in vitro paternity test of Crystal's baby.

"Hello?" She could feel the tremor in her voice.

"Mrs. Culhane, this is Dr. Morgenstern. I have the results of Miss Carter's paternity test." He paused. "She took so long coming in, I was afraid she'd changed her mind. But she finally showed up, very confident and cheerful."

"I don't mean to sound impatient, Doctor, but what did the test show?" Eternities seemed to slide away as Lila waited for the answer that could shake her world.

"The markers showed a definite match between the baby's DNA and your late husband's," the doctor said. "I've already emailed the test results to you. Of course this information will be held in strictest confidence. Do you have any more questions for me?"

"No . . . that's fine. Thank you," Lila murmured, ending the call. Nausea churned in her stomach. Her knees threatened to collapse beneath her. She made it back to the patio and sank onto a chair.

This was her new reality. The husband who'd never been able to conceive a child with her had managed it with a cheap little tramp he'd met in a bar.

But that was past history now. The real question was what would happen next. Crystal would have an agenda. She would undoubtedly want money. But what else would she want? That remained to be seen. Only one thing was certain. If this situation were a poker game, there was just one player holding the aces. And it wasn't Lila.

Roper finished the training session with his client's bay gelding, dismounted, and passed the horse off to a waiting groom. The morning sun, slanting rays in through the arena's open sides, was already warm. The day was going to be another scorcher.

He'd paused to drink from the water bottle he kept by the arena entrance when he saw Lila standing in the shadows. His pulse quickened. Relief, mixed with apprehension, flooded his emotions. After a three-day absence, she had finally come to him. But his instincts told him something was wrong.

As he walked toward her, she stepped into the light. "Hello, Boss," he said. "Are you all right?"

Her faint smile appeared forced. "Just sore. My daughter came to babysit me and keep me resting. She just left."

"I know. I recognized her from Frank's memorial service."

They stood facing each other in what was becoming awkward silence. He had made love to this woman. Yet, in many ways, he scarcely knew her at all.

"So, how are things going?" she asked. "Has One in a Million settled down?"

"He seems fine. I've been working with him every day. But we're keeping him away from Fire Dance."

"And Fire Dance? Is he going to be all right?"

"He's doing better. I think he's beginning to trust me again, but he had a bad scare. We've got a long way to go and not much time."

"Have you kept your word about training him on your own time?"

Her question stung. "If you've been watching me, you already know that I have."

"I haven't been watching," she said. "I trusted you, and I've had other things on my mind. But since I've got a stake in this, I'm saying take the time. Do whatever you need with him. The assistant trainers can take on more responsibility."

"Thank you, Boss. That'll help." The sunlight deepened the shadows on her face. She looked tired, he thought.

Maybe more distressed than tired. “Is something the matter?” he asked. “If there’s anything I can do—”

“No. Just a family issue. I’ll deal with it.” She turned to leave.

“Boss?”

She turned back, her eyes questioning.

“Would you like to see Fire Dance in action? It won’t take long to get him ready.”

There was a beat of hesitation, when Roper almost regretted asking. But then she nodded. “Yes, thanks, I’d like that very much.”

Perched on a rail across from the stable entrance, Lila waited while Roper and the grooms readied Fire Dance for his workout. With so much weighing on her mind, she needed the diversion. And she needed to do her job, which was overseeing the entire horse program. As capable as Roper might be, she mustn’t depend on him to do it all.

She’d promised to continue Frank’s legacy. But there was more to that legacy than she’d realized. Frank had betrayed her and their marriage in the most uncaring way. She owed him nothing. Going forward, anything she did to keep the stables running and the horses winning would be for her own satisfaction.

As for the unborn child Frank had left . . . But she wouldn’t think about that now. She needed time to recover from the shock and make an intelligent plan. The confrontation with Crystal would come. But not now. Not today. She wasn’t ready.

Roper led Fire Dance into the arena, mounted, and warmed him up with an easy lope around the ring. They made a striking pair—the stallion with his regal body and gleaming chestnut coat, and the handsome rider who moved as one with the horse.

Stopping, Roper began the routine, starting with the spin in place and moving into the patterns and direction changes. As Frank's wife, Lila had watched years of reining competitions. She knew what to look for, and she knew good work when she saw it. Roper was good. He was more than good. As he cued the horse with subtle movements of his hands, knees, and body, he was superb.

Still, she sensed a flicker of distrust in the stallion's response. Fire Dance had been trained to depend on his rider for guidance and safety. When the other horse, bigger and more aggressive, had attacked him out of nowhere, he'd been shaken and scared. Unless Roper could make him feel safe, he might never fully trust again.

The young stallion's quality showed in his every movement. But Lila's gaze was drawn to Roper. His expression was calm and focused, his posture erect, his hands light on the reins. Only the patch of damp sweat between his shoulder blades betrayed the physical effort that went into his control of the horse. That kind of grace couldn't be learned. It had to be second nature.

Frank had been an excellent horseman, winning multiple contests over the years and taking home some handsome prizes. Much of his success had been due to One in a Million. But on the right horse, Roper would have bested him every time.

Watching him now, Lila understood why Frank had refused to let Roper compete. And she could imagine how Roper, ambitious man that he was, had chafed under that restriction. Had Roper's frustration been powerful enough to drive him to murder?

But where had that thought come from? Just because Roper possessed the perfect combination of motive, means, and opportunity didn't mean he was a killer. She knew him. He'd never given her reason not to trust him.

The memory flooded through her as she watched him ride—Roper's arms around her, his mouth on hers, her body burning with need as they'd shed clothes and given themselves to total abandon. Since then, he'd hadn't mentioned that forbidden encounter or laid so much as a lustful hand on her. But he had to be thinking about it, just as she was.

Her face was still flushed with the memory when the routine ended with a sliding stop in front of her. Pulling her thoughts back to the present, Lila slipped off the rail and applauded. "He's beautiful," she said. "I can see why you chose to ride him."

"He can be spectacular when he's focused," Roper said. "But when he's nervous and distracted, the performance falls apart. What we're working for now is consistency—when I depend on him and he depends on me. We'll have one run at the big money. It's going to take both of us giving all we've got."

His expression didn't flicker—the steely gaze, the resolute mouth. She'd been wrong. He hadn't been thinking about her at all. Out there in the arena, he had scarcely been aware of her. His attention had been riveted on his connection with the stallion, every move, every breath.

That was as it should be, Lila told herself. And she was through making a fool of herself over an episode that was best forgotten.

"I'm going to take him through it again at a slower pace," he said. "You're welcome to stay and watch."

"I'll leave you to it," Lila said. "Good luck, and thank you for the show."

She walked out of the arena, not the way she'd come in but through the entrance to the stable. She hadn't planned it that way, but now that she was in charge, she needed to show more of a presence here.

Restless and feeling slightly out of place, she wandered along the line of stalls, stopping to examine a horse or give an occasional smile and greeting to a worker. Everything appeared to be in order, as she knew it would be under Roper's stewardship. How would she have managed if he'd decided to leave?

But she couldn't allow herself to think like that. She couldn't depend on a man who wasn't family, a man who could leave anytime the fancy struck him, and probably would.

She could offer him the partnership, as she'd planned to do earlier. But what if he didn't want to be tied down? What if he said no?

The partnership was no longer a sure solution. Only one choice made sense—learning to manage the whole operation on her own.

I can do it, Lila told herself. She was already running the business end of the ranch. The rest—care and training of the horses, maintenance of the facility and pastures, dealings with employees, clients, and service providers such as vets and farriers—Frank had done it, and he wasn't a genius. She could learn to do it too. It would take time and effort, but the thought of being prepared to do it all made her blood race.

The stable bustled with activity—stalls were being cleaned, horses were being readied for exercise or grooming. A worker pushed a wheelbarrow loaded with dirty straw and manure toward an exit. Lila stopped outside the box stall where One in a Million had been moved after his attack on Fire Dance. Recognizing her, the big roan nickered for attention.

"Hello, big guy." She reached over the stall gate and stroked the satiny neck. "Sorry, no treats today, but I'll remember next time."

He butted her with his head. He was an affectionate horse, a devoted horse. The fear of being replaced by a rival stallion must have been very real to him—just as the trauma of watching his master die must've been. Now he was in exile, at least until after the Run for a Million when Fire Dance would be returned to his owner.

"Sorry, old boy. Life hurts sometimes, doesn't it?" Lila pressed her cheek against the noble face. A tear trickled a salty path down the side of her nose.

It wasn't just the horse. It was everything. Damn!

"Boss?" The voice from behind her was a low murmur. She turned to find Roper standing at her shoulder. "Are you all right?"

Lila ignored his question. "What are you doing here? I thought you were training the stallion."

"We finished. One of the grooms told me you'd gone this way."

"Is that a problem? After all, I do own the place."

"As I'm well aware. But until your shoulder heals, you shouldn't be here. With horses and people coming and going, you could get jostled and injure it again."

"I'm fine. Stop babying me." Turning away from him, she wiped her damp cheek with her sleeve.

"You're not fine. You're crying."

"It's nothing. I was just feeling sorry for this poor horse who's given his all and doesn't understand why he's being cast aside. He deserves better."

"I'm planning some time with him this afternoon," Roper said. "Meanwhile, let me walk you back to the house."

"I told you, I'm fine. I don't need an escort."

He exhaled slowly, as if counting to ten. "Then do it for me. Just this once, let somebody be here for you."

Something in his voice told Lila he was in no mood to argue. His fingertips touched her back, guiding her lightly but insistently toward the open door at the far end of the wing. They stepped outside to a sunlit view of the pastures. The morning breeze cooled Lila's damp face. In the near paddock, the brood mares grazed on watered grass while their leggy foals bucked and frolicked.

To get her back to the house, they would have to walk partway around the long wing of the stable. Roper fell into step beside Lila as she strode ahead. "Talk to me, Boss," he said. "We haven't had much time for that lately. What's on your mind?"

She slowed, then stopped, gazing past him at the expanse of pastureland, dotted with horses and cattle. They were alone here, the closed side of the stable behind them. His nearness stirred little whorls of heat inside her. Lila willed herself to ignore them.

"That depends on what's on *your* mind," she said. "I've been thinking about what I need to do when you leave."

"Who says I'm leaving?" He sounded genuinely surprised.

"Don't play games with me, Roper. You almost left once before. It could happen again—and probably will. You're bigger than this ranch, and you know it. You could go anywhere, do anything."

"I would argue against that." His tone was neutral, giving her no clue. "But tell me what you're thinking."

"I'm thinking that when—or if—you go, I'll need to do your job. For that, I'll need to know everything that you know."

Roper didn't reply. Was he skeptical? Was he amused? She gazed across the pastures, avoiding him with her eyes. From here, Charlie's game farm could be seen as a faint line of buildings and fences along the horizon.

"I know it can't happen right away," she said. "We've got the Run for a Million coming up. Then there's the battle with Frank's children for my right to keep this ranch. That's bound to get even nastier than it already is. And Frank's killer has to be found and brought to justice. And now—" Lila stopped herself. She wasn't ready to talk about the latest development. Not until she had a plan to deal with it. Even telling Sam might have been a mistake.

She took a breath and continued. "I guess what I'm saying is, I hope I can count on your help."

"Of course you can," Roper said. "But unless you fire me, I have no plans to leave. I like to think that we're building something here, a good program that will last. Apart from that, my family needs me. My father's disabled, my brothers and sister are going their own ways. My mother's strong, but she's not getting any younger. Working here, I can live at home and be close by when they need my help."

"That may be true," Lila said, "but when we discussed your bringing Fire Dance here and I gave you my terms, you almost left."

"But I didn't leave. And I just told you why."

"Is there any other reason?" She raised her head to look up at him. His expression hardened.

"You know better than to ask that question." He stood so close that she could hear the low rush of his breathing. His smoky eyes blazed into hers. The urge to be in his arms and feel his mouth on hers heated her blood like a fever.

Don't make a fool of yourself, the voice in her head scolded. *You know better. Didn't you learn anything before?*

The voice was fading. As she met his gaze, warm and tempting desire uncoiled in the depths of her body. If she were to stretch on tiptoe and lean toward him, would he respond or would he push her away?

The jangle of the phone in her pocket left the questions unanswered.

Even without picking up, Lila sensed who the caller would be. She left the phone in her pocket, letting it ring again and again.

Roper had stepped back, breaking the tenuous connection between them. "Aren't you going to answer it?" he asked.

"It can wait. They'll call back."

Before she could reach the phone, the call went to voice mail, which she'd set on speaker for convenience when she was driving her car. The all-too-familiar voice was a young woman's. "Mrs. Culhane, you know who this is, and you know why I'm calling. Call me back, please."

This was the last thing Lila needed, a reminder that Crystal was calling the shots, or at least trying to. She bit back a curse, feeling like a fighter on the ropes. Before she returned the call, she needed to get herself and the situation under control.

In the silence that followed, Roper gave her a concerned look. "I know it's none of my business, but—"

"You're right. It's none of your business," she said, cutting him off. "It's something I need to take care of myself. And I don't need you fussing over me. Go on back to work now, with my blessing."

She turned away and stalked up the path. Roper kept an eye on her until she'd crossed the patio and gone into the house. She'd seemed vaguely troubled when she'd come out to the arena. Roper had assumed that he was the cause of her anxiety, and he'd done his best to smooth things over. He'd even been foolishly tempted to take her in his arms. But then the phone call had come.

He'd heard the voice message clearly. The woman had

sounded young, with a Texas drawl. Whatever her business was, the phone call had been enough to throw Lila off the rails.

Had the call been about Frank? Maybe from a girlfriend?

Now Roper remembered Sam showing him a photo of Frank standing in the doorway of a motel room. The woman in his arms, visible only from behind, had a cloud of dark hair. Sam had wondered if she might be Cheyenne.

Roper had been quick to confirm that the woman wasn't his sister. But the picture had been taken by a photographer working for Lila. Suddenly he couldn't stop asking silent questions. Had Lila tracked down the mystery woman? Was that who had called her?

Lila may have conquered his heart, but a world of secrets lay beyond what he knew of her. Would she ever trust him enough to unlock that world? Or would it be safer for things to remain as they were now, with unspoken words building a wall between them?

Sam had spent the past few days poring over bank records, land title histories, news articles, and any written accounts he could get his hands on. This work wasn't his favorite part of the job. But somebody needed to do it—and only Sam knew his subjects well enough to do it effectively.

Now he sat at the computer, in the bungalow, organizing what he'd discovered. So far, he'd found no earthshaking revelations. But he was learning more about the principal suspects in his murder case.

The McKennas were exactly what they appeared to be—honest, hard-working, and frugal. They'd been poor until the four young rodeo stars had started raking in prize money. Now the family had a sizeable nest egg in the bank, but they still lived as if they were on the edge of poverty. The mother made regular donations to her church. Most of Roper's income went into supporting the ranch, including the mortgage payments. The younger family members paid for their rodeo fees, their horses, and their top-of-the line hauling equipment. They were allowed spending money, but none of them lived lavishly. The girl had a contract to do a modeling spread for *Vogue* magazine. The second boy was out on bail pending a charge of cocaine possession. Too bad, but it happened in the best of families.

All Sam could conclude from the evidence was that if any of the McKennas, including Roper, had killed Frank Culhane, it hadn't been over money.

But he couldn't rule out other reasons.

Sam hadn't forgotten the signs that Darrin Culhane was abusing his pregnant wife. Darrin's explosive temper was something to consider, but there were no surprises in their financial records. As a small-town lawyer, he didn't earn much, but the money from the management of his mother's cattle herd and from serving as her attorney made up the difference. Their house in Willow Bend was a rental. They'd made no move to buy a home, because their ambitions were set on booting Lila out of the family mansion and taking over the ranch.

None of this information had come as a surprise. Darrin could have killed his father in a burst of anger. But that was unlikely. Frank's murder had been carefully planned. And if Jasmine's claim was to be believed, Darrin didn't have the balls to carry it out.

Then there was Charlie Grishman. Sam had done a thorough search hoping to find incriminating evidence—anything that would cause that horror of a game ranch to be shut down. But Charlie's record was as clean as the man had claimed, every financial transaction accounted for. Legally, he didn't have so much as a parking ticket, and he held clear title to the land he'd inherited from his grandmother nine years ago. On paper, at least, Charlie was almost too good to be true.

But the man reeked of evil intent. There had to be something that wasn't showing up—something Charlie was clever enough to hide. Maybe Frank had discovered a secret that could get Charlie in trouble, that could be motive for murder. But Sam was grasping at straws now. He had no proof of anything against the obnoxious little rat.

He had a mountain of work left to do. But he was getting tired, which could put him at risk of missing something important. It was time for a break.

The time was just past eleven thirty—early for lunch, but he'd skipped breakfast to get an early start on work. Mariah had given him leave to rummage up his own snacks in the kitchen. With luck he could make himself a quick sandwich and get out of her way before she got impatient with him.

He entered the kitchen through the back door. Mariah, a handsome, middle-aged woman with a buxom figure and graying hair, was cutting up meat and vegetables for the slow cooker. She glanced up as Sam closed the screen door behind him.

"Missed you at breakfast." Her deft hands didn't pause. "I figured you'd be hungry, so I made your sandwich. It's in the fridge, middle shelf. And help yourself to a couple of cookies from the blue jar."

"Thanks. That's kind of you, Mariah." Sam moved past her to get to the fridge, poured himself a glass of chilled water, and took a seat at a corner of the cluttered kitchen table. Most of the time Mariah, who'd been with the family since the early days of Frank's first marriage, treated him like a bothersome child. But now and again she surprised him with a small favor, like this one.

In the one interview she'd given him, she'd made it clear that family secrets would be off-limits. But as Sam ate his sandwich, taking his time, it occurred to him that what he was looking for now had little to do with the Culhane family. But it was about someone she knew.

What harm would it do to question her? The worst she could do was order him out of her kitchen.

"Maybe you can help me with some research, Mariah," he said. "This has nothing to do with you or the family, but I've come to a dead end. I need some answers, and I was thinking you might know something."

Mariah looked back at him, over her shoulder. She wasn't smiling, but he caught a glint of curiosity in her expression. "Try me," she said.

"It's about your neighbor, Charlie Grishman. How well do you know him?"

In the silence, her knife blade whacked onto the cutting board, beheading a carrot. "I know him," she said. "But I'd be happier not to. His grandmother was a good friend of mine, a fine old woman. She took Charlie in and raised him after his parents died. You think he'd have been grateful. But the way he treated her . . . I've always believed it drove her to her grave. Just thinking about it makes my blood boil."

Sam laid his sandwich on the plate and turned his chair in her direction. "Tell me more," he said.

CHAPTER NINE

Lila pulled into the parking lot on the south side of the Trail's End restaurant. The battered Hyundai, parked in one of the spaces, told her that Crystal was waiting for her.

She could feel the nervous tension as she parked the white Jeep Liberty next to the dumpster at the back of the lot. She'd decided against driving the Porsche into town. The last thing she wanted was to be noticed, and the sleek luxury car was a flag for attention.

Meeting at the restaurant had been Lila's idea as well. Crystal had suggested a spot by the old railroad bridge, where teenage lovers liked to park at night. But Lila had insisted on a safe, public place where words and actions would be limited to a civil exchange. She'd also chosen lunchtime, when the place would be crowded and too noisy for their conversation to be overheard. She'd even reserved a booth in the far corner, where they could talk in relative privacy.

So far, everything was under control.

Walking around the corner to the front door, Lila reminded herself to be cool, confident, and in charge. Crystal mustn't be allowed to call the shots.

Walking through the door was like diving into a sea of noise. Dolly Parton's "Jolene" blared from the speakers. *Appropriate*, Lila thought as she wove her way through the busy dining room. But Crystal was no Jolene. She was just a greedy little tramp who'd been impregnated by a married man and was out to profit from it.

She could see Crystal now, sitting in the booth, sipping a drink and watching her approach with a faint smile on her pretty, made-up face, which struck Lila as odd. Surely the woman didn't think the two of them could be friends.

Lila slid into the opposite side of the booth. There was an untouched Coke with ice, a straw, and a lemon in front of her. A basket of French fries with paper cups of ketchup sat in the middle of the table. "I ordered Cokes for us," she said. "Yours is diet. And you can help yourself to the fries if you want. They're to share."

Lila sipped her Coke but ignored the fries. "Let's just get this over with," she said. "I accept that the baby you're carrying is my late husband's. If it's money you want, tell me what you expect, and we'll take it from there. Frank wouldn't want his child to go without. But you must understand there are limits. You're not going to get rich just for sleeping with a married man."

Crystal selected a fry, swirled it in the ketchup, and ate it. Her expression revealed nothing.

"What is it?" Lila asked. "Are you thinking you want to terminate your pregnancy?"

"No! Heavens, no!" Crystal showed emotion for the first time. "I loved Frank, and I love our baby. I want him—or her—to have a good life. A better life than I can provide."

"I can't help you if I don't know what you're thinking," Lila said. "Suppose you tell me."

"I will, if you'll listen." Crystal nibbled another fry.

"All right, I'm listening. Go ahead."

"You probably think I'm just a bimbo," Crystal said. "But I'm smarter than I look. I've done my homework. I happen to know that you're fighting Frank's kids for your ranch. They're claiming that you're not entitled to stay there because you didn't give Frank any children."

Shocked, Lila stared across the table at her rival. "How did you—?"

"Let's just say that I got lucky. I work as a hostess at Jackalope's, usually the afternoon shift. Most of the customers are men. Some are just looking for peace and quiet. Others want to talk about their troubles—their jobs, their marriages, whatever. If I have time, I'll listen."

Crystal dipped another fry in the ketchup, gazed at it thoughtfully, and left it there. "Your lawyer stepson is a regular in the afternoon. Mostly he just drinks and then leaves. But when I realized who he was, I started paying him extra attention, encouraging him to talk. It took a little time, but I finally got the story out of him."

Lila stirred the ice in her drink, her thoughts scrambling. *That's not surprising*, she told herself. Darrin was never the sharpest pencil in the pack. Still, it was hard to believe that he would share such private information with an attractive stranger in a bar. Maybe he'd had too much to drink.

Whatever the reason, Lila had underestimated the woman who sat across the table with a triumphant gleam in her eye. Crystal Carter was an adversary to be reckoned with.

"I've heard enough," Lila said. "Just cut to the chase and tell me what you want."

"All right," Crystal said. "As I told you, I want the best life for my baby. I also know that you'd do anything to keep from losing your ranch. So here's what I'm proposing." She paused, taking a breath. "How much would it be worth to you to adopt Frank's child?"

Lila stared at her, stunned into silence.

"Think about it," Crystal said. "You'd be adopting a Culhane, a child who could continue Frank's bloodline. And with the baby legally yours, Frank's other children would have no case. I'm due in February. That should give you plenty of time to make the arrangements."

"Wait—" Lila found her voice. "I need to understand. Your question—you asked me how much it would be worth."

Crystal nodded. "That's right. I'm thinking a million dollars. I know you're good for it."

The clamor of sound in the dining room coalesced into a roar that filled Lila's head. How could she process this now? She forced herself to speak.

"You mean to say that you're offering to sell your baby? That's illegal. It's also wrong."

Crystal shrugged. "So are a lot of other things. But this is a win-win situation. The baby gets a good home. You get your genuine Culhane heir. And for my part, I deserve something, too. Take it or leave it."

"And if I say no? If I refuse to take part in this travesty?"

"Then I'll decide what to do. I can't picture myself as a good mother. But if I decide not to have this baby, I'll need to make arrangements soon. I can't wait months for you to make up your mind. If it's yes, I'll need a down payment now and the rest when the baby comes. If it's no . . ." Crystal let the implication hang.

Lila opened her purse and whipped out her checkbook and a pen. "This isn't a down payment. For the welfare of the baby, I was prepared to pay for your basic expenses and set up a trust fund for when he—or she—is older. I'm giving you fifteen thousand to start—enough for a health checkup, some vitamins, a decent place to rent if you need it, and a cheap used car to replace that death trap you're driving."

"What about the rest?" Crystal's disappointment showed in her pretty, painted face.

"The rest?" Lila gave her a sharp look.

"You know, the adoption and all." For the first time, she sounded uncertain.

"I'm still thinking about that." Lila pushed the check across the table and slid out of the booth. "Meanwhile, if I find out you've had an abortion, you'll never get another cent from me. Understand?"

Crystal nodded.

"We're done for now. I'll be in touch." Lila turned away from the table and made her way through the crowded dining room to the front door. She stepped outside without looking back.

Crystal gazed down at the check Lila had left on the table. Fifteen thousand dollars was more money than she'd ever seen at one time, let alone possessed. The cash would get her into a small apartment, buy her a usable car, and allow a few nice things to wear. She could even get her hair and nails done in the beauty salon that had opened next to the grocery store.

But that was all. And it wasn't enough. Not when she'd hoped to come away with the down payment on a million dollars.

She had foolishly believed that the money would come easily. But Lila Culhane was one tough bitch. Frank's widow would probably make her earn every cent—on her knees.

Crystal's threat to end her pregnancy hadn't been serious. She'd only wanted to put pressure on Lila. But what if it hadn't been enough? What if, for whatever reason, Lila refused to go through with the adoption?

If the baby had been Judd's, deciding what to do would have been simple. But this baby was Frank's. She had the results of the paternity test. Frank's name would be on the birth certificate. That alone had to be worth something.

A chance like this one would never come again. If things didn't work out with Lila, she was going to need a Plan B, and maybe even a Plan C.

Crystal selected a cold French fry, dipped it in the ketchup, and chewed it slowly, thinking. She could always get a lawyer and sue the family for her child's share of the estate. It would take time and money, and she might not be able to start legal action until after the baby was born. She would have a good case; but the settlement, whether in property or cash, would go to the baby, probably in a trust, not to her.

There had to be another way, an easier way that would get her the money sooner. If the adoption didn't happen, who else might be interested in Frank's baby?

What about Frank's son, Darrin, and his pregnant wife?

Crystal's pulse skipped as the thought struck her. They might not want the baby, but they'd do anything to keep Lila from adopting a Culhane heir and securing her claim to the ranch. They should be willing to pay—either for an end to Crystal's pregnancy or a guarantee that the newborn would be sent out of Lila's reach. Maybe they'd even want the baby themselves, to raise with their own child.

For now, she would keep her arrangement with Lila. But it was comforting to know that, if anything went wrong, she had a backup plan.

A splatter of ketchup had dripped onto the check. Crystal dabbed it away with a corner of her napkin, but the crimson stain had soaked into the paper, blurring part of her name. Never mind, the check was still good. She slipped it into her purse. She would take it to the bank now and open a checking account with a debit card.

Her head swam with plans as she laid a $10 bill on the

table and left the restaurant. Until now, things had been tough for her, living in a dump at the Blue Rose, thrift shopping for clothes, and driving her ex's junk car. But those hardships were over. Starting now, her dead-end life was about to change.

Lila gripped the Jeep's steering wheel, her hands damp with nervous sweat as she sped through the open country between the town and the ranch. Had she done the right thing, giving money to Frank's pregnant mistress? What if instead of writing that check, she'd turned her back and walked away? Would Crystal already be seeking some back alley abortionist to end her baby's life?

This was blackmail, pure and simple. But what about Crystal's adoption offer? There was no way Lila had seen that coming. She still didn't know what to make of it, let alone what she should do.

She was driving too fast. Her foot slammed the brake as a family of feral pigs trotted across the two-lane road. The Jeep screeched to a halt, just short of hitting one. Blasted animals. They were dangerous and had ways of turning up anywhere. Charlie Grishman sometimes killed them to feed his menagerie. But he was allowed to shoot them only on his own property.

The pigs moved down into the grassy bar ditch and vanished from sight, but Lila could still hear them grunting and squealing. She felt shaky and needed to get home. She started the engine and continued on down the road.

What did she want to do about the baby? Common sense told her to walk away. Get involved and she'd be facing worry, expense, possible legal issues, and heartache. Even if Crystal had offered to give her the baby for free, Lila would have hesitated. She wasn't ready to be a mother—especially not to the child of her husband's affair.

But what if Crystal was right? What if adopting a Culhane baby could secure her inheritance?

How could she even entertain such a coldhearted, mercenary, utterly despicable idea?

But she was already involved. She'd opened that door when she'd met with Crystal and given her the check. She should at least talk to her lawyer and discuss her options before she took another step.

Ahead, she could see the ranch, the stately house rising above the barns, stables, and pastures that spread behind it. In the eleven years she'd lived here, she'd come to love this place. It would break her heart to lose it. But what if the price for keeping it was too high?

Still feeling shaken, she drove in through the front gate, rounded the house, and parked the Jeep in the vehicle shed. For a moment, she sat in the driver's seat, gazing toward the back door. She wasn't ready to go inside yet. She needed to talk to someone—not a lawyer, just someone who'd listen without judging while she talked things out.

Mariah wouldn't do as a confidante. Her actions when Madeleine was around had made it clear where the cook's loyalties lay.

Sam would be the better choice. He knew about the baby. He'd interviewed Crystal. With him, Lila wouldn't have to start her story at the beginning. But she couldn't tell Sam about the woman's offer to sell her child. Such a transaction, if she actually decided to go through with it, was highly illegal. Sam would have no choice but to report it.

His SUV was parked next to the bungalow. She would probably find him inside.

The midday sun felt like the open door of a furnace as she climbed out of the vehicle. She was exhausted from the battles she was fighting on every front—alone, with no one she could trust to stand beside her. Even Sam, behind his mask of friendliness, was a man doing his job. A man who still suspected her of murder. How could she trust him with her secrets?

She had started for the house when she glanced the other way and happened to see Roper come out of the stables.

He appeared to be taking a short break from work. His sweat-dampened shirt was plastered to his torso. His dark hair lay flat against his head. He raked it back with one hand while the other hand raised a jug of water to his lips. He drank long and deep. Lowering the jug, he turned to go back into the stable. He stopped as he caught her watching him. Would he come to her or go back inside?

As she waited, something inside her seemed to break. She felt the strange, warm pain of it, like a dam washing away in a spring thaw. It wasn't Sam she needed to talk with. It was Roper.

He wasn't the easiest person to understand, but he'd been honest with her even when it made her angry. She had struggled to keep him at a distance, especially after they'd lost control and made love. Could she keep that distance if she took him into her confidence?

He walked toward her. She waited for him to come within speaking distance.

"Boss?" He stopped a few paces from her. "Is everything all right?"

"Not really," she said. "Have you got a few minutes to talk?"

He frowned. "I can arrange it. Give me a minute to put somebody in charge."

He vanished inside the stable, leaving Lila to wait and wonder. What if Roper was driven by motives she wasn't even aware of? Could she trust him?

But she was overthinking now. She wanted to trust him. She needed to trust somebody.

A few minutes later, he reappeared. He had splashed his

face and hair with water. Drops glistened on his sun-weathered skin. "If you want to talk, maybe we should get out of the heat," he said.

"The Jeep's still cool, and the AC is working. Let's take a ride. You can drive." Lila tossed him the keys and led the way back to the vehicle shed. Inside, the Jeep was already warming, but when Roper started the engine, the air conditioner kicked in with a cooling blast.

"Where to?" he asked as he backed out of the shed.

"Anywhere." She fastened her seat belt. "Just drive."

At the gate, Roper made a left turn onto the road that would lead past the McKenna ranch and down the lane where Lila had driven him the night she'd picked him up to offer him a job. After hours in the stifling heat of the arena, the blowing air felt deliciously cool on his damp face. But he was here for other reasons.

In his side vision, he could see Lila's profile, a tendril of pale hair fluttering against her cheek. Her silence lay between them, weighing on his concern. Was he in trouble? Should he say something, or wait for her to speak?

But waiting wasn't his way.

"What is it? Have I done something wrong?"

"No, not you," she said. "This is just something I need to talk about. There's nothing you can do to help. All I'm asking is that you listen."

"That sounds easy enough." He slowed the Jeep as they passed the gate to the family ranch. He could see his mother outside hanging sheets on the clothesline. The house had come with a dryer, but Rachel liked to do some things the old-fashioned way. And the air-dried sheets did smell fresh.

Rowdy's pickup was parked in the yard. Roper could only hope the young rascal was getting along with his parents and helping with the work.

Ahead, the lane cut off to the right. Without asking,

Roper swung off the main road and followed the unpaved pathway through the overgrown tangle of brush and trees to where it ended next to a wide curve in the creek overhung with willows. He pulled into the shade, switched off the engine, and opened the windows far enough to let in the sound of water babbling over stones.

After unfastening his seat belt, he turned toward her. "Take all the time you need, Boss. I'm all ears."

She shifted in her seat and took a deep breath. "I know you thought a lot of Frank. Did you know he was cheating on me?"

"I didn't know until Sam showed me the photo you had taken. He was wondering whether the woman could be my sister, Cheyenne. As soon as I saw the woman's hand in the photo, I knew that she wasn't."

"I can't imagine she was the only one," Lila said. "I know he cheated when he was married to Madeleine—and not just with me. Sorry, I can't say I'm proud of that, but I had my reasons."

"No need to apologize. I'm not here to judge you."

She leaned back in her seat. "When Frank died, I tried to put the past behind me. I told myself the cheating didn't matter anymore. Then I got a phone call from the woman in the picture. Her name is Crystal Carter. She's pregnant."

Roper had seen the photo and was aware of the woman. He wasn't surprised that she would contact Lila. But pregnant? That was a stunner. For a moment he was lost for words. *I'm sorry* didn't seem appropriate here.

"And she claims the baby is Frank's?"

"I insisted that she take an in vitro paternity test," Lila said. "The doctor called me with the results. Guess what?"

She'd spoken calmly, but there was a broken undertone in her voice. For all her cool demeanor, Roper sensed that she was devastated.

"I take it the woman wants money," he said.

"Yes. I wrote her a check today, just to help her out. But that's not the half of it."

She nodded, her lips pressed together, visibly battling emotion. Roper waited for her to go on.

"She knows about the legal fight for the ranch," Lila said. "She offered to let me adopt her baby—making the child my legal heir and Frank's—for a million dollars."

Roper pretended not to be shocked. "So the dispute over the will would go away."

"In theory." Her tone was laced with irony. "I have yet to talk to a lawyer."

He mouthed a silent curse. "That's monstrous," he said. "I don't know the law, but I think an offer like that could be illegal as well."

She gave him a fragile smile. "Thank you. I'm glad you agree with me. But the situation isn't that simple."

"I can imagine."

"It's not the money. Even if I couldn't bargain for less, I could manage it if I had to. It's not even the legality. Things like that can be done under the table if you've got a smart lawyer."

She was struggling now, her voice on the edge of breaking. "It's the baby, Roper. That poor, innocent little thing. If I walk away from this, she's threatening to get rid of it."

"My guess is that she's playing you," Roper said. "The baby's a Culhane. As long as the child lives, she'll have that connection to Frank's family and whatever money or influence it can buy her. Without it, she'll have nothing."

"But imagine the baby growing up with that woman as a mother—a woman with no resources, a woman who'd exploit her own child. If I were to go through with the adoption—yes, I'd be giving the baby every advantage money could buy. But how would you feel if you were that child and you found out you'd been bought like a piece of property for reasons that had nothing to do with love?"

"But surely you'd come to love the baby."

"Would I?" she demanded. "What if I couldn't—because of my guilt or because I couldn't forgive Frank? I'd be no better than the woman who sold me her child. Maybe that's really what scares me."

The tears had begun to flow, salty rivulets accompanied by muffled sobs, as if something had broken inside her, releasing her tightly guarded emotions.

Lila had stood alone in the storm since Frank's death, and even before that. Frank's family was against her. Even the cook had sided with her rival. And the FBI agent would arrest her in a heartbeat if he could find a reason.

Here on the ranch, Roper realized, he was her only hope of an ally. But he'd done a pitiful job of being there for her, behaving as if he cared only about the horses and winning the upcoming contest. She needed a champion. So far, he had failed her.

Lila was a proud, independent woman who hid her tender heart. He was seeing that heart now, and it was breaking.

Her hands balled into fists as she struggled to stop her tears. "I'm sorry . . ." she muttered. "You shouldn't have to see me like this. It's not in your . . . job description."

"It doesn't matter. Come here." He wrapped her in his arms and drew her against his chest. She went rigid for an instant. Then she softened and pressed her damp face into his shirt.

Overcome by tenderness, he cradled her, his lips nibbling a trail of kisses along her hairline. Holding her felt right. Maybe too right. But for now, that didn't matter.

She released a long tight breath.

"Let it go," he murmured. "You don't have to be the boss all the time."

"Then who's going to make the decisions—and live with the consequences? It can't be you—you work for me. And I won't let it be Darrin. He'd sell the horses and turn the whole place into a cattle operation. Sometimes I think about how easy it would be to give up and walk away. But I can't. There's nobody else. And now, with so many decisions to make, I feel paralyzed. You can't imagine what it's like. I've watched you, Roper. You always seem so sure of yourself."

A shudder passed through her body. His arms tightened around her. His lips brushed her temple as he spoke. "You don't know how wrong you are. Once, you asked me to tell you a story. At the time, I wasn't ready to share it. But maybe the time is now."

She nestled against him, her breath warm against his throat. Roper took her silence as consent to go on.

"If you don't like me by the time I'm done, that's a chance I'll have to take," he said. "It's about a decision, the worst one I ever made."

He took a deep breath as the memory returned—the high valley, the ragged skyline of the mountains above it. "You know my family came here from Colorado," he said. "We had a small ranch there. Times were hard, especially with the cold winters, but we were happy enough. We survived.

"There was a town nearby, with a school. I had a sweetheart. Her name was Becky. She was a good girl, from a religious family, but I was wild, and she wanted to please me. You can guess what happened. She got pregnant. I did the honorable thing and married her."

Lila's body tensed slightly, but she didn't speak.

"It wasn't as bad as you might think. We were young and crazy in love. We were excited about the baby. But her parents had kicked her out, and we had hardly any money at all. We had to move in with my family.

"We wanted to be on our own before the baby came. For that, we needed cash, and I knew of just one way to get it. I left Becky with my folks, renewed my PRCA card, and went on the rodeo circuit.

"It was the summer season, Cowboy Christmas, with rodeos every week. I got an old truck running and hit the road. Becky wasn't due till fall. I promised her I'd be back in plenty of time for the baby, but she was having a rough time of it. I still remember how she cried when I left."

Lila stirred, shifting against him. When she looked up, he caught a fresh glimmer of tears in her eyes. By now she would have guessed how the story ended. Still, he felt compelled to finish it.

"I slept in the truck and ate out of cans to save all the money I could. There was no cell phone service at the ranch, so it was hard to keep in touch. I did manage a few collect calls, but the connections weren't the best, so I focused winning money to bring home.

"I was a pretty good bronc rider, both bareback and saddle. I didn't always win, but I usually finished in the money. As the weeks passed, I could tell that I was getting better and better.

"The time came when I'd promised Becky to be home. But there was one big rodeo left the following weekend—with a ten thousand dollar first prize for bronc riding. Winning could make all the difference for my new family. I decided to stay and drive home after the rodeo."

"And did you win?" Lila asked.

"Not a nickel. The horse bucked me off out of the gate, and I broke my ankle when I hit the dirt. The medic taped me up so I could drive home, but on the way out of town, the clutch went out on the truck. It cost me two days and a chunk of my savings to get it replaced, but I was finally on my way again. If I didn't lose any more time, I figured that I could still make it back in time for the baby." He fell silent for a moment, remembering. "I came back to a grave."

"Oh, Roper," Lila whispered.

"Becky's labor started early. My mother had planned to help her with a home delivery, which was how she'd had all her own children. But with Becky, there were complications, and not enough time to get her to a hospital. She died in the truck. The baby—a little girl—didn't make it either. Maybe if I'd been there, I could have done something to save her. I still blame myself for that. At least I would have started for the hospital at the first sign of trouble."

"What happened wasn't your fault," Lila protested.

"Wasn't it? My mother said it was God's punishment because we'd sinned. But I don't believe God had anything to do with it. It was my decision not to come back when I'd promised to." He shook his head. "It's not a pretty story, but I'm telling it because if you see me as a man who's too cocksure to make a mistake, you couldn't be more wrong—"

"Stop beating on yourself, Roper!"

Her lips blocked his words. His heart slammed as she pressed upward, deepening the kiss. He circled her with his arms, feeling her warmth, her yielding softness and his own racing pulse. Need, like hot pain, surged in him—not just need for her body but for her tenderness, her understanding, and her love. He kept his response gentle. His kisses were slow and deep, as if his soul was reaching for hers. Her fresh tears wet his face. He ached to love her. But this wasn't the time or the place.

Reluctantly, he eased her away. "We need to get back to

the ranch, Boss," he said. "Back to where we were—and who we were."

"Yes." She brushed back her hair, her lips curving in the slightest hint of a smile. "But only for now."

Her words triggered a surge of hope. This could be the beginning of something real. But hope was a fragile thing, and there was a world out there that could shatter it like a blown glass ornament. Roper was no fool. He knew.

CHAPTER TEN

Darrin was reviewing case files when his wife walked into his office, unannounced. He gave her an annoyed look. "Simone, I told you to knock before you come in here. Can't you remember anything?"

"Sorry." She was flushed and slightly breathless. "I just got a call from Mariah. She saw something. Something that could be important."

Darrin swiveled to face her. "All right. What did she say?"

Simone sank into a chair. "Lila went out at lunchtime. But she didn't take the Porsche. She took the Jeep. When she came back, Roper came out of the stables. They got into the Jeep together, drove out of the gate, and turned left toward where his ranch is." She paused for breath. "They were gone a little over half an hour. Then they came back and parked in the shed. He opened the door for her, touched her shoulder, and went back to work."

"Interesting," Darrin said. "But it all sounds pretty ordinary to me. I don't understand why—"

"Don't you see? He touched her shoulder. *Touched her shoulder!* She's his boss. Why would he do that if it didn't mean something? And they'd just been somewhere alone, plenty long enough to—"

"Okay, I get the picture," Darrin said. "I've still got to prepare my case against Lila."

"But you might not need it. They're lovers—and I'd bet my life that one of them killed your father. I'd rather it had been Lila, but I think it was more likely Roper. He wanted a chance to compete in the Run for a Million, and he wanted Lila. Now he's got both. And his only alibi is his parents. They claimed he was home all night. You know they'd lie for him."

Simone pushed out of the chair and stood quivering. "I'm going to call that FBI man right now. If Roper McKenna isn't behind bars by tomorrow, I'll be demanding to know why!"

Working in the bungalow, Sam sighed as Simone ended the phone call. He'd agreed with much of what she'd said—yes, it was possible that Roper and Lila were involved. And yes, it was possible that one of them, most likely Roper, had murdered Frank. But only possible. Nothing she'd told Sam was proof. As for the alleged affair, even if the two had been caught in bed together, any bearing on the crime would be circumstantial at best.

He needed evidence—blood, prints, a weapon, a witness, an admission of guilt, or something else of equal weight. When he'd explained all this to Simone, she'd ended the call in a huff.

Sam understood. He even felt sorry for her. She was pregnant and married to an abusive man who gave her no validation. Taking over the ranch house was likely her one hope of happiness. In her helpless condition, she was fighting for it any way she could.

At times like this, all Sam wanted was to throw up his hands and leave. But for him, giving up would be unthinkable. It wasn't just that his reputation hinged on solving Frank Culhane's murder. He wanted the truth. He wanted justice. He wanted honor. He couldn't walk away. Not even to be with Jasmine again.

He'd followed every clue, done interviews and background checks on every suspect. What was he missing? He needed a breakthrough.

He was reviewing the notes from Mariah's interview about Charlie when he heard a knock. After closing the computer screen, he got up from the table and opened the door.

Mariah stood in the doorway. She was shepherding two boys who appeared to be brothers, in their early teens. They were dressed in faded jeans with mud-stained knees. The smaller boy wore a Dallas Cowboys T-shirt. The other boy was bare chested. Their feet were clad in worn, soggy sneakers.

Both of the boys were tanned and freckled with sun-bleached hair from long summer days spent outdoors. Their bicycles lay at the end of the driveway. Sam guessed that they were from one of the ranches that bordered the McKenna spread.

"These boys came to the house and asked to speak to the FBI man. They say they have something to show you." Mariah, her duty done, turned away and headed back to her kitchen. Only then did Sam notice that the older boy was carrying something bundled into a damp gray shirt.

He ushered the boys inside, introduced himself, and gave them cold sodas to drink. "You must've had a long, hot ride to get here," he said. "Let's see what you brought to show me."

The older boy handed Sam the rolled shirt. "We were fishing in the creek when we found this. Our mom said we should bring it to you."

It occurred to Sam to wonder how the boys' mother had known he'd be here. But this rural ranch country was not so different from a small town. Word would have spread.

Wearing latex gloves, Sam laid the shirt on the table and unrolled it to expose what was inside. His breath caught.

Lying amid the damp folds, coated with mud and moss, was a veterinary-sized hypodermic syringe.

Pulse galloping, Sam covered the syringe and turned to the boys. "Tell me exactly where and how you found this," he said.

The older boy spoke. "Like I say, we were fishing in the creek—mostly for fun. There aren't many fish there now that the water's so low. My hook snagged on something. I waded into the water to get it loose. That's when I saw this needle. It was stuck between two rocks."

"How did you get it out?" Sam asked. "What did you touch? Did anything stick you?"

The boy shook his head. "I was careful. I used my pocket knife to work it loose. I just touched the end when I put it in my shirt. At first, I thought maybe some junkie had tossed it out of his car. But then I saw that it was too big for that. It looked more like something for a horse or cow. I took it because I didn't want some little kid to find it."

Smart lad, Sam thought. A find like this in the wrong hands could have led to a bad outcome. Had the boys just brought him the murder weapon? That remained to be seen.

He couldn't count on the local crime lab for this. The syringe would have to be delivered, preferably by hand, to the FBI lab to check for any prints, DNA, and any trace of fentanyl. Given its muddy condition, finding anything useful would be a challenge. But even a small clue could crack this case wide open.

Sam drew a $10 bill out of his wallet. "I'll need to keep your shirt," he said, handing the boy the money. "This should buy you a new one. Now, what I want to do is drive you boys home and let you show me exactly where you found this. We can put your bikes in the back of my vehicle. All right?"

The boys nodded, clearly excited to be involved in solving an actual crime. They watched while Sam photographed the syringe, covered it with the shirt again, and zipped it into an evidence bag before stripping off his gloves.

"One more thing," Sam said. "You need to promise me you'll keep all this a secret. Not a word to your friends or anybody, understand?"

"Can we tell our folks?" the younger boy asked.

"All right. But they'll need to keep the secret, too. It's very important. Do you promise?"

Wide-eyed, the boys promised. Sam loaded the bikes into the back of the SUV, made sure the boys were buckled into their seats, and set out to follow their directions.

He knew the road. It was the one he'd taken when he went to interview the McKenna family. The creek, which flowed south, meandered on the right-hand side through a shallow wash. The creek was low in the dry summer, with boulders emerging from the water. Redwing blackbirds flitted among clumps of overhanging willow.

A sturdy wooden bridge, supported by thick logs, crossed the creek bed where a dirt road cut off to the McKenna ranch. Sam had driven across it when he'd visited Roper's family. But at the time he'd paid the crossing scant attention. The bridge blended into the landscape as it likely had for decades.

They had driven past the bridge when the older boy touched Sam's arm. "Stop," he said. "It was here. I remember that dead stump by the water."

Sam braked and pulled off the road. The bridge was a dozen yards back—a distance from which the syringe could have easily been thrown by a good arm or dropped into the water and washed downstream.

His heart drummed as he climbed out of the vehicle with his phone ready to take pictures. Roper McKenna had been high on his list of suspects. The horse trainer had just been moved to the top.

Charlie sat at his office computer, pasting the new photo of Jasmine the elephant into his website. He'd caught her at a moment when she was lunging at one of her tormentors with her ears spread like wings and her eyes blazing fury. The tusks he'd photoshopped into place made a nice addition, even though he would have to explain their absence later.

Of course, he'd cropped the bottom edge of the photo to hide the leg irons that kept her from moving more than a few steps. He'd also removed the log fence from the background and replaced it with a fiery sunset. The result was a dramatic photo guaranteed to stir the pulse of any big game hunter. Photoshop was a wonderful invention.

Bids to shoot the elephant were still coming in. Charlie knew enough about the market to single out the serious customers—hunters who were decent shots and wouldn't freeze when the critical moment came. They would also need the cash to pay up-front.

With a click, he saved the photo to the page. This image should bring in even more high rollers. He would wait another week, then close the bidding and pick an offer that was both high and safe. With such a big, dangerous animal involved, he couldn't afford to let anything go wrong.

Too bad Miss Jasmine Culhane wouldn't be here to see her namesake go down. Charlie had lusted after Jasmine for years, ever since she'd sat in the front row of the high school algebra class he'd taught. But after she'd become involved with the animal rights group that had raided his ranch, he'd been cured of his obsession. He had her red

Corvette as a consolation prize. And there were plenty of other women out there who'd appreciate a good man with money.

After sending the image out to his potential clients, Charlie shut down the computer, rinsed out a glass, and poured himself three fingers of Jack Daniel's. Sipping, he meandered out onto the wide verandah and stood at the rail.

His kingdom spread before him, a modest stretch of untrimmed grassland dotted with clumps of sage, mesquite, and a few acacia trees he'd planted himself—not so different from the African savannah where animals such as lions, leopards, giraffes, and zebras roamed free.

Two vultures, then a third, circled against the cerulean sky, riding the warm updrafts. Charlie had never been to Africa. As far as he knew, neither had any of his clients. But he'd done plenty of reading—books by men such as John Hunter, Jack O'Connor, and Peter Capstick. And he'd watched all the movies. He was selling the big game safari fantasy. That meant making the experience as realistic as possible.

Ten years ago, when he'd first told his grandmother that he wanted to quit teaching and start a game ranch, the old woman had been horrified. She'd even threatened to disinherit him and donate the property to a nature sanctuary. These days, he seldom thought about the old woman. When he did, he wondered what she might think of her grandson's successful business. Would she be proud or ashamed? But that no longer mattered.

A band of feral hogs trotted across the yard, as bold as you please. Almost a dozen sows, piglets, and rank, husky boars were so close that Charlie could have hit them with the toss of a stone. Attracted by the smells from the compound, the hogs were a nuisance. But since they were on his property, Charlie's hired men could legally shoot a couple to feed the big cats. He would let them know, or maybe do the job himself.

Tonight he'd be turning out an aging lioness for the hunt. Her teeth were mostly gone, but she still had enough spunk to put up a fight. The hunter was starring in a new TV adventure series and wanted the experience of killing a dangerous animal. It would be Charlie's job to see that he got his money's worth.

After that, it would be time to prepare for the elephant shoot.

Sam drove back to Abilene with the syringe wrapped in the shirt and sealed in the evidence bag. The chain of custody required that it remain in his possession until logged into Evidence. And even without that rule, he couldn't trust the mail service to protect it from loss or contamination.

After photographing the spot where the syringe had been found, he had driven the boys home and taken their fingerprints, along with their mother's. The prints would be used to eliminate any that might be found on the evidence.

The task of collecting Roper's prints from his truck in the parking lot had left Sam conflicted. Until now, he had liked and respected the man. Part of him still hoped to find Roper innocent. But he had a job to do. And assuming the syringe was the murder weapon, any trace of Roper's fingerprints or DNA on it would make an ironclad case for his guilt.

Still, there were questions. Why would a man as smart as Roper dump the weapon so close to his home, where it could be easily found? Maybe he'd needed to get rid of it in a hurry. Maybe he'd been missed at home and someone had come out looking for him.

Or maybe he'd been framed. Maybe the real killer had dropped the syringe in the creek for a reason. Sam hoped the lab would find some answers. But there were no guarantees.

Nick met him in the parking garage. By then the workday had almost ended, but the evidence desk was manned around the clock. "So you think you've finally got a breakthrough," he said.

"That remains to be seen." Sam took the evidence bag, along with the fingerprint samples, out of a cooler in the vehicle. "I'm trying not to get excited until we hear from the lab. It's spent weeks in the water, so we'll be lucky to find anything on the outside. But there could be traces of fentanyl inside the syringe. That's what I'm hoping for. That, and any DNA in the needle that could be Frank's."

"Let's get this logged in and routed to the lab," Nick said. "I can try to rush them, but they're busy down there. You may not hear for a few days. Will you be staying in town?"

"I planned to drive back tonight. It'll be late when I get there, but I've got a good place to stay. I can't fault Mrs. Culhane for her hospitality, though I know she'll be glad to see the last of me."

"Well, a man's got to eat. Share a pizza with me before you start back. There's a good little place around the corner. My treat."

"I won't turn that down." Sam sensed that his boss and former mentor wanted to talk. He was curious and more than a little apprehensive. Was he about to get some bad news?

After logging the syringe into Evidence, they left the building and walked to the small restaurant. It was early for the dinner hour, and the place was quiet. The décor was traditional, with red-checked tablecloths, candles in wine bottles, and travel posters of Italy on the walls. In their booth, Nick ordered a large deluxe pizza and two Michelobs to sip while they waited.

"Have you made any big plans for your retirement, Nick?" Sam asked.

Nick's expression shifted, deepening the furrow between his thick gray brows. He shook his head. "Sometimes life has a way of making plans for you," he said. "But never mind that. It can wait. What I want to talk about now is your case."

"That's what brought me here."

"Do you expect to have it wrapped up soon? I'm asking because you can't stay on that ranch forever. The bureau needs you here in Abilene."

"I'll have a better answer for you when we hear from the lab. If that syringe turns out to be the murder weapon, and it has any trace of prints or DNA, that should tell the story."

"And if it doesn't?"

"Then I'll keep trying. Somebody planned Frank Culhane's murder and carried it out in cold blood. If you need to pull me off the case, I won't argue. You're the boss. But I'll be damned if I'm going to quit on my own."

"And you're looking at the horse trainer?"

"Everything fits. If the evidence points to Roper McKenna, we'll have our murderer."

"What about Culhane's widow? I get the impression they're lovers. Could she have been involved in her husband's death?"

"We can't rule her out. There's no evidence, but Frank was cheating on her. If we nail Roper, he might give her up under pressure. You know how that works."

The pizza had arrived, heaped with toppings and still sizzling from the oven. Sam and Nick helped themselves to generous slices and waited a moment for them to cool.

"And the girlfriend? You told me she was pregnant."

"That's right. If Frank knew, and he refused to marry her or even support her, that would give her a reason to kill him."

"I'm of two minds about that. But why would she kill the father of her baby, especially if there was a chance he'd change his mind later on? Besides, if the syringe turns out to be the murder weapon, it doesn't make sense that she'd toss it in the creek. As far as I know, she doesn't even know Roper."

"What about Frank's son? Have you cleared him?"

Sam took a bite of his slice, savoring the taste of sausage, onion, peppers, and melted cheese. "Darrin is still on the list. From all indications, he had issues with his father. And he hates Roper. If Darrin did kill Frank—or even if he didn't—he could have planted that syringe to frame the man. I'm hoping the lab can give us answers."

"And the girl? Frank's daughter? Is she out of the picture?"

Sam willed his expression to freeze, betraying nothing. But Nick was looking at him as if he already knew about his secret relationship with Jasmine.

"She loved her father, and she had nothing to gain by killing him," Sam said.

"But she could have been working for her mother. She's with her mother now." Nick drained his glass and leaned forward, across the table. "Be careful, Sam. The Culhane family is toxic. You're a good man and I'd hate to see you get burned, especially when it could jeopardize your case and affect your career."

Sam's stomach clenched. He should have known that Nick would guess the truth. He was being warned before the axe fell.

"Thanks, I understand." Sam hid his reaction as he helped himself to more pizza. "We were going to talk about your retirement."

"Were we?" Nick hadn't eaten much.

"I'm aware that you need me here," Sam said. "I'll do my best to make that happen."

"Thanks. We're shorthanded as it is, and I can't bring myself to leave until you're back. None of the other agents have the experience to run this place. If we can't do our jobs here, we'll be shut down. Everything will be transferred to Amarillo."

"Can you give me a rundown on your case load?" Sam asked.

"Mostly the usual, not much different from Chicago. Drugs. Kidnappings and human trafficking across state lines. Conspiracy groups. Mob activity—and before you ask, I'm still trying to nail Louis Divino. I may have to turn that case over to you."

Sam studied his old friend across the table. In the flickering candlelight, Nick looked old and weary. He appeared to have lost weight over the past weeks. Sam didn't like what he saw.

"You've told me about the case load," Sam said. "What can you tell me about yourself?"

Nick sighed. "You'll find out sooner or later, so I guess it might as well be now. I've got prostate cancer, Sam. And it's not the slow kind that can last inside a man for years. It's a fast mover, already spreading. My doctor's pushing me to start chemo. But first, I want to leave things here in good hands."

The news struck Sam like a blow to the gut. How could that be right? Nick had always been so strong, so wise. This was the last thing he'd expected to hear.

"Nick, don't put this off," he said. "I'll quit the ranch and come back tomorrow if I need to. Your life matters ten times more than finding the person who killed Frank Culhane."

Nick shook his head. "It's my call to make. I'm scheduled to start treatment the first of September. I'll be needing you here before then. Otherwise . . ." He left the thought for Sam to finish.

Sam calculated the time in his head. The need to be here and free Nick for treatment gave him just a few weeks to find Frank Culhane's killer. If the lab found incriminating evidence on the syringe he'd turned in, the case could be wrapped up early. But he couldn't count on that. He only knew that from here on out he would need to work harder and smarter. Otherwise he'd be forced to walk away with the case unsolved and his own reputation tarnished.

But in light of Nick's illness, none of that could be allowed to matter.

"Don't worry, Nick, I'll be here," he promised. "I won't make you wait. But meanwhile, I'll do whatever it takes to put Frank Culhane's killer behind bars."

Roper took the chestnut stallion from a full gallop to a perfect sliding stop. Fire Dance was a natural performer. He'd racked up good money for his owners. But learning to trust a new rider in a new place, especially after the attack from a rival, had taken time. At last, the horse was coming around. When he was good, he was flawless. The only question now was one of consistency. With the Run for a Million less than two weeks away, some intensive work lay ahead.

He walked the stallion around the arena to cool him, then dismounted and turned him over to a groom to be showered and put away. He still needed time with One in a Million, who'd be coming to Vegas as his backup horse. The big roan had settled down since his assault on Fire Dance. But it remained to be seen whether the two stallions could be trailered to Las Vegas together.

As a professional trainer, Roper was allowed to bring

three horses. His second backup horse for the event was a filly, a daughter of Million Dollar Baby via embryo transplant to a brood mare. Her sire had been Blood Diamond, a stallion from the Four Sixes Ranch. Her registered name, Million Dollar Diamond, reflected her pedigree. But around the stable, she was known by her nickname, Milly. Already a futurity winner, with her mother's white face and blazing talent, Milly was full of promise. But she was young and inexperienced—a long shot, if needed, to fill in for one of the stallions.

Waiting for One in a Million to be brought out, Roper paused to drink from his water bottle. From where he stood, he could see the house, with its patio and pool in the rear. He hadn't seen Lila since yesterday when he'd brought her home after their talk.

He remembered the sensual magic of their long, deep kisses. Things were finally good between them, with the promise of more, Roper told himself. But a buried instinct whispered a warning. Something was just waiting to go wrong.

Maybe that was the trouble. Life had taught him that nothing could be counted on. And the higher your hopes, the harder you'd fall when fate came along to send everything crashing down around you.

For now, he would keep his distance, letting her come to him if she needed him. Lila had enough on her mind, with her fight to keep the ranch and the demands of Frank's pregnant mistress.

He remembered the photograph Sam had shown him—the woman's dark hair and her hand, bedecked with cheap rings and long fake nails, resting against Frank's jacket.

Something clicked in Roper's memory. He had seen her someplace else, and he suddenly remembered where.

The jail—he'd been waiting to speak with his brother,

and she'd been there ahead of him to visit the prisoner in the next cell. He remembered the shouting and the swearing from the adjoining room before she'd stalked out and fled into the night.

Had she spoken to him on the way out? Maybe not. The memory had faded. But Roper was sure of what he'd seen—the hair, the nails, the rings . . . it had to be her.

He had to let Lila know.

After opening a bank account, Crystal had used her new debit card to get her hair and nails done at the beauty salon. She'd opted for eyelash extensions, too, even though she didn't really need them. When she looked in the mirror, the woman gazing back at her was as glamorous as a movie star—well worth the money she'd spent.

She'd also spent a few hundred dollars on clothes and shoes. Not that Willow Bend had the classiest selection. She could do more shopping later at the big mall in Abilene. She was going to need maternity clothes, too, but that could wait. At least she wouldn't be needing them for long.

Still driving Judd's piece-of-crap car, she passed a white Ford Focus pulled off the road with a hand-lettered For Sale sign on it. She called the phone number. An hour later she was driving to the courthouse to register the title. Crystal was no stranger to cars. This one was in decent condition, and she'd talked the price down from $10,000 to $7,500. It wasn't a Porsche like Lila Culhane had, but at least it was white.

She'd parked Judd's car on the shoulder of the road and left it there. As far as she knew, Judd was still in jail, awaiting trial. The least she could do was tell him where to find the car. And she wasn't above letting him see how far she'd come in the world. She would enjoy laughing in his face and walking away.

The waiting room at the jail was empty. After the woman at the desk patted her down and took her new knockoff designer purse, Crystal walked back to the room that contained the cells. Today, Judd was the only prisoner. Rumpled and unshaven, with a ketchup stain on his orange jumpsuit, he glared at her through the bars.

"Well, look at you, missy," he said, sneering. "All gussied up like a hundred-dollar whore. Did you rob a bank, or find yourself a new sugar daddy?"

"Neither, you butthead. I'm making better choices, that's all," Crystal said. "I just came to tell you I won't be needing your car anymore. It's parked on the shoulder, out by the power station. I gave the key to the lady at the desk. You can pick up your old junker when you get out of jail, if it hasn't been towed."

For an instant, he looked as if he wanted to strangle her. Then his anger fell away. He gazed at her through the bars with the hangdog expression she'd once thought was cute. Now Crystal found it annoying.

"Come back to me, baby," he said. "I wanted to die when you left me. Some rich old bastard can't love you the way I do. Nobody can."

"Go to hell, Judd." Crystal turned and walked out of the room.

Behind her, she could hear him cursing, calling her every vile name a man could use against a woman.

She didn't look back.

Chapter Eleven

Lila was at her desk, updating the stable accounts, when her cell phone rang. Her pulse cartwheeled as she saw Roper's name on the caller ID. But it wouldn't be like him to call her in the middle of a busy workday. Maybe something was wrong.

"Roper? What is it?" she asked.

"I'll make this quick, Boss," he said. "I just remembered something—thought I'd better pass it on, in case you haven't made a decision about that woman's baby."

"I haven't. What is it?"

"I saw her, in the jail when my brother got arrested. She was there to visit a boyfriend. From what I heard, I got the impression she was breaking up with him. But I could be wrong."

"You're sure it was her?"

"Positive. I recognized her jewelry from the photo. I know you told me the baby was Frank's, and DNA doesn't lie. But you need to know that there's another man involved. He could be part of a scheme to get money from you."

The news wasn't surprising. A woman who looked like Crystal would be a magnet for men. That was one of the reasons Lila had insisted on a paternity test.

Was the boyfriend pulling Crystal's strings? Had he been using her in a scheme to take advantage of Frank and get money? It was possible. But this information couldn't be allowed to influence Lila's decision. What really mattered here was the future of an innocent baby—Frank's child. She was still torn.

"He may have mentioned something to my brother," Roper said. "I can ask him."

"Thanks. That can wait for now. But I should probably share this with Sam. He disappeared yesterday, but his car's outside the bungalow this morning. I'll find him later. Is everything else all right?"

"Fine. Fire Dance is performing like a champ. I should let you go." He paused. "Boss, I just want to say—" He broke off as if he'd changed his mind.

"What?" she asked.

"Nothing. I need to get back to work."

He ended the call, leaving Lila to wonder what he'd almost said to her. Had it been something tender, some hint that he might even love her?

But that would be too much to expect. It was too soon for love. She was still raw from Frank's betrayal and death. And Roper was a man who guarded his heart behind a wall of stone.

Steeling herself against the memory of his mouth on hers, his arms clasping her close as his body filled her urgent need, Lila went back to work on the accounts.

Sam was making his second coffee of the morning when he got the call from Nick. "Surprise," he said. "I didn't expect to hear from you so soon. Have you got any news?"

"Yes," Nick said. "The lab folks rushed it for me. I bribed them with a dozen donuts. Anyway, I've got good news and bad."

"Go on." Sam's pulse kicked into overdrive.

"First the good. They found traces of fentanyl in the syringe. Given where it was found, there's a good chance we've got the murder weapon."

Sam exhaled. "And the bad news?"

"There were no fingerprints, DNA, or anything else that could ID the killer. Whoever it was, they were probably smart enough to wear gloves. The mud and other detritus from the creek bed didn't help either. So we still don't have anything that would hold up in court."

"Thanks, Nick. At least it's a good lead. My money's still on Roper McKenna. If the lab finds anything else, let me know."

"That's not likely, but if they do, you'll be the first to hear. Keep me posted."

Nick ended the call. Lost in thought, Sam stood gazing down at the phone. Zeroing in on Roper too soon would be a mistake. He needed to consider anyone who might have a reason to frame the horse trainer and who would know where to toss the syringe.

Charlie? He was still a long shot, but Frank could have been holding a threat over him. And he would know where Roper lived. Even if he and Roper weren't enemies, Charlie could have planted the syringe to deflect suspicion.

Darrin? He had already tried to frame Lila with a clumsily planted syringe in her car. Only Madeleine's insistence that her son was acting on her orders had saved him from arrest. But he could still use a different version of the same trick to target a man he hated.

As for Simone, Sam knew better than to underestimate Darrin's wife. Beneath her fluttery charm-school demeanor, the woman was strong-willed, determined, and possibly smarter than her husband. He couldn't count her out—especially if the two were working together.

And then there was Lila . . .

Sam's musings were interrupted by a knock. He opened the door. As if the thought had summoned her, Lila was standing on the porch.

"I need to talk to you," she said.

"Come on in." He stepped aside. "Can I get you some coffee?"

She shook her head. "I'm good, thanks. I just wanted to give you an update. We can talk on the porch."

"Sure." Sam pulled the two Adirondack chairs into the morning shade and invited her to sit. He would listen, but he resolved to tell her nothing. The discovery of the murder weapon would remain a secret. He settled in the opposite chair.

Speaking in terse sentences, she told him about the paternity test results and Crystal's ongoing demands for money. Sam kept his responses neutral, trying not to judge. It made sense that Crystal would need help, although it didn't seem fair that Lila would be on the hook to support her late husband's mistress.

Lila seemed uneasy, as if holding something back. But Sam knew better than to push her. He listened and waited.

"There's something else," she said. "Crystal's got another man. His name's Judd. He's in the county jail. Crystal went to visit him, and Roper saw her. He didn't realize who she was until later, when he remembered the photo you showed him.

"Is Roper certain that's who he saw?"

"He said he recognized the rings on her hand."

"And what was Roper doing there?"

"His brother was locked up for drug possession. Roper had gone to help him out. Roper said that Crystal and Judd were having a loud argument, like she was breaking up with him. Judd swore at her, and she went storming out of the jail. That's all I know."

Sam already knew about Roper's brother. But the news about Judd opened up a world of possibilities. He needed to check the date of Judd's arrest. If Crystal's boyfriend had been free at the time of the murder, he could have killed Frank out of jealousy.

"Thank you, I'll definitely look into this," he told Lila.

"Would it be asking too much for you to tell me what you learn about him?" she asked. "I need to know. It's important."

"Important why?"

She glanced away before returning his gaze. "I need to know whether he and Crystal were involved in a scheme to get money from Frank—and then from me. I know you're not allowed to discuss your case. But this is a separate matter."

"I understand," Sam said. "But I can't make any promises. What I tell you will depend on what I learn."

"Of course."

"Is there anything else you wanted to tell me? Anything at all?"

Again, there was a beat of hesitation. "No. Nothing."

Her voice had taken on a chilly note. They weren't friends, Sam reminded himself. In his line of work, making friends was against the rules—rules he'd broken in spades when he'd fallen in love with Jasmine.

His thoughts strayed to Jasmine as Lila left the porch and headed back to the house. Damn, but he missed her—her husky Liz Taylor voice, her mischievous laugh, and the heat of her silky, suntanned skin against his.

He remembered Nick's warning. Until this case was closed, he mustn't see her or even try to contact her. Even the burner she'd bought wasn't completely safe. For now, the best he could do was find her father's killer and hope that once he was free, she would still be waiting.

Lila had just brought him a new lead—and one more suspect to add to his list. The idea that Frank had been killed by a jealous boyfriend, one who'd have easy access to fentanyl, made sense. The murder weapon's location didn't fit the profile, but there could be an explanation for that—some connection he had yet to discover.

Meanwhile, he would start with a call to the court. The right person should be able to give him Judd's last name and the date of his arrest. If Crystal's paramour had been behind bars when Frank died, he'd have a perfect alibi. But that didn't mean he was innocent of scheming against the Culhanes.

Keying in the number of the court clerk, Sam made the call. After several rings without an answer, a voice mail recording came on. The clerk wouldn't be available until tomorrow. He would have to try again in the morning.

Jasmine's fingers shook as she entered Sam's cell number on her burner phone. She was about to complete the call when she realized she'd misdialed a digit. She deleted the number and tried again. But her grip was unsteady. The phone slipped from her hand and clattered to the kitchen floor.

Trembling, Jasmine retrieved the phone. What had she been thinking? She'd been told not to call Sam. Not even after what had happened tonight. The consequences of even one phone call could get him suspended or killed.

Her memory relived the events of the past hour. That evening, her mother and Louis had eaten a sunset dinner of coq au vin and champagne on the condo balcony before going to a music concert in downtown Austin. Madeleine had complained of a blinding headache that morning and spent the afternoon sleeping in her room. The nap had done wonders. For a terminally ill woman, she was radiant—laughing, tossing her abundant auburn hair, and flashing the diamond earrings Louis had given her for her recent birthday.

After the meal, they had left in Louis's vintage black Lincoln Town Car, with his driver at the wheel. The driver was undoubtedly armed, the car chassis and windows reinforced against attack. Still Jasmine couldn't help worrying about her mother—not only because of Louis Divino's dangerous lifestyle but because of his character.

True, Louis seemed to care for her. He treated her like a queen. But he was a cold-blooded killer who dealt in drugs, weapons, human trafficking, and murder for hire. And under his influence, perhaps, Madeleine had thrown all caution to the wind. She had stopped seeing doctors, stopped any medical treatment. It was as if she wanted to go out in a blaze of self-destruction. And there was nothing Jasmine could do to change her mother's mind.

Jasmine had stood on the balcony and watched the big black car drive away. She could tell from the way Madeleine had clung to Louis's arm that she'd be coming home late. It was almost as if the two of them had reversed roles, with Jasmine as the mother and Madeleine as the reckless daughter.

The urge to call Sam was an ache inside her. She missed the gentle wisdom in his voice and his way of reading her emotions even when she was silent. She could tell him anything, even her concerns about her mother. But with his career on the line, she knew better than to try. Until her father's killer was arrested, even calling on the burner would be a risk. And the last thing she wanted to do was put him up against Louis Divino.

The maid had left after preparing dinner. Jasmine didn't

mind cleaning up and running the dishwasher. Maybe after that, she could find a good movie to stream on TV.

She'd almost finished clearing the outdoor table when she noticed Louis's brown leather jacket hanging on the back of his chair. He must've taken it off before dinner, then forgotten it when he left with Madeleine for the concert.

A breeze had sprung up from the west, raising whitecaps on Lake Travis. Sooty clouds billowed above the horizon. The coming storm would probably bring nothing but wind and dust, but she could hardly leave an expensive jacket out in the weather.

Balancing a pair of wineglasses in one hand, she draped the jacket over her arm with her free hand and carried it inside. As she laid it over the back of the sofa, where it could be easily seen, something slipped out of a pocket and dropped behind a seat cushion.

After placing the glasses on a side table, Jasmine reached behind the cushion. Her fingers closed around something hard—a cell phone.

She pulled it out. The phone was an older style, well used and fully charged. Jasmine knew she should put it back where it had come from, but she couldn't keep her imagination from running wild. What if the phone was the modern version of a crime boss's black book, with lists of contacts, payments, debts owed, and more—evidence that, in the right hands, could crush Louis Divino's organization and put him behind bars? If she could take it to the police, or to the FBI . . .

There was no time for that. Maybe she could get into the account and see what was there. But what was she thinking? Louis was a dangerous man. If she tampered with his phone, he would know.

Jasmine remembered the conversation she'd overheard

earlier, mentioning FBI Agent Nick Bellingham. She could try to get in touch with Bellingham—but no, that same conversation had revealed that Madeleine was involved in her lover's drug and money-laundering activities and that Frank had learned about them—which would have gotten him murdered if someone else hadn't killed him first. Calling in the FBI would get her mother arrested. She would spend the rest of her days behind bars, however brief that time might be.

Jasmine stared down at the phone, imagining the evil that innocent-looking device could contain. *Put it back*, she told herself. *Put it back now!*

She picked up the coat from the back of the sofa. There were four pockets—one on each side, an outside breast pocket on the left, and an inside breast pocket on the right. Which pocket had contained the phone? A chill of dread prickled the skin on the back of Jasmine's neck. If she replaced the device in the wrong pocket, Louis would know she'd handled it.

If he were to ask, she could tell him the truth, that the phone had fallen out of his jacket. But would he believe her? Louis hadn't survived this long by trusting people.

A drop of perspiration trickled down her temple as she decided to take a chance on the inside breast pocket. She was about to slip the phone into it when the device rang, loud and piercing in the silence of the room.

In the same moment, she heard the front door open. She froze as heavy footsteps approached down the hallway and Louis stepped into the living room.

The phone had stopped ringing, but Jasmine was still holding it. At the sight of her, his face turned livid.

"What the hell are you doing with my phone?" He snatched it from her hand.

"It fell out of your jacket. I was putting it back." Jasmine tried to keep her voice level, but she was genuinely afraid.

He didn't contradict her, but his expression made it clear what he thought of her reply.

She held out his jacket. "I didn't want to leave this outside," she said. "Believe me, I wasn't snooping."

"Sure you weren't." His voice dripped sarcasm as he took the jacket. "Just mind your own business, girl," he said. "Do that and we'll get along fine."

Without another word, he stalked down the hall toward the door. As he opened it, his phone rang again. He answered it, slamming the door behind him as he left.

Jasmine sank onto the sofa, her knees too weak to support her. Louis had dismissed her. But that didn't mean he'd believed her story. It didn't mean he wouldn't be planning some ghastly accident for her in the near future. She couldn't contact Nick Bellingham without implicating her mother. And she couldn't involve Sam without risking his life.

Was Madeleine in danger, too? Louis appeared to care for her, maybe because he knew she didn't have long to live. But that could change in a heartbeat if he decided she knew too many of his secrets.

Jasmine could try to run. But running would only cast her into suspicion. And Louis had a web of contacts that could reach her anywhere. Even if she could get away, as long as her mother lived, she was duty bound to remain here. Madeleine hadn't been a paragon of perfect motherhood, but she didn't deserve to die alone.

Jasmine stood up and walked out onto the balcony. The sunset had darkened to twilight. Windblown clouds were scudding in over the lake. Jasmine could taste the grit in the air. She thought about Sam. She knew he loved her. But she couldn't call and ask him to keep her safe. He had his own worries, and the risk was too great.

The wind had taken on a chill. Jasmine stepped back inside. She didn't need sharp instincts to tell her that once

Madeleine was gone, Louis would have no more interest in keeping her alive. He might even choose to get rid of her sooner.

Protecting herself—and possibly her mother—would be up to her. She would have to be smart and alert. And she was going to need an escape plan.

The next morning, Sam was able to reach the court clerk. A few weeks earlier, he'd spoken with her in person and presented his FBI credentials. She remembered him and had no problem giving him the information he needed.

"The prisoner you're asking about is Judd Proctor. For now, he's still locked up, charged with dealing controlled substances, mostly cocaine. He was remanded to custody because he has a history as a flight risk. So there he sits, at least until his trial, which is on the docket for Tuesday."

"And his arrest date?" Sam asked.

She gave him the arrest date—three weeks ago today. Well after Frank Culhane's murder. Sam's pulse surged. The timing could mean nothing. Or it could be the key to unlocking this case.

"How do I arrange to talk with him?" Sam asked.

The clerk gave him the number to call for an appointment. "Don't be surprised if his lawyer shows up."

"I'd be more surprised if he didn't show up." Sam thanked the woman and called the number she'd given him. He was able to get an appointment for that afternoon, with Judd Proctor's attorney present.

The interview was conducted in the jail's interrogation room with the usual table and one-way mirror in the back. Judd and his counselor were waiting on the far side of the table when Sam walked in.

The lawyer, Calvert Watson, was a lanky, professorial type with a balding head, prominent hooked nose, and glasses. As he stood, Sam noted the expensive cut of his tailored suit. He remembered walking past a new Lexus in the parking lot. The man was clearly no bargain basement public defender. He was being well paid, perhaps with drug money.

Judd Proctor was not handcuffed to the table, but he looked surly enough to bite. Rangy and muscular in his ill-fitting orange jumpsuit, he glowered at Sam from beneath bristling eyebrows. His hair was shoulder length, his jaw coated with stubble. The nails of his outsize hands were overgrown and permanently stained with grease.

Following procedure, the interview would be recorded. Sam switched on the machine; noted the date, time, and place; and named himself, the lawyer, and Judd Proctor as individuals present.

Watson spoke up. "Permit me to add, Agent, that Mr. Proctor is here as a courtesy, by his own consent, and that this interview has no bearing on his present case. Agreed?"

"Of course," Sam said, and began with the routine preliminary questions before getting to the reason he'd come.

"Mr. Proctor, were you acquainted with the late Frank Culhane?"

Judd glanced at the lawyer. "Not in person. But I knew who he was. Everybody did. And I don't care that he's dead. Whoever killed the rich old bastard did the world a favor."

"Did you ever speak with Mr. Culhane?"

"No. Not even after he stole my girlfriend. I was mad enough to kill him, but I didn't do it. I swear to God."

Watson cleared his throat. "Agent, if you wouldn't mind stopping a moment, I'd like a private word with my client."

Sam turned off the recorder and stepped outside. Through the one-way window, he could see the two men talking. It didn't take lip-reading skills to know what Watson was telling his client. Whenever possible, Judd was to confine his answers to yes and no. He was not to volunteer anything.

Sam returned to the interview. He'd been right about Watson's warning to his client. Most of Judd's answers to his questions were now given in monosyllables.

"Do you know a man named Roper McKenna? Do you know where he lives?"

"No and no."

"Are you acquainted with Miss Crystal Carter?"

"Yes."

"Was she the girlfriend you claim that Frank Culhane stole from you?"

"Yes."

"Are you still in contact with her?"

"She says we're done. But we'll see about that."

Watson gave his client a scowl. Sam wondered what kind of rise he'd get out of Judd if he were to mention Crystal's pregnancy. He decided against it.

"Mr. Proctor, can you tell me where you were between midnight and six a.m. on the night Frank Culhane was killed?"

"Probably drunk. I don't remember that far back. But I sure as hell wasn't anywhere near Frank Culhane. And I didn't kill him—even though I wanted to. Somebody else did me that favor." Judd was ignoring his lawyer's advice.

"Think about it," Sam said. "Where would you have been that night? Did you go home? Did you have anybody with you who can verify where you might have been?"

"Like a woman, you mean? Like maybe the bitch that threw me over for an old prick with money? Maybe she was with him. Maybe you ought to talk to her."

"Are you saying you don't have an alibi, Mr. Proctor?"

Watson stood. "I think we're done here, Agent. My client needs to go back to his cell. Unless you have probable cause, I don't see any need for you to talk with him again."

"Fine for now." Sam knew when to keep his tone polite. "I'll let you know if anything changes."

Sam ended the recording, left the jail, and headed back to the ranch. The interview had gone about the way he'd expected it would. It had also left him wondering whether Judd Proctor was as unsophisticated as he appeared to be, or if his crude manner was a clever pose. Either way he remained high on Sam's list of suspects. He'd hated Frank, and he looked strong enough to easily overpower the older man. As a drug dealer he'd have ready access to fentanyl; and the large syringe could be ordered online or bought at a veterinary supply store. Only one piece of the puzzle didn't fit. Why had the syringe been found in the creek near the McKenna place?

The crime lab had found traces of fentanyl but no prints or DNA. Sam swore out loud as the thought struck him. What if the syringe had been a decoy? What if it hadn't been the murder weapon after all? He needed to call Nick.

Crystal was broke again. She'd spent the last of her $15,000 windfall for the deposit and first month's rent on a shabbily furnished one-bedroom apartment in the basement of an old house that had been converted into rental units. The plumbing clanked and she'd already killed two cockroaches. This was all she could afford until more payments came in. At least it was better than living at the Blue Rose Motel.

Days ago, she'd been celebrating her newfound fortune. Now she couldn't even afford to put gas in her car. At least she'd had the good sense to keep her job at Jackalope's.

Until Lila came through with another check, she was going to need the work.

Every day, she'd waited for the ring of her cell phone, hoping the wretched woman would call. But the phone had remained maddeningly silent. Crystal was growing desperate. It was time to take matters into her own hands.

She pulled her bathrobe tighter as she sat down on the sagging Naugahyde couch and scrolled her phone to Lila's number. She hesitated for the space of a breath. What if something had gone wrong? What if Lila had decided not to adopt her baby or even help with expenses?

Summoning her courage, Crystal made the call.

At Lila's chilly hello, she almost lost heart. Something about the woman's Grace Kelly looks and ice queen manner always made Crystal feel low class. But with her need so desperate, giving up was not an option.

"Is this a good time to talk, Mrs. Culhane?" she asked.

"As good as any. Didn't I say I would call you?"

"Yes. But I need to know if you—?"

"If I plan to adopt your baby?" Her voice was emotionless. "I haven't decided yet. That's why I haven't called you. But there's another matter. Someone told me you have a boyfriend."

Crystal felt her stomach clench. "I *had* a boyfriend. We broke up before I met Frank." It was true except for the timing. "He's in jail. I'm totally through with him."

"I'm glad to hear that. A man like that wouldn't be good for you or the baby. If I hear you're back with him, we're done. Do you understand?"

"Absolutely. I told you, I already broke up with him. But that's not why I'm calling."

"Let me guess. You need more money. I gave you fifteen thousand dollars. Are you saying you've already spent it?"

Was Lila going to say no? Crystal began to babble. "It wasn't like I wasted it. I bought a car—not new but safe and reliable, and I had to get it licensed. I bought maternity clothes and some things for the baby." That last wasn't quite true. The clothes weren't maternity, and the baby could wait. "Then I rented an apartment—it's a dump, but it was all I could afford on what I had left. That's it. If you don't believe me, I can show you the receipts. I still have my job, but it doesn't pay much, and I won't get a check for another two weeks."

Lila sighed. "All right. If you'll give me your bank account number, I'll transfer ten thousand."

Not fifteen? Crystal felt a pang of disappointment, but she knew better than to ask for more.

"Thank you," she said. "I really appreciate it."

"Make it last this time," Lila said. "The money should be in your account by tomorrow. I'll let you know about the adoption when I make up my mind. And don't call me. I'll call you. Any questions?" There was a brief silence on both ends of the call before it ended.

Crystal began to breath normally again. At least Lila wasn't cutting her loose. But $10,000 was a lot less than the easy million she'd dreamed of getting.

She checked the time on her phone. In less than an hour her shift at work would be starting. She felt sluggish and slightly crampy. All she wanted to do was curl up in bed and sleep. She hadn't realized how tired pregnancy would make her. But calling in sick, which she'd already done too many times, could get her fired. Until she could be sure of a big cash payment from Lila, she needed that job.

With effort, she pushed off the sofa and stood. She just had time to wash her face, do her hair and makeup, and put on the tight jeans, black tee, and boots she wore to work. Thank goodness she wasn't really showing yet. But that was due to change. She would get as big as a cow before the baby came.

She was already counting the months—six of them. Then,

if all went as planned, she would be free, with enough money to buy the life of her dreams.

She was walking toward the bathroom when a sharp pain, like the stab of a knife, struck low in her body. As she doubled over, her pulse going crazy, something warm and wet began trickling down her legs. "*No!*" Her mouth formed the word. *No! No! No! This couldn't be happening!*

When she raised the hem of her robe, Crystal saw the blood dripping onto the linoleum raining crimson drops that pooled around her bare feet. She knew what it was, but she was powerless to stop it.

A scream of pain, frustration, and rage ripped from her throat. She was losing Frank's baby.

Chapter Twelve

The next morning, when Crystal went online to check her bank account, the $10,000 payment was there.

She took deep breaths as the panic eased. Last night, after the bleeding and the worst of the pain had stopped, she'd cleaned up the mess and curled into a blanket on the sofa, shaking and whimpering until dawn. Frank's baby had been her one chance at a new life. Now it was gone.

But the sight of those numbers in her account had boosted her hopes. It wasn't too late to carry out her plan. All she had to do was convince Lila Culhane that she was still pregnant.

That wouldn't be easy. First she'd have to account for the changes in her appearance—not just in front of Lila but everywhere, the whole time. No one could be allowed to see her without the padding she'd have to wear. And the disguise would have to be perfect. Maybe there were fake pregnancy kits she could order online, inflatable or made in progressive sizes. Now, while she wasn't yet showing, she could do some research.

But there would be other challenges. She would have to fake doctor visits. And when the time came, Lila would probably demand to see a sonogram. Surely it would be easy enough to borrow or buy copies of someone else's.

In time, one of two things would happen. Either her fake pregnancy would become suspect, or she'd be expected to give birth and produce an actual baby. One way or the other, that would be the time to flee—take her money and disappear without a trace. For that, she'd have to be ready on a moment's notice—plans made, cash on hand, and a bag packed to go.

Could she do it? She had to try. Otherwise she'd be forced to choose between leaving now with the $10,000 or confessing to the miscarriage while returning the money. Faced with those choices, how could she pass up the chance to be rich beyond her dreams?

Sam sat on the porch of the bungalow, drinking his morning coffee. From the direction of the game ranch, he could hear the whine of heavy power tools. Even from a distance the sound, which had started at first light, was loud enough to be irritating. It didn't help to imagine that the work had something to do with Charlie's plans for that poor, miserable elephant.

Staging a hunt for such a creature would involve a high degree of danger. Maddened by fear and rage, perhaps wounded as well, the huge animal could crash through the present fences and rampage across the countryside, destroying property, killing stock, and even taking human lives. A businessman like Charlie Grishman would want to keep that risk to a minimum. He would need to reinforce walls and fences, perhaps build an area of containment for the hunt.

Damn Charlie! The bastard deserved the same fate as his wretched animals. Nobody would miss him, except maybe a few bloodthirsty idiots who'd pay to act out their big game hunter fantasies and post the kills on Instagram.

Believing that Charlie had killed Frank was a stretch. There were higher names on Sam's mental list. But nothing would give him more satisfaction than cuffing the odious little man and putting him behind bars for life.

From where he sat, Sam could see Lila seated on the patio, sipping her coffee as she gazed across the pastures. She didn't look as if she wanted company, but he had some forthright questions to ask her. She might not like him for it, but this wasn't a popularity contest. It was his job. And with Nick needing him back in Abilene, he didn't have the luxury of waiting. It was time to kick this investigation into high gear.

Leaving his coffee mug on the porch, he crossed the distance to the house and entered the patio by the outside gate. Lila glanced up as he approached. She wasn't smiling.

"May I join you?" Without waiting for a reply, Sam pulled up a chair.

"It appears you already have," she said. "But as long as you're here, what can I do for you?"

"I just need answers to a few questions. Forgive me for intruding on your privacy, but I'm as anxious to wrap this case up as you must be to get rid of me."

"I can't say you're wrong. Sorry if I'm a little raw around the edges. That god-awful racket"—she gestured toward Charlie's place—"woke me up early with a headache that's only gotten worse. And now, here you are. So, fine. Let's get this over with."

"I appreciate your honesty."

She sipped her coffee. "I'll take that for what it's worth. I know I haven't been a gracious host, but I've never lied to you, Sam."

"I believe you." But that didn't mean she'd told him the whole truth, Sam reminded himself. In talking with Lila, what remained unsaid could be as revealing as her words. "This is why I'm here now," he said. "I've done everything

I can think of to solve your husband's murder. I've interviewed suspects and witnesses, analyzed data, made up scenarios in my mind . . ." Sam shook his head. "So far, all I've got is a tangle of loose ends. I'm hoping you can help me tie a few of them together."

For a long moment, she didn't reply. The distant scream of power tools, cutting and drilling, filled the silence between them. At last she spoke.

"You can ask me anything. But I won't promise to answer."

"Fair enough." Sam shifted in his chair, leaning toward her. "First question. If you were in my place, who's the top person you'd suspect of having killed Frank?"

"Darrin, I suppose. But my guess is tainted because I can't stand him. If he turned out to be the killer, and you arrested him, my troubles would be over."

"And Simone?"

"The same. I can't picture her taking on Frank. But she could bully her husband into doing it. He only pretends to be the man of the family."

Sam remembered Simone's bruised face. Something was going on between the couple, but he decided not to mention it now.

Roper's truck had been in the parking lot since first light. He was working all hours to prepare the stallion and his backup horses for the big event. Sam had wanted to get Lila talking. Now, risking her anger, he went for the answers he really needed.

"Simone insists that you and Roper were having an affair before Frank's death," he said. "Is that true?"

Her coppery eyes blazed. "Absolutely not. Roper was Frank's employee. I barely knew the man then."

"What about now?"

Her brief hesitation spoke volumes. "Roper works for

me. He calls me Boss. We've become friends, but only since Frank's death. I assume there's no law against that."

"Of course not. But according to Simone, you're more than friends. She claims that someone saw the two of you going into the sprinkler shed together."

"Someone?" Heat flushed Lila's face. "Who? And what does that have to do with Frank's murder?"

"Simone claims that Mariah was ordered to spy on you."

Lila exhaled sharply. "That would be Madeleine's doing. Mariah would do anything for her."

"Would Mariah kill for her?"

"God, no. Frank was always good to Mariah, especially after she lost her husband and baby. She practically worshipped him. She would never have hurt him." Lila ran a hand through her hair, raking it back from her face. "I know she'd be happy to see me gone and Frank's children back in the house. But it does surprise me that she'd risk her job by spying on me."

"You'd actually fire her?" Sam asked.

"Not for that. But I do expect a degree of loyalty from the people I pay."

"I assume that includes your horse trainer. Are you sure you can trust him?"

Lila's gaze went cold. "Nothing that happened after Frank's death is any of your business. That includes my relationship with Roper." She stirred in her chair as if preparing to get up and leave.

"Not even if Roper fits the profile of the person who killed your husband?"

She went rigid, as if he'd drawn a pistol and aimed it at her heart. "That's ridiculous," she said. "Roper and Frank respected each other. They weren't close friends, but they got along well."

"So you say. But Roper wanted to compete. He was

frustrated because Frank wouldn't allow it. And let's say that I believe you, Lila, when you tell me there was nothing between you and Roper before Frank's death. But that wouldn't keep him from seeing you. That wouldn't keep him from wanting you and making plans. Now that Frank's gone, Roper's wishes have come true. He's taking Frank's place in the Run for a Million, and now it appears that he's staking a claim to Frank's widow."

"Is that what Simone told you?" Lila was visibly seething. "That conniving little princess would say anything to get her hands on this house. And Roper couldn't have killed Frank. He was home all night. His parents vouched for him."

"I know what he claims," Sam said. "But think about it, Lila. How many parents would lie to protect their children? And even if they weren't lying, what they said was that Roper got up to chase a skunk off the porch. Maybe they were asleep when he went out and they woke up when he came home. They could easily have believed him when he said he'd gotten up because of the skunk. So, you see, his alibi has some holes in it."

"That's enough. Why are you telling me this?" Lila pushed to her feet. She stood over him, quivering.

"I'm telling you as a warning. If you trust Roper, you could be in danger, or he could take advantage of your situation. I can't tell you what to do. I can only caution you to be on your guard."

"Are you going to arrest him?" she demanded.

"Not until I have more evidence. I need something solid that will hold up in court. Sooner or later, I'll find it. In fact I may have found some damning evidence already. But that remains to be seen."

"In other words, you've got no proof at all," she said. "It's just as likely that I killed Frank myself. Have you thought of that?"

"I have," Sam said. "Frank's death has brought an avalanche of trouble down on your head—trouble you wouldn't have knowingly brought on yourself. You might have divorced your straying husband and taken him for whatever you could get. But you didn't kill him, Lila. You're too smart for that."

"Smart enough to know when I'm being played. I've heard enough. Let me know when you have some real news. Until that happens, I hope you'll leave me in peace." Lila turned away and stalked into the house.

Sam stood, watching her go. Yes, he had played her deliberately. It was part of a method he sometimes used on challenging cases—when you come to an impasse, throw a rock at the hornet's nest and see what flies out.

Lila's impassioned defense of Roper confirmed that she was in love with the man. She would almost certainly warn him. The question was, What would Roper do next?

Would he run? But that would be a sure admission of guilt. Roper was no fool. And with the Run for a Million coming up, he would risk anything to compete.

Sam's mention of evidence had also been deliberate. If Roper had tossed the murder weapon into the creek, he might check to see whether it was still there. If he left fresh tracks at the bankside, that would be proof enough to justify an arrest. For Sam, that would be a matter of watching and checking.

He felt the familiar adrenaline rush as he walked back to the bungalow. He hadn't wanted Frank's killer to be Roper, and he could still be wrong. But his suspicions felt right, and he had a job to do.

The distant whine of power tools had paused. But as Sam mounted the porch, the racket started up again. Sam's thoughts shifted to Charlie and his plans for that pitiful elephant. Time was growing short. If there was anything he could do to shut the vile man down, it would have to happen soon—perhaps now, while he waited for Roper to make a suspicious move.

What would Jasmine have done about Charlie? But Jasmine had already tried. She'd reported him and gotten nowhere. And then she'd joined the disastrous protest that had wrecked Charlie's compound, freed a murderous animal, and almost gotten her arrested. Charlie was already back in business, driving her car and planning a brutal death for another innocent creature.

There had to be a way to stop him. He would find it, Sam resolved. He would do it because it was right. And he would do it for Jasmine.

With the distant construction noise ringing in his ears, Sam took a seat on the porch and forced himself to concentrate. Satisfying as it might be, he had yet to find a solid reason for Charlie to have murdered Frank. His business, tax, and bank records were all within regulation, and he had legal title to the property he owned. Sam had verified that when he'd checked the records in the County Clerk's office. A copy of Charlie's grandmother's death certificate had been attached to the title, indicating that the transfer of the deed was due to inheritance, not to sale or default.

Sam had made a mental note of the woman's name—Ethel Mae Hibbert Grishman—and the fact that she'd died at seventy-four of natural causes. Nothing to raise suspicion there.

But the recent conversation with Mariah had stayed with him—how dismayed Ethel had been that Charlie wanted to turn the property into a game ranch. While she lived, she'd refused to consider the idea. She'd even threatened to disinherit him if he tried to go ahead with his plans.

Sam recalled Mariah's description of their last visit.

"*The poor woman had bruises up and down her arms,*" Mariah had said. "*I asked her if Charlie had been abusing her. She swore he hadn't. The bruises had just appeared, and she said she had other bruises on her body. She insisted that she must've gotten up in the night and fallen or bumped into something and couldn't remember it the next morning. A week after that, I heard that she'd passed away—a surprise, since she'd been healthy for as long as I'd known her.*"

Sam remembered an incident back in Chicago involving bruises. A four-year-old boy had ingested rat poison. The poison had contained warfarin, a blood thinner used in humans to prevent blood clots. The much higher dosage in the rat poison was deadly to rodents and had almost killed the child. Sam and his partner had rushed the boy to the ER, where his life had been saved. But Sam remembered the mottled bruises on the boy's arms and body, caused by bleeding under the skin.

He needed to look at Ethel's medical records, or at least talk with her physician.

He remembered the signature on the death certificate and the name typed underneath—Leonard Warburton, MD. Probably local. Maybe he'd acted as coroner. A quick call confirmed that he'd worked at the Willow Bend Clinic nine years ago and had since retired. The receptionist, who remembered Sam from an earlier visit, gave him the doctor's phone number.

Dr. Warburton answered Sam's call on the first ring and readily agreed to a visit. Sam drove to Willow Bend and followed the doctor's directions to a quiet street on the far side of town.

The single-story brick house was modest in size, the casually tended yard overhung by willow trees and bounded by a low picket fence. A vintage Pontiac Firebird with expired plates was parked at the side of the house. As Sam climbed out of the SUV, a black Labrador retriever, lounging on the shaded porch, lifted its graying head, stretched, and trotted down the path to meet him.

Soon after he rang the doorbell, a gravelly voice spoke from the other side. "Come in, Agent. It's unlocked."

Sam opened the door. An elderly man, dressed in jeans and a faded flannel shirt, sat in a brown leather recliner. A metal walker stood within reach. A side table held glasses, a book, a phone, and a TV remote.

"Forgive me if I don't stand to welcome you," he said. "Getting out of this blasted chair takes a lot of effort these days. I have a young man who comes in to help me, but he's only part-time. Have a seat, Agent Rafferty. What can I do for you?"

Sam positioned a lightweight wooden chair for easy conversation. As he sat down, he took a few seconds to study the man facing him. Leonard Warburton appeared to be in his eighties. He was stoop-shouldered, his finger joints swollen with arthritis. His prominent nose and chin were softened by furrows of age. Below a thatch of iron gray hair, the pale blue eyes that returned Sam's gaze were sharp and alert.

"Thank you for seeing me, Dr. Warburton," Sam said. "I have questions about a woman named Ethel Grishman, who died nine years ago. Your name is on the death certificate. Do you remember her?"

"Hell, yes, I remember. I'm not senile. She was a good woman, and strong. It surprised me that her health deteriorated so fast. But that's the way it goes sometimes."

"According to the death certificate, she died of natural causes. A friend I spoke with mentioned a lot of bruising. Did you notice that?"

The doctor scowled, then nodded. "Understand, I hadn't

seen Ethel as a patient for almost a year before she died. When I filled out the certificate, it was after she'd passed. I did question the bruising. But without an autopsy, including blood work, there was no way to know the cause. I suggested to her grandson that he might want to have it done. But he declined."

"Charlie Grishman declined the autopsy and blood work?"

"That's right. Since she was already gone, he didn't see much point in it. It wasn't a police matter, and as her next of kin, he had the right to make that decision. So I signed off, and he buried her on the ranch the next day. No funeral. The poor woman deserved better." The doctor's frown deepened. "What are you thinking?"

"A few years ago I saw a case of warfarin poisoning in a child who'd ingested rat poison. I remembered the bruises."

The doctor's eyes narrowed. "You're saying that Ethel might have been poisoned?"

"That's what I'm hoping to find out. Rat poison could have killed her—or it could have been an overdose of blood thinners. Was she on any of those?"

"Not that I'm aware of. And I would have known. She was my patient for years."

"Charlie had a reason to do it. He wanted to start his game farm, and his grandmother wouldn't allow it. Maybe he got tired of waiting. Did that occur to you after she died?"

"It might have, briefly. But I dismissed the idea. She was an elderly woman, and there are autoimmune conditions that can cause bruising. I grant you that Charlie might have been capable of it—he's a cold chap. He didn't shed a tear when Ethel died, and I know she raised that boy. But there's no proof, not even if you were to exhume the body. Warfarin doesn't last that long in the system."

Sam sighed. "I'm just looking for a reason to put Charlie away and shut down that damned game farm."

"You'd be doing a lot of people a favor. But I understood you had come back to the ranch to find out who murdered Frank Culhane. Word travels fast in this small town."

"That's right. I'm still working Frank's murder. This is just something that needs to be done, and there's no one else to do it." Sam stood and extended his hand. "I won't keep you any longer, Doctor. Thanks for your time."

"As you see, I've plenty of time to spare. I'll call if I think of anything else that might help you." He accepted Sam's handshake, his arthritic fingers knotted like the limbs of an ancient tree. "Oh—Ethel was a churchgoer. First Community, on Main Street. You might want to talk to her minister. Sorry, I can't recall his name, but he lives in that house behind the church. Ethel might've said something to him about her health or her grandson."

"Thanks, I'll check that out."

After leaving, Sam drove down Main Street. He found the small frame house behind the church. But there was no vehicle in the driveway, and no one answered when he rang the doorbell. He would check back later. For now, it was time for him to return to the ranch.

Lila had watched Sam drive away, headed for town. There was no telling what he planned to do or how soon he'd be back. For the past couple of hours, she'd kept herself busy, trying not to think about what he'd told her. But she couldn't keep the worries from pushing into her mind.

Now, in her room, she sank onto the bed and forced herself to ask the dreaded question. What if Sam was right in suspecting that Roper had murdered Frank?

But how could that be? She *knew* Roper, knew his gentleness, his wisdom, his integrity.

She loved him.

But had that love blinded her to who he was and what he was capable of doing?

Even with the window closed, the construction noise from the game ranch pounded in her head, echoing the pain of the headache that had awakened her that morning. Her hands splayed over her ears, failing to block the sound as she struggled to think.

Innocent or not, Roper would need to be told about Sam's suspicions. But hadn't that been Sam's intent—to see that Roper was warned and then watch for his reaction? Would he run? Would he try to cover his tracks, or maybe do something else to hide his guilt? Sam would be counting on it.

But if Roper was innocent, as Lila believed him to be, what then? Even without solid evidence, the case against him was strong. If he were arrested, he wouldn't be the first person to go down for something he hadn't done. She had to make him aware of the danger and warn him that his every move was being watched.

As hers would be also. Sam had told her she was above suspicion. But she would be a fool to believe him.

Her first impulse was to find Roper in the arena, where he'd been working with the horses since dawn. But that could be risky. Sam had been gone for almost two hours. He could return at any time—or someone like Mariah could be watching. It wouldn't do for them to be caught together right now. A phone call would be safer.

Strange, for as long as he'd been here, Lila had considered Sam an ally, almost a friend. Now suddenly, he'd become the enemy. Maybe he had been the enemy all along.

Lila called Roper's cell phone. It rang several times and went to voice mail—not surprising, since Roper usually silenced his phone or left it in his office when he was training. Lila left a short message, asking him to call her. As she ended the call, she saw Sam's SUV come in through the front gate.

Her body tensed with a hunted animal's wariness. For now, she would have to watch her every move, guard her every spoken word. Her enemy had returned.

Roper took the call on his break. The message was brief, just a few words, but the anxiety in Lila's voice set off alarms. He called her back. She answered on the first ring.

"Roper, thank goodness."

"What is it, Boss? Are you all right?"

"For now. But we need to talk."

"What's wrong?" he asked, picking up on her distress. "Where are you? Can you talk now?"

"I'm in my room. I'd come to you, but I don't think that's wise right now."

"Just tell me. Whatever it is, I'm here for you."

In the silence, he could hear her breathing. "It's Sam," she said. "He believes it was you who killed Frank."

The words struck him like a shotgun blast. There had to be some mistake. "I didn't do it," he said. "I swear to God, I didn't—I wouldn't. You've got to believe me, Boss."

"I believe you," Lila said. "I tried to tell him that. But Sam seems to think all the pieces fit. He said that he just needs a critical piece of evidence and he'll be ready to make an arrest."

"What kind of evidence? Did he tell you?"

"No. But I'm sure he meant for me to let you know. He wants you to react and give yourself away." She lowered her voice, as if she feared someone might be eavesdropping. "Listen to me, Roper. You've got to behave as if you know nothing about this. Go on with your training as if nothing's happened. If you try to leave—"

"I understand," he said.

"There's more." She continued as if he hadn't spoken. "Mariah's been spying on us and reporting to Darrin and Simone. They claim that you and I were having an affair while Frank was still alive. Sam believes you killed Frank because of me—and he suspects that I might've helped you. And now you're competing in his place. You can see how this looks."

"Yes. It looks like hell." Roper felt as if he were drowning in the flood of her words. "I'll deal with this, Boss. What's most important is that you believe I'm not a murderer. Can I count on that?"

Was there a beat of hesitation? "Of course you can," she said. "But there's one more thing. You and I mustn't be alone together. Someone might see, and that could be bad for both of us."

"Agreed." That brief pause in her reply had cut deep, but at least he knew where she stood. "I'll just keep training the horses and hoping for the best," he said. "Keep me posted. I've got to get back to work."

Roper ended the call, laid the phone on the desk, and turned away. A shudder passed through his body as he realized that his whole life could change in a heartbeat.

He had long since stopped believing in happy endings. Fate could be fickle, and there was no compassion in justice. He hadn't killed Frank, but that didn't matter—not when one stroke of bad luck could put him behind bars for good.

Chapter Thirteen

On Sunday morning, Sam drove into town for the ten o'clock service at First Community Church. He'd never been much of a churchgoer, but he was hoping to speak to the reverend about Ethel Grishman. Showing up for the meeting would be his best chance.

Arriving early, he took a seat in the back pew, where he could see the people who came in. Most of them were strangers, although he recognized a few he'd seen in town. Some had already taken their seats. Sam studied them from behind. One woman with her graying hair pulled into a bun looked vaguely familiar. At first, he couldn't place her. Only when she turned her head, giving him a view of her profile, did he recognize Rachel McKenna, Roper's mother.

For now, he abandoned his intent to meet with the reverend. That could wait. Questioning Rachel about her son could be the key to wrapping up this murder case.

Did Rachel know that Roper was the target of his investigation? Sam would bet against it. Even if Roper knew, it wouldn't be like him to tell his mother. He wouldn't want her to worry.

Sam wasn't about to tell her either. He just wanted her to relax and talk to him. If he could get her to admit that Roper might've left the house the night of Frank's murder, that would be pay dirt.

The service began with an opening hymn that Sam didn't recognize. The sermon, delivered in a droning voice by the middle-aged minister, was mostly lost on Sam because his mind was racing ahead to the hoped-for encounter with Rachel. How would he approach her? How could he question her in a way that would encourage her to talk about her son?

What he planned to do wasn't kind, but getting information from family members was part of his job. He'd long since learned to steel himself against any twinge of guilt. But the guilt was there, below the surface. Maybe that was why, when the collection plate was passed, he laid down a $20 bill.

After the closing prayer, the parishioners rose and began to file out of the chapel. Sam kept his eyes on Rachel. As she passed him on the way out, he fell into step behind her.

"Fancy meeting you here," he remarked as they cleared the front steps of the church.

Rachel turned to look at him, one eyebrow shifting upward. She was a tall woman, almost as tall as Sam. Roper may have gotten his height from her. "I didn't know you were a God-fearing man, Agent Rafferty," she said.

"Calling me that is probably a stretch." Sam adjusted his stride to hers. "I don't usually have time for church. But today I just needed a bit of spiritual refreshment."

"Since you're still around, I take it you're still looking for Frank's killer," she said. "How is that coming along?"

"Not as well as I'd hoped. I've been going over my notes, looking for something I may have missed. And I've been following up with people I interviewed earlier. But I seem to have hit a dead end. That's why I'm especially glad to see you this morning. I hope you don't mind answering a few questions—just to help me tie up some loose ends."

Her expression was distrustful. Maybe he'd come on too strong. He could have already struck out with her. "I won't keep you long," he said. "I just need to verify some things I've already been told."

Her mouth tightened, the lips narrow and bare of makeup. "You can walk me to my car," she said. "But I can't talk long. I need to get home and start dinner."

"Is your family at home?"

"The younger ones are gone. They'll be back tonight. If I make ham and beans, I can warm everything up when they get home." She began walking toward the curb, where the cars were lined up in front of the church. As Sam fell into step beside her, he recognized the older sedan he'd seen in the McKennas' yard.

"I need to verify the alibis of the people in your family," he said. "It's just procedure."

"That's easy enough," she said. "Cheyenne and the boys were on the road. Kirby and I were in bed. And Roper was home, too."

"In my notes, I have something about Roper getting up to chase a skunk off the porch. Do you remember that?"

She nodded. "The dog barking woke me up. I'm a light sleeper. Not like Kirby—an earthquake wouldn't wake him. I called to Roper in the next room. A couple of minutes later he came back in and said the dog had been barking at a skunk. He'd chased the skunk away and put the dog in the barn so he wouldn't go after it."

"What time was that?"

"After midnight. I didn't look at the clock, but it was still dark."

"You say you got up. Was that when you heard the dog or later?"

"It was right after I heard the dog. I put on my robe and waited for Roper in the kitchen."

"When Roper came inside, did you see what he was wearing?"

Rachel shook her head. "Neither of us turned on the light. No need. But I could hear his boots on the floor. He would've put them on before he went outside. It's not safe to walk around barefoot in the dark. Anything could be out there—stickers, scorpions, maybe even a rattler."

"You say you heard him outside. Did you hear anything earlier, like the sound of a vehicle?"

They had reached her car. She stopped and turned to face Sam. Her eyes were slits of anger. "That's enough. If you think my son would kill Frank, you're dead wrong. Roper's a good man. I raised him by the holy book. He's honest to the bone. He loves his work, and most of what he earns goes to help our family. You keep coming back to that skunk story. I could see skunk tracks the next morning. The dog was shut in the barn, just like Roper said."

She fished her keys out of her purse and opened the car door. "Our family never did think much of the Culhanes—Frank and that fancy-pants wife of his, with their big house and their cars and their money. But the McKennas are God-fearing people, and murder is a sin. If you want to find out who killed Frank, maybe you should look closer to home."

With that, she climbed into the car, slammed the door, and started the engine. Sam stood looking after her as she drove away. She'd put up a passionate defense of her son. Had she protested too much? That remained to be seen. The story of the skunk sounded plausible, but Sam didn't know enough about skunks to judge.

Still, Rachel's account had left some openings. Evidently, she hadn't heard Roper go outside. So he could have gone out earlier and awakened the dog when he came home. The skunk story could have been real or a fabrication.

Also, she said she hadn't seen what Roper was wearing. If he'd been fully dressed, that would argue for his having gone to the Culhane place, killed Frank, and returned.

How much did Rachel know? How much was she hiding?

Only one person could give him more answers—Roper McKenna.

When he got back to the ranch, he would find a time to corner Roper and ask some probing questions. Meanwhile, he would put that issue on the back burner while he spoke with the reverend about the death of Ethel Grishman.

After working with Fire Dance and Milly for most of the afternoon, Roper decided to take a break and go home for supper. He was tired and hungry. Besides, Cheyenne and the two boys were due back this evening. He looked forward to hearing about the rodeo and talking with Cheyenne about her future plans. Rowdy, still on bail awaiting trial, would be sulking as usual. Roper could only hope the young man had learned his lesson. So far, that didn't seem to have happened. Rowdy was surly and defiant, insisting that the lawyer he'd hired would get him off and then he'd be free to do whatever he wanted.

By now, the workers had gone. Roper was about to leave the arena, thinking he might come back after the meal and spend more time with One in a Million, when his eyes caught a movement in the shadows near the entrance. His pulse leaped with the hope that it might be Lila. But the tall figure stepping into the light was Sam Rafferty.

Roper's nerves clenched. Lila had already told him that

the agent had zeroed in on him as Frank's most likely murderer. Was Sam planning to spring a trap on him? Whatever was about to happen, Roper would need to be prepared.

Stopping in the middle of the arena, he waited for Sam to come to him. The agent crossed in the fading light, his shadow falling long across the trampled floor.

Roper kept his silence until the two were within speaking distance. "Is there something I can do for you, Sam?" he asked.

"This won't take long," Sam said. "I just want to clarify some things your mother told me earlier. Is there somewhere we can talk?"

"Right here is good enough for me," Roper said. "For starters, I'll answer one question before you ask. Whatever you might be thinking, I'm not a murderer. I didn't kill Frank."

"Then you won't mind accounting for your time on the night in question." Sam kept his gaze level and his voice flat, like a TV cop. Roper had once viewed him as a friend. He should have known better.

"Go on," Roper said. "I have nothing to hide."

"Fine. Where were you between midnight and four a.m.?"

"At home. Mostly asleep. My parents vouched for that. They were in the next room. Nobody had a reason to leave the property."

"Your mother mentioned that you were outside."

"I was. I heard the dog barking in the night. We get coyotes, feral pigs, and skunks around the ranch. I pulled on my boots, grabbed the pistol I keep by the bed, and went out through the kitchen to see what it was.

"A skunk was on the back porch, eating the dog food. The dog was about to go after it. I grabbed the dog, hauled him to the barn, and shut him in."

"And the skunk?"

"It ran off. I left the dog in the barn, took the food dish, and went back into the kitchen."

"And your mother was in the kitchen when you came in?"

"Yes. She'd gotten up after I went outside. I told her about the skunk, and we both went back to bed. You know all this. Why go over it again?"

"I just need a few more details," Sam said. "You say she didn't hear you leave the house."

"I can't say what she heard. But she was up when I came back in."

"Were there any lights on?"

"No. But the moon was up. That's how I could see the skunk."

"And in the kitchen? Was the light on?"

"No. I could've turned on the light, but I wasn't dressed. I sleep in my skivvies. My mother's a modest woman. It would've made her uncomfortable to see me like that."

"You're saying that when you heard the dog, you pulled on your boots and ran outside in your underwear."

"I needed to stop the dog from tangling with whatever he was barking at. He's an old dog. If I'd taken the time to get dressed, he could have been sprayed, bitten, or even killed."

"So even if you'd been dressed, your mother wouldn't have been able to see what you were wearing?"

"Probably not." Roper's patience had begun to fray. "What are you getting at? I told you I didn't kill Frank. If you don't believe me, just say so, and we'll take it from there."

Sam took a moment, as if to organize his thoughts. "I believe you killed Frank because he was standing in the way of what you wanted. As of now, I have no solid proof. You claim you didn't kill him. But you could have left your ranch without being heard, killed Frank, then accidentally awakened the dog when you returned. The skunk story may have been true or invented to satisfy your mother."

"But how would I have known Frank would be in the stable at that hour?"

"That's an easy question. You could have called him about an emergency—maybe some trouble with the stallion. Or maybe you wanted to talk about your relationship with his wife. Any number of things could have gotten him there."

Roper bit back a curse. "Anybody else could have done the same. I told you, I didn't kill him."

"That's what you say. Only you can't prove it—no more than I can prove you did kill him. But I'm on the trail of something that could change that. All I can tell you now is, don't leave town. That would only make things worse for you." Sam turned to go.

"Anything else, as long as you're here?" Roper's question was tinged with sarcasm.

"If you want to talk more, you know where to find me." Sam walked out of the arena and disappeared into the twilight.

Roper stood alone in the darkening arena, waiting to make certain the agent had gone. Sam's accusation had shaken him to the core. But that was something he couldn't change. He could only hope that Sam would discover the truth for himself. Meanwhile, all he could do was focus on preparing the horses and himself to score high in the Run for a Million.

Even though, when the time comes, I might not be free to compete.

Roper was about to walk out and go home when something stirred in the shadows. His breath caught as he realized it was Lila. She paused for an instant, then flew across the distance that separated them and flung herself into his arms.

Roper caught her close. He could feel her heart pounding against his chest as he held her, breathing in the fragrance of her skin. He knew he should scold her for being here. But right now he needed her, more than he'd ever imagined he could need anyone.

"You heard?" he asked her.

"I followed him when he came out here. I heard everything." She raised her head for his kiss. Her lips clung to his, warm and damp and passionate. He drank in her sweetness and her reckless courage.

"It doesn't look good, Boss," he said. "Sam needs to wrap up this case and find somebody to charge. He's picked me as an easy target."

"Then we'll fight him!" Her arms tightened fiercely around him, her fingers gripping his back. "I'm here for you, Roper. I know you're innocent. I'll stand by you—with my lawyers if it comes to that."

"We agreed not to be seen together," he reminded her. "I might go down, but I'll be damned if I'm taking you with me. You know what people will say—with Frank gone just a few weeks and me a suspect in his murder."

"They're already saying it—and the ones who are talking were never my friends. I don't care."

"But you will care. Don't be a fool, Boss. I love you too much to drag you into this mess."

She gazed up at him, a hint of a smile tugging at her lips. "Say that again."

He sighed, surrendering. "I love you, Lila. God help me, if things were different, I'd give anything for what we might've had. But I've got to face this alone. I'd rather go to jail than see you hurt by the vicious things people would say—not just behind your back but to your face."

She touched a finger to his lips. "Enough. We can't know what lies ahead. The future will have to take care of itself. Just kiss me, Roper. Just love me. For now."

Straining upward, she pressed her eager mouth to his. Roper tasted the saltiness of summer sweat and fresh tears. Deepening the kiss, he felt the heat going through him, igniting the hunger that had been simmering in him since their first meeting. And he felt the ache of knowing that he had nothing to offer her—no promises, no security, no future. All he could give her was his love.

Taking her hand, he led her out of the arena, back toward the stable wing. Silent and trusting, she let him guide her. Roper knew that possessing her, with all her passion, wouldn't be enough. He wanted her to be his. But more than that, he wanted to be completely hers, to give her love and pleasure as if this might be the last time.

The stable was silent except for the chuffing and nickering of horses and the low murmur of the ventilation fans. The security lights, which had come on at dusk, glowed softly above the corridor.

The vacant stall, prepared for the next new horse, had been scrubbed, the floor layered with fresh straw. A clean blanket hung over one side. Roper spread the blanket over the straw. Something prompted him to apologize for bringing her to such a place. But when Lila pulled him close and melted against him, he forgot about everything except wanting to make love to this woman.

Their first time together, in the sprinkler shed, had been frantic, with clothes yanked aside and bodies jammed against the wall. This time would be different.

Kissing her, he unfastened the front of her blouse, sliding each button through its silken hole until the garment fell free and slid to the floor. The lacy bra fastened in front, held by a tiny clasp. She undid it herself with a mysterious flick of her fingers, freeing her breasts. Roper lowered her gently to the blanket and moved to kneel over her.

Bare above the hips, she lay in the soft glow of the security light. She had a mature woman's body. The slight sag of her breasts and the faded stretch marks from the long-ago birth of her daughter made her even more beautiful to Roper than she might have been as a young girl. She gazed up at him, her eyes soft with desire, with need, and with love.

He buried his face between her breasts, burrowing into their softness, inhaling the heavenly womanly fragrance of her skin. Her breath caught as he found a nipple and sucked it into his mouth. Her flesh hardened against his tongue, her body arching upward to deepen the sensations.

Roper's arousal threatened to burst through his jeans, but he willed himself to make the pleasure last. She whispered his name, twisting and thrusting beneath him as he unfastened her slacks.

"Please, I'm . . ." The words trailed off as he bent to work her slacks off her feet and ease his way between her legs. His tongue caressed the moist honey folds and the sensitive nub in their center. She gasped. Shudders passed through her body as she came, then came again. Breaking the intense contact, she reached down, pulled open his belt buckle, and tugged down the zipper. He gasped as her seeking fingers found him. His jeans came down. After taking an instant to protect her, he entered with a gliding thrust.

He was home.

Moist, warm, and welcoming, she cradled him as he moved inside her. She met his every thrust, pulling him deeper into the sweet, dark mystery of her body. He felt her giving everything she had to give, and he gave in return—in desire, in passion, in bittersweet joy as the sensations swirled, mounted, and burst.

As they lay spent in each other's arms, he felt the wetness of tears on her face. He knew what she must be thinking. He feared it too. He was innocent, but with so much circumstantial evidence against him, he could be arrested as soon as tomorrow. Any hope for the future would be gone as if it had never existed.

Sam had seen Lila enter the arena after him and slip into the shadows. Later, when she didn't come out, it was easy enough to guess what was happening. *Let it happen*, he told himself. He already knew that Lila and Roper were lovers. Sam's focus now was on proving that Roper had killed Frank Culhane. If he could establish that, the only remaining question was whether Lila might have helped him.

What if Simone's wild claims about the pair had been spot-on?

He settled into the chair on the porch of the bungalow. The air was cooler after the torrid heat of the day. A light breeze whispered through the oleanders that bordered the driveway. A train whistle echoed through the distant darkness. Bittersweet memories of Jasmine in his arms and in his bed tormented his thoughts. What if their forced separation had changed her mind about him? What if he'd already lost her?

But brooding over a woman wouldn't helping him wrap up his case here. He had a solid lead. But he needed to follow through with evidence that would hold up in court.

The construction noise from Charlie's ranch had ceased for the night. Would Charlie be getting ready to hunt that wretched elephant? Sam listened for vehicles and scanned the distance for lights. But there were no signs of activity. Ending the man's cruelty was not in Sam's job description.

But if there was a way to stop him, Sam couldn't walk away—especially when it would mean so much to Jasmine.

His conversation at the church, after Rachel's departure, hadn't given Sam all that he'd hoped for. But he had learned something new. The reverend had mentioned that Ethel Grishman had been in good health for most of the time he'd known her. A few weeks before her death, she'd stopped coming to church.

Concerned, the reverend had finally called the ranch. He'd reached Charlie, who told him his grandmother was resting and couldn't talk on the phone now. In the background, the reverend could hear a woman's voice, which seemed to be calling for help. When asked, Charlie said it was only the TV, which Ethel turned up loud because she was hard of hearing.

Charlie had ended the call, saying he needed to go. The reverend hadn't called back, but he'd had an uneasy feeling about the situation. A few days later, he heard that Ethel had died. Charlie had declined his offer to conduct a funeral service. Ethel hadn't wanted one, he'd said. She'd already been buried on the ranch.

"About that feeling I had," the reverend had told Sam. "I think the good Lord was trying to tell me something. Sadly, I didn't listen. I may have to answer for that when I meet Ethel in the hereafter."

Had Charlie murdered his grandmother to get his hands on the ranch? The reverend's story sounded plausible. But again, the woman's voice he'd heard might have really been the TV. Charlie could have declined an autopsy because it was inconvenient, or because he didn't want to subject the body to the indignities of cutting and opening. There was no proof of how the good woman had died.

But if Charlie had killed Ethel, and Frank somehow

knew about it, that could throw a whole new light on Frank's murder.

Why couldn't things be simple for once? But Sam knew better than to ask that question. He also knew that he mustn't be blindsided by his need to close this case.

A mosquito settled on Sam's arm long enough to sample his blood. Sam flattened the pesky insect with a slap, but another one was buzzing around his ears. With a muttered curse, he rose, walked back inside, and closed the door behind him.

The air inside the bungalow was warm and stale. Sam was about to turn on a fan when his phone rang. The caller was Nick.

"Is everything all right, Nick?" Sam's first concern was for his boss's health.

"If you're asking about me, everything's on track. No need to fuss." Nick sounded tired. "How's the investigation going?"

"Complications around every corner. But my money's still on Roper McKenna. All I need is solid proof."

"Then I might have some good news for you," Nick said. "I asked the folks in the lab to take a closer look at that syringe from the creek. Still no prints, but they did find a trace of blood in the needle. There wasn't enough of it to run a DNA test, but the B-negative blood type is the same type as Frank's. It's rare enough that I'd say we can assume our syringe is the murder weapon. Now, if our techs can trace the serial number, then track where it came from and who bought it, the search could give us the evidence we need."

After the call ended, Sam walked back outside. Ignoring the mosquitoes, he gazed toward the horizon, where the moon was rising above the distant hills. If Nick was right, he could be making an arrest in days. He should be excited, even elated. But his instincts told him that something was missing from the picture—something he should have noticed earlier.

What was it?

What the hell was it?

CHAPTER FOURTEEN

Roper finished taking Fire Dance through his early-morning paces. The chestnut stallion was performing flawlessly, responding to the lightest pressure of Roper's hands and knees. At last, the horse's trust issues seemed to be fading.

"Good boy." Patting the sweat-dampened shoulder, Roper spoke as if nothing had changed since yesterday. "Keep doing what you just did, and we'll have a good chance of winning our million."

The stallion snorted and tossed his head, as if in agreement. But Roper had to force himself to focus on the coming event. After yesterday's confrontation with Sam, he wasn't even sure he'd be allowed to compete.

Last night, after making love to Lila, he'd insisted that they stay apart until he was cleared. She'd wanted to fight for his innocence. But Roper knew that her involvement would only strengthen Sam's case against him. It could even implicate her in the crime.

This morning he struggled to keep her out of his thoughts. But as always, she was there. In his imagination, he pictured her in her bed, yawning herself awake, her hair tousled, her body a little sore from his loving . . . Roper blocked the image with a silent curse. Nudging the stallion to an easy walk, he began the cooldown.

Last night he'd arrived home late to find his supper of ham and beans warming on the stove. The rest of the family had already eaten. Cheyenne had an ugly bruise on her cheek, from a barrel-racing accident, she'd said with a shrug. Rachel had made a fuss over the injury, forcing her daughter to sit with an ice pack on her face. Rowdy had been sulky as usual, especially when his brothers described their winning rides. His trial was scheduled for tomorrow morning. Roper would sacrifice needed training time to be there for him.

Roper had been thinking about how he'd miss Lila if he went to prison. But what about his family? Rachel was showing early signs of the arthritis that had crippled her late mother. Kirby was going to need more care as time passed. The young rodeo stars had their own plans, and Rowdy, with his defiant attitude, could be headed for trouble. For years, Roper had been the lynchpin of the family. What would they do without him?

They didn't know, of course, that he was the prime suspect in Frank's murder. He would keep that worry from them for as long as he could.

Roper was about to dismount and turn the stallion over to a groom when a petite figure, perched on a rail at the far side of the arena, jumped to the ground and walked toward him. It was Cheyenne.

No member of his family had ever visited him here, at work. Had something happened at home? Suddenly anxious, he swung off the horse, dropped the reins, and strode to meet her.

"Is something wrong?" he demanded.

Cheyenne didn't answer. She stood facing him, the top

of her dark head barely reaching his shoulder. Dark lashes veiled her eyes. The bruise on her cheek had faded from livid purple to blue.

A groom had come out to take the stallion. Roper studied his sister. "How did you manage to hit yourself there on a barrel?" he asked. "Did you come to tell me what really happened?"

"No," she said. "I just wanted to talk. We didn't get a chance last night. But since you're wondering about the bruise, I'll tell you the real story. You just can't tell Mom, okay?"

"You know me better than that, Little Sis." He walked her to the side of the arena and offered her a bottled water. She twisted off the cap and took a long, deep drink.

"It was a drunken cowboy." She touched the tender bruise. "He grabbed me under the stands as I was shortcutting my way back from the ladies' room. When I scratched his face, he slapped me so hard that I saw stars. I got him with a boot between the legs. When he doubled over, I ran."

"Do your brothers know what happened?"

Cheyenne shrugged. "What do they care? Mom thinks they're still protecting my virtue. That's the only reason she let me go on the circuit when I was sixteen. But I've been on my own for a long time." She finished the water and crushed the plastic bottle in her fist. "I want a different life, Roper. I need it."

"Are you serious about cutting? It's going to take a lot of work and a champion horse to get you to where you are now in the rodeo standings."

"That's what I wanted to talk to you about, Roper," she said. "I really want to do it. And I need to start soon. Will you help me?"

"As much as I can." Roper wasn't ready to tell her what

he was facing. Maybe he could at least get her started. "Are you still doing that photo shoot for *Vogue*?"

"It's set for next month, after the Run for a Million. After they pay me, along with what I've saved, I should have enough money for a horse. But I want to start looking now. You said you could get me into the cutting events. Can I count on that?"

"I'll do my best, but no promises." Silently, Roper cursed the twist of fate that had turned him into a murder suspect. He would do anything to help his sister, but lying now would only make things worse.

"What's the matter with you, Roper?" She frowned up at him. "The last time we talked, you offered to take me and even to get me behind the scenes. Now you're saying no promises. Is something wrong?"

"I said I would try. And I will. But it might not be easy. Roper was saved from saying more by the sound of a truck pulling up outside. A door opened and closed. The tall, well-dressed cowboy who walked into the arena was Hayden Barr.

"Hey, Dad asked me to come by and check on Fire Dance." He greeted Roper, but his gaze had already singled out Cheyenne. "Don't I know you from somewhere?"

"Do you follow women's mixed martial arts?" Cheyenne's reply dripped sarcasm as she touched the unsightly bruise.

Hayden looked puzzled, then laughed. "Heck, I know you. You're Cheyenne McKenna. I've seen you ride."

Roper made the introductions. "Cheyenne, Hayden Barr. His father owns Fire Dance. Hayden, my sister."

"I should've guessed," Hayden said. "But I never made the family connection until now. I can see the resemblance."

"Actually, I'm only his half sister. Same mother. I've been told I look like my dad." Cheyenne appeared unimpressed.

"Fire Dance is coming along fine." Roper knew better than to mention the attack. "If you'd come a few minutes earlier, you could've watched him perform. By now, he should be getting his shower. If you want to see him, I can take you back to where he is."

"I'll take your word for it. I'm just passing on a message from my dad. He said to tell you he's counting on that horse, and on you, to win some big money."

"Fire Dance is a great horse. I'll do my best." Roper tried not to imagine what Chet Barr would say if it turned out that his stallion couldn't compete because the rider was in jail.

"Are you coming to the Run for a Million?" Hayden was talking to Cheyenne now. "I'll be in the cutting event, with my horse, Steely Dan. If you're watching, maybe you can cheer me on."

"I'd cheer if I had a ticket. But I hear they're sold out."

"I can fix that. There might not be any seats, but I can get you a pass for the stables behind the arena. If you're interested, you'll even get to see the horses and meet some of the riders."

"If I'm interested?" Cheyenne grinned. "Mister, you've got yourself a deal. I'll give you my phone number. But remember, I don't take kindly to cowboys who make promises and let me down." Her gaze darted toward Roper. "Got a pen, big brother?"

Roper had a Sharpie, which he used for marking the charts posted outside each horse stall. He took it out of his pocket and passed it to his sister.

"Roll up your sleeve," Cheyenne ordered Hayden.

Hayden obliged, a look of amusement on his clean-cut features as she wrote her number in two-inch letters on the tanned flesh of his arm. "I promise not to wash until I've copied it somewhere else," he said.

Cheyenne gave him an impish look. "No need. I believe

the ink is permanent. Just so you won't forget how much I want that pass."

"Got it. Don't worry, I'll remember."

"You'd better not let your girlfriend see it," she teased.

"No girlfriend. Not for now, at least."

Hayden was grinning when he walked out to his truck and drove away. Cheyenne had clearly made a conquest. "There, that's taken care of," she said, returning the pen. "But you've got me worried, Roper. I can tell something is bothering you."

"Nothing I can't handle, Little Sis," Roper said. "Let's get the next few weeks over with. Once things are back to normal, after you've done the photo shoot and picked out a horse, we'll figure out your training. Okay?"

"Okay." She turned to leave. "But if you need to talk—"

"Don't worry, I'll be fine." Was that a lie? Roper asked himself as his sister walked out to her SUV. Maybe not. Maybe he really would be fine. Or maybe what he'd told her was a lie and he would never be fine again.

Crystal had promised herself that she'd be careful spending the $10,000 Lila had given her. But that was before she saw the ring.

She'd seen it in the window of a jewelry store in the Abilene mall, where she'd gone to buy a few practical things, like sheets and towels for her apartment. She'd also needed a new purse, and the red sandals she'd loved on sight were on sale. Small purchases—she hadn't spent much. She had plenty of money left for things like food and rent.

The ring was marked down—a three-quarter-carat solitaire mounted in white gold. Still, $5,500 was an unimaginable amount to pay. She'd only meant to try it on and leave. But when she slipped it on her finger, it fit perfectly.

It made the other rings on her hand look like the cheap trinkets they were. She had slipped them off and dropped them into her pocket so they wouldn't detract from the spectacular diamond.

The effect of the ring was magical. Wearing it, she no longer felt like a girl who'd come from trash—or a woman whose only hope of getting a leg up in life lay in convincing some rich bitch she was still pregnant with her husband's baby. The diamond on her finger made her feel equal to the people who lived in nice homes, wore expensive clothes, and drove flashy cars. It made her feel like *somebody*.

Before she knew it, she'd presented her debit card, waited while the clerk checked her bank account, then walked out of the store with the ring on her finger and the receipt in her purse. But now her account was getting low, and she still needed to put some emergency cash aside. She was going to need more money.

By the time she'd driven back to Willow Bend, she'd made up a story to tell Lila.

In her shabby basement apartment, she took time to guzzle a cold beer, try on her new red sandals, and admire her ring. Then, summoning her courage, she made the call.

"Why are you calling, Crystal? Is something wrong?" As usual, Lila sounded annoyed.

"Well, sort of. For one thing, I've lost my job. When my boss found out I was pregnant, he fired me. I'm starting to show a little, and he said it wasn't good for business." Actually, Crystal still had her job, but she planned to quit when she had enough money. As for showing, she'd practiced walking around her apartment with a folded dish towel tucked into the front of her underwear. When she found something more realistic, she would try wearing it in public.

"That's too bad," Lila said. "But at least you've got enough money to last awhile."

"I'm afraid not," Crystal said. "There's this black stuff growing inside the walls of my apartment. I found out it was mold, and that it's really bad for the baby. I've signed up for a better place, but the rent's more, and they want a big deposit, with first and last month's rent in advance. Oh—and it isn't furnished. I'll need to buy a good bed and some other things.

Lila's sigh could be heard over the phone. "We'll talk about that. Right now, I'm more concerned about your health and the baby's. Are you taking prenatal vitamins?"

"Every day," Crystal lied.

"And are you seeing a doctor? If we decide to do this adoption—and I'm still making up my mind about it—I'm going to want a report after every checkup."

That, Crystal realized, could become a problem. She thought fast. "Actually, I've found this woman—she's a birth doula, like a midwife, only she guides you through the entire pregnancy. Food, vitamins, everything wholesome and natural. She's even got me doing exercises to make the baby come easier."

"Oh? And does this woman have a name?" Lila's sharp tone told Crystal she was skating the edge of trouble.

"The woman goes by Eve. I met her through somebody at work. But she keeps her contact information private. She's got some important clients—celebrities and all—who wouldn't want the press trying to question her. Know what I mean?"

The story sounded far-fetched, even to Crystal. She spoke again before Lila could respond. "Anyway, here's the real reason I called. I'm getting anxious to settle my baby's future. I called an adoption lawyer. He knows a couple who'd be happy to take my little one. They've got money and would pay all the fees and my living expenses. You have first claim, of course. But I can't wait forever. Neither can the people who want to adopt my baby."

"Stop giving me the runaround, Crystal. What do you want? Is it more money?"

"I can always use more money," Crystal said. "But what I need is security. I want a signed agreement with a ten-percent deposit to guarantee that, when the time comes, you'll pay the balance and take this baby. If you change your mind, the deposit will be mine to keep."

There was silence on the other end of the call. Was Lila about to say no?

"Think about it," Crystal said. "Frank's baby—his very last child—could save your right to keep the ranch. Force me to walk away and you'll never have another chance. What's the price of that?"

"Ten percent of a million." Lila spoke slowly, as if weighing each word. "That's a hundred thousand dollars."

"For you, that's pocket change," Crystal said.

"Be still and listen. I'm not saying I'd agree to your terms. But if were to say yes, I'd insist on a sonogram to make sure the baby was healthy. If you can promise to do that, we'll talk about the rest."

This wasn't good. Crystal thought fast. "I'd be fine with that. But I'm not even four months along. The baby won't look like a baby yet—more like a little tadpole. I've seen pictures on Google. A sonogram would be useless."

Crystal's pulse raced as she waited for a reply. After a long silent pause, Lila spoke.

"All right, here's what I'm proposing. For now, I'll give you five thousand dollars a month to live on. That should be plenty. When you're ready for the sonogram, if everything looks good, we'll negotiate. Meanwhile, you're not to accept offers from anybody else. Understood?"

Crystal twisted the diamond ring on her finger. Five thousand dollars a month was nothing! She'd have to keep her job. She'd have to stay in the same creepy apartment with the dingy furniture and lumpy bed. But she was in no position to argue for more. If Lila discovered she'd had a miscarriage, it would be game over.

Lila had outfoxed her. But Crystal wasn't beaten yet. Her pulse danced as a new idea—a perfect Plan B—sprouted in her mind.

"I asked you if you understood." Lila made no effort to hide her impatience.

"Yes, ma'am. Could I have the five thousand by tomorrow? I really need it."

"All right. I'll transfer the funds. But that's all you're getting until next month. Don't ask me again."

"I understand." Already thinking about her new plan, Crystal ended the call.

The next morning, Roper drove his brother into Willow Bend for trial. Rowdy was putting on a confident face, bragging about how his lawyer was going to get him off. But Roper could see the fear in his eyes and in the way his hand shook when he drank the coffee they'd picked up on the way to the courthouse.

The lawyer met them there—the same man Roper had seen on his visit to the jail. He was as good as his reputation. Rowdy's case was swiftly dismissed by the judge on the grounds that the arrest had involved entrapment and an unlawful search. Rowdy walked out of the courtroom grinning.

"I hope you've learned your lesson, young man," the lawyer admonished as they left the building. "If you get into trouble again, you might not get off so easily."

"Yes, sir." For once, Rowdy was on his best behavior. "I

have one question. What happened to my jail buddy, Judd Proctor? I haven't seen him since I got bailed out."

The lawyer frowned. "If you're smart, you'll steer clear of that fellow. His trial is set for this afternoon. I'm hoping for an acquittal, but with a jury, you never know. If they don't like him, he'll be facing prison. That's all I'm allowed to tell you. Now go home and live a good life, Rowdy McKenna. Don't ever let me see you here again."

Roper drove his brother home. On the way, Rowdy was already talking about how he was going to grab his gear and clothes, load his truck, and head out on the circuit.

"I hope you'll take time to set things right with Mom before you go," Roper said. "It's not a good idea to leave with bad blood between family members."

"Tell that to Mom. She told me I was going to hell for disgracing the family name. Maybe that's where I'm headed. I don't care, as long as I don't have to listen to her sermons anymore."

"You'll break her heart, Rowdy."

"Hell, her heart's made out of granite, if she's even got one. She'll probably be glad to have me gone. That way, she can make up any damn story she wants about me—like maybe I'm off saving souls in Borneo or someplace. Since I won't be coming back, it won't matter what she says."

Roper sighed and settled into silence. He'd tried to put things right at home, but Rowdy was determined to go his own way. The young man had some hard lessons to learn. There was nothing to do but let him. Right now, Roper had enough trouble of his own.

Crystal crossed the unkempt lawn and mounted the front porch of the large house. Her hand trembled as she raised it to the doorbell and heard the loud chime from the other side. Light footsteps approached the door. The door opened.

The woman in the entry was petite, blond, and visibly pregnant. Her doll-like face wore a sour expression. "Whatever you're selling, we don't want any," she said.

"No, please, I'm not selling anything." Crystal placed a booted foot across the threshold so the door couldn't be closed. "Your husband knows me, Mrs. Culhane. I have some important business to discuss with the two of you. It concerns your right to inherit the Culhane Ranch."

"Who is it, Simone?" Darrin Culhane appeared from the next room. "What do they want?"

Simone stepped aside, revealing Crystal in the doorway. "*This woman* claims to know you. She says she's here to discuss business. Something about the ranch."

"Oh." Darrin looked startled. Crystal suspected he'd never told his wife about his visits to the Jackalope Saloon. "Well, come on in," he said. "What can I do for you?"

"It's what I can do for you," Crystal said, stepping through the doorway. "I have a story and a business proposition, for both of you. If you're interested in getting control of your family ranch, you'll want to hear me out."

Darrin switched off the TV and motioned her to an armchair. After clearing magazines off the sofa, he took a seat with his wife to face Crystal. "Well, let's hear it," he said.

Crystal took her time, telling her rapt audience how she'd met Frank and they'd become lovers. "He promised to divorce Lila and marry me. He even gave me this." She held out her hand, displaying the diamond ring. "Look all you want. I guarantee it's real." She dabbed at her eyes with a tissue from her purse. "Of course you know what happened. I didn't even get a chance to tell Frank that I was pregnant with his baby."

Simone gasped. "You're *pregnant*? How do you know the baby is Frank's?"

Her tone made Crystal want to slap the woman. She bit back an angry response. There was nothing to be gained by losing her temper. From her purse, she took out a copy of the test results the doctor had sent her. "Take a look. DNA doesn't lie."

She passed Darrin the paper, which she'd printed off her email. He showed it to his wife. Crystal could see their disbelief turn to resignation. "Keep it," she said. "It's a duplicate."

Darrin folded the paper and put it in his shirt pocket. "So what's the rest of the story? Where are you going with this?"

"I needed money, so I made a call to Lila," Crystal said. "I'd planned on keeping the baby, but she offered to adopt it and pay me for my trouble. At first I was shocked—that would be like selling my baby. But what kind of life would that baby have with me? Lila could give him—or her—everything. So I agreed."

Crystal paused to gauge the effect her story was having on Darrin and Simone. They were transfixed.

"Of course, I know why Lila wants my baby," Crystal said. "As the legal mother of Frank's child, she'd be meeting the terms of Frank's will. You two would no longer have a case."

Crystal could tell the news had hit them hard. Simone's mouth had hardened into a thin line. Darrin looked as if he'd been slapped across the face.

"So what are you doing here?" he demanded. "What do you want?"

Again, Crystal took her time. "To tell you the truth, I'm having second thoughts about Lila. She only wants the baby to help her keep the ranch. She wouldn't love Frank's child by another woman. Not the way I would love him—or her. I want to keep this baby. But look at me—I work in a bar. I have no education, no family support. If I can't afford to give my child a decent life, I'll have no choice except to take Lila's offer."

"How much is she planning to give you?" Darrin asked.

"We're still negotiating. But my baby could save the ranch for her. That has to be worth a lot. Of course, I won't get the full amount until I give birth and turn over the baby."

Crystal gave the words time to sink in. Darrin and Simone exchanged uneasy glances.

"Here's my offer," she said. "What would it be worth to you if I were to leave town and disappear? I could move out of the state, start a new life somewhere, raising my baby on my own. Lila would never hear from me again, and you'd have a good chance of getting your family ranch back."

"We're not millionaires like Lila," Darrin said. "How much would you need?"

"For moving expenses and a new start, a hundred thousand dollars cash up-front." It wasn't a million, but she needed it soon. From these people, it was as good as she was likely to get.

Again, the couple exchanged glances. "We'll need to talk this over," Darrin said. "Can we let you know?"

"Of course." Crystal stood. "But don't make me wait. I need to make a decision, and I'm running out of time. Here's my number." She handed them the card she'd prepared and left before they could ask her more questions.

"What do you think?" Darrin asked his wife as Crystal drove away. "A hundred grand is a lot of money."

"But what if Lila adopts that baby?" Simone demanded.

"If she becomes the legal mother of your father's child, our lawsuit is dead in the water."

"I don't trust her," Darrin said. "For all we know, she could be scamming us."

"Maybe. But that report from the doctor looks real enough. And you know how your father loved the ladies, especially the young ones. He fooled around when he was married to your mother, and he didn't stop after he wed Lila, especially now that she's older."

"But he never got one of them pregnant before."

"You don't know that," Simone said. "You could have an army of half brothers and sisters out there who you've never met. I'm surprised that none of them showed up for the memorial service."

"Stop it!" Darrin checked his hand, which had risen to slap her. She flinched and drew back, then released a breath when the blow didn't come. "My father was who he was," Darrin said. "But that doesn't mean you can disrespect his memory." He studied the card Crystal had given him. "Right now we've got to figure out what to do about that woman and her baby."

"You could pay her," Simone said. "Yes, it's a lot of money, but it's better than giving Lila a weapon to use against us."

"But what if we give her the money and she doesn't leave? Or what if she sneaks behind our backs and strikes a bargain with Lila? I don't trust her."

"Well, we've got to do something." Simone picked up the remote and switched her reality show back on. "By the time we get our court date, that baby could be born and adopted."

"I'm going to do some research," Darrin said. "If Lila can legally adopt that baby, we need to stop her—any way we can."

* * *

Crystal popped the tab on a can of Budweiser and settled onto her sagging couch. The visit to Frank's son and daughter-in-law had left her emotionally drained. She could only hope the couple had bought her story and that they were worried enough to come through with the money.

Lila had made good on her word to transfer the $5,000 to Crystal's bank account. But the woman was clearly getting suspicious—making too many demands, asking too many questions. Sooner or later, she was bound to guess the truth. By then, Crystal would need to be on the road to her new life. A hundred thousand dollars wouldn't last forever. But it should at least keep her in style until she could find a man with money.

It would probably be a good idea to keep her bags packed, her car gassed, and her account converted to cash. That way she could be ready to leave at a moment's notice.

The thought of leaving Willow Bend was both frightening and exhilarating. She would be all alone with no home and no friends. But she would be free—free to do and become anything she wanted.

The sound of the doorbell broke into her thoughts. Hardly anyone knew she'd moved here. Maybe it was her landlord to fix the constantly running toilet she'd complained about.

She got up and opened the door. Judd Proctor grinned as he stepped across the threshold.

"I'm back, babe," he said. "Now we can be together, just like before."

CHAPTER FIFTEEN

The more Sam learned about Ethel Grishman's death, the more convinced he became that Charlie had murdered her. His last interview with Mariah had solidified that belief.

"Ethel was your friend, Mariah," he'd said. "You've already told me that Charlie mistreated her. When she died, did you have any reason to think he might have killed her?"

Mariah had sighed. "At the time, I couldn't imagine it. She loved her grandson, in spite of his ambitions. And she'd never mentioned any fear that he might harm her. But she seemed tired all the time and so confused that she'd had to stop driving. When I mentioned it and suggested she see a doctor, she said it was just old age. The next time I went to visit her, Charlie met me at the door and said she was sleeping and couldn't be disturbed. A few days later, I learned that she'd died. It did seem strange that he wouldn't have taken her to the clinic. But murder? I never thought of that. Not until now."

"Is there any chance that Frank discovered what Charlie had done and Charlie killed him for it?" Sam had asked.

"I can't imagine that. Nobody expected foul play. And

Frank wouldn't have known anything. If he had, he would have told me."

Recalling the conversation, it was easy for Sam to believe that Charlie had poisoned his grandmother. But that wasn't evidence. The only evidence, if any, lay under six feet of earth on Charlie's ranch.

Now Sam had a choice. He could walk away from the whole dirty business and get back to his real job. Or he could confront Charlie face-to-face.

He already knew what he would choose. He would go to the game ranch, face Charlie, and hope to get answers he could use. He would do it for the sake of those wretched animals, yes, but mostly for Jasmine.

Charlie stood on the terrace sipping Scotch from a crystal glass—the last of a set that had belonged to his grandmother. The sun's dying rays cast long shadows over the scrubland. Insects fluttered around the porch light. A coyote's yipping wail echoed through the dusk.

Everything was in readiness for the hunt.

In less than an hour, the client would arrive. Hubert Greenway was a retired Texas businessman who'd hunted here before. For the thrill of gunning down an elephant, he'd put down $20,000, which was less than half of what a bare-bones African hunt would cost. Others had bid higher, but Hubert had experience with shooting big game. He also had the cash to pay up front.

Charlie couldn't afford for anything to go wrong. When the old female wasn't riled, she was as docile as a milk cow. But an elephant was an elephant, powerful enough to kill a man with a stomp of one foot. Her size alone was imposing enough to strike terror into a hunter's heart. Faced with a five-ton animal, even experienced marksmen had been known to freeze, too thunderstruck to shoot.

When Hubert stalked his elephant, Charlie would be standing backup with his 577 Nitro Express, a gun with the power to kill anything on four legs. Charlie had never shot an elephant, but he trusted the weapon, which was the favorite of the world's most celebrated big game hunters.

The elephant—which Charlie still called Jasmine—was tethered behind the big mesquite clump by an ankle chain, with a flake of hay to keep her quiet. When the hunt started, she'd be turned loose and herded out by Charlie's workers dressed as bearers. They would make a racket and prod her in the right direction. Charlie hoped she'd be mad enough to put on a good show.

A bonfire had been laid in the front yard and would be lit to welcome the client when he arrived. To add to the ambience, a recording of African night sounds would play on a speaker from inside the house.

Charlie was about to pour himself another finger of Scotch when he noticed something out of place in the carefully raked yard. It was a pile of reeking pig dung, left behind like a gesture of contempt. The blasted feral hogs had been hanging around most of the day. He'd shot a couple of them for cat meat and driven the rest off. But now they'd come by again, as if to leave him a calling card.

Using the walkie-talkie clipped to his belt, he called an employee to bury the mess and make sure the hogs were gone. The workman had come with a shovel and was just digging the hole when Charlie saw headlights moving through thc main gatc.

Had his client arrived early? Swearing, Charlie put down his Scotch, switched on the speaker with the African night sounds, turned off the porch light, and hurried down the steps to ignite the bonfire. The kerosene-soaked wood had begun to blaze before he realized his mistake.

The driver of the approaching black SUV wasn't Hubert

Greenway. It was that God-cursed, trouble-making FBI man, Sam Rafferty.

Wearing the Glock under his jacket, Sam pulled onto the gravel strip alongside the house and stepped out of his vehicle. From where he stood, he could see the dancing flames in the front yard and hear what sounded like the track from an old Tarzan movie. In the yard, a man dressed like someone's idea of an African native was shoveling dirt into a hole.

As Sam rounded the corner of the house, the porch light came on. The sound effects abruptly ceased. Dressed head to toe in big game hunter regalia, Charlie strode across the veranda toward him. Only then did Sam realize what must be happening. The elephant hunt was set for tonight, complete with costumes and sound effects. The star of the production—the old lady elephant—would be somewhere out of sight, awaiting the arrival of the client who'd paid big money to kill her.

Sam felt vaguely sick. He should have come here sooner. As it was, he might be too late to stop the travesty.

"This isn't a good time, Agent," Charlie said. "If you have anything to say to me, you'll need to come back later."

"You don't seem too busy now, Charlie," Sam said. "I can tell you're waiting for somebody. Is it your client? Is that why you turned the light on when you realized it was me? Are you about to stage your elephant hunt?"

Charlie's small eyes gleamed with hatred. "I told you, what I'm doing here is perfectly legal. I have a licensed business on my own property. And I have a bill of sale for the animal. Killing it is no more illegal than slaughtering a steer or a hog."

"It may not be illegal, but it's inhumane," Sam said. "That poor elephant belongs in a sanctuary."

"Now you're talking like your bleeding-heart girlfriend." Charlie glanced past him, looking toward the gate as if expecting to see headlights.

"Maybe so," Sam said. "But that's not why I'm here. I've learned some things about your property and how you got your hands on it." Sam was bluffing now. He'd learned nothing that could be proven. He could only hope that Charlie might slip and give him more.

"What are you talking about?" Charlie sputtered. "I inherited this land from my grandmother. It was in her will."

"Your grandmother, Ethel Grishman, was a healthy woman who sickened and died under suspicious circumstances. You didn't even take her to a doctor or let her friend visit her before she died. When she was gone, you buried her here on the ranch, without an autopsy or even a service. But the last friend who saw her described bruising and weakness consistent with an overdose of blood thinners, possibly warfarin."

"You're out of your mind!" Charlie had gone rigid. "Even if that was true, which it isn't, you wouldn't have a chance in hell of proving it." He glanced uneasily toward the gate, where a pair of headlights could be seen, coming closer. "I didn't kill my grandma. And I didn't kill that sonofabitch Frank. Now get out of here and let me get back to work."

Using a remote device, Charlie turned off the porch light and switched on the jungle sound effects. As the headlights cleared the gate, Sam remained where he was. He'd been ordered to leave, but Charlie wouldn't create a scene in front of an important client—especially a confrontation with a federal agent.

Sam had no power to stop the hunt and no grounds for arresting Charlie. But at least he could witness the sad event and sneak a few shots with his phone camera to share on social media. Jasmine would be glad to help with that. Maybe the photos would stir up enough outrage to get something done about Charlie.

The worker with the shovel had vanished. As the vehicle parked and the driver turned off the engine, Sam moved back into the shadow of the overhanging roof to watch and listen. Charlie swaggered down the steps to meet the newcomer, a scarecrow figure of a man in his late sixties, dressed in khakis and carrying an outsized gun case. He walked with an awkward limp.

The two shook hands. "You're right on time, Hubert," Charlie said. "Are you ready for some action?"

"Ready to go." The man spoke with a Texas drawl. "With my bad knees, I'd never survive an African hunt. But I've vowed to shoot an elephant before I die. This will be my last chance."

"You told me you had a rifle that would do the job." Charlie glanced at the heavy carrying case.

The man looked old, his youthful vigor long faded. If this was to be his last hunt, he clearly meant to go out in a blaze of glory. "I brought my new Heym Express bolt action," he said, setting down the case. "I hope it'll do the job."

"It should," Charlie said. "I've never shot that model, but I've read some good reviews. If anything goes wrong, I'll be behind you with my 577 Nitro."

"You won't need it. In fact, I don't want you there, Charlie. I know that this hunt is staged. But I want it to be as real as possible. That means me against the elephant with no backup. I'm an old man. If I lose, I lose. There are worse ways to die."

"I understand," Charlie said. "But I can't risk the bad press if a client get hurt—or worse."

"This isn't about bad press. I paid to hunt and kill that elephant. For twenty thousand dollars, I should be allowed to do it alone, without a damned babysitter."

"All right. If you insist," Charlie lied. He would keep his distance, but there was no way he'd allow Hubert to face a deadly animal without backup. "But you'd better be prepared to kill that beast with a single shot, or we'll have a wounded elephant on our hands."

Hubert didn't appear to be listening. He was staring up toward the porch where Sam had just stepped into sight. "I didn't know you had company," he said.

Charlie shot Sam a look of pure hatred. "I believe my visitor was about to leave," he said.

"Actually, I've changed my mind," Sam said. "I've never seen one of your hunts, Charlie. I'm looking forward to some excitement." He came down the steps and approached the client.

"Sam Rafferty," he said, extending his hand.

With an awkward expression, the man accepted his handshake. "Hubert Greenway," he said. "I wasn't aware that we were going to have an audience."

"Neither did Charlie. Don't worry, I'll stay out of the way. You won't even know I'm here." Sam could feel the hostility radiating from Charlie like heat from a blast furnace. But as he'd expected, Charlie wouldn't make a scene in front of a paying client.

A gibbous moon, just rising in the east, cast its pale light over the landscape. Mounting the steps again, Sam stood at the railing and watched Charlie usher his guest toward the fire and offered him a camp chair. With the gun case laid open on a folding table, they removed and inspected the heavy-duty weapon. As they were loading the ammunition, Sam heard a sound from somewhere beyond the firelight—a sound that chilled his blood. Ringing through the darkness, it was the trumpeting cry of the doomed elephant.

The creature was probably chained somewhere out in

the brush. When the man with the giant gun was ready, she would be released and prodded forward into the open. Sam could only hope the ending would be swift and merciful.

There was nothing he could do to save her. But if he got some clear photos and posted them where they'd be seen, maybe the poor old lady wouldn't have lost her life for nothing.

Unsettled, perhaps, by the unearthly cry, Greenway dropped a high-powered shell into the dust at his feet. He scooped it up and, without cleaning it, crammed it into the breech. Hefting the weapon to his shoulder, he peered through the scope, which probably wouldn't be needed. The elephant would be too close for that.

Greenway took his place. Charlie stood a dozen yards behind him with his own rifle. Sam recognized it as a 577 Nitro Express, the traditional gun used for big game hunting. Sam had heard Charlie tell his client that he wouldn't be standing backup. Either he'd lied or changed his mind. Greenway appeared not to notice. To Sam, he appeared nervous as he braced for the elephant's charge.

The risen moon hung above the horizon, lending enough light to see clearly now. Greenway chambered a shell in readiness. Charlie did the same, then took a flare pistol from his belt and fired a signal into the air.

The flare whined upward and burst against the dark sky. As the sparks fell and faded, the beaters in the brush began their clatter, pounding on drums and pans, shouting and chanting. The elephant's scream shattered the night as the huge animal, driven by the beaters, crashed through the scrub.

Sam could make out the elephant now, a hulking shape lumbering through the brush, maybe fifty yards distant. Greenway raised his rifle, aimed carefully, and squeezed the trigger.

The gun didn't fire.

From where he stood, Sam couldn't hear the ominous click, but he could imagine the sound of it, followed by more clicks as Greenway pulled the trigger again and again. Shrieking a curse, he flung his rifle to the ground.

Charlie charged forward, the 577 Nitro Express raised to his shoulder. With a shout of "No!" Greenway snatched the rifle away from him and swung it into position. The elephant was less than forty yards away now, lumbering head-on, trumpeting in fury, or maybe fear, as Greenway aimed.

That was when the unthinkable happened. A dark, bulky shape barreled across the elephant's path, followed by another, and another. Feral hogs, spooked by the commotion, were racing around in panic, grunting and squealing.

Startled and scared, the elephant bellowed, swung to the right, and charged off at an angle, moving away from the shooter The workmen tried to turn her with their pointed sticks, but they were clearly afraid of being trampled. Nothing was going to stop the giant animal from going her own way.

Greenway, who had Charlie's 577 now, swung the weapon to follow her, but now he could aim only for her side and rear. Any bullet that hit her would only deliver a wound, driving her mad with pain and rendering her deadly dangerous. Still, it appeared that Greenway was determined to get his quarry.

Sam sprinted down the steps and launched himself into the melee of milling hogs and yelling men. If he could keep Greenway from shooting the elephant, there might be a chance of saving her. But he couldn't get close enough, and even if he could, his Glock would be useless. He was helpless to stop what was happening. He could only watch with his heart in his throat.

Unarmed now, Charlie flung himself at his client. "Don't shoot, you fool!" he shouted. "Give me the gun."

But Greenway, like a man obsessed, was intent on finishing what he'd come to do. He swung the barrel hard, hitting Charlie with a blow that knocked him backward to sprawl in the dust. Charlie struggled to stand, but the fall had injured him. One leg buckled beneath him. He collapsed to his knees, blocking Greenway's line of fire.

"Don't shoot, Hubert!" Charlie yelled. "You don't want to wound her! We can try again later!"

At the sound of that hated voice, the elephant stopped in her tracks. With a scream of rage, she swung back in Charlie's direction. Her raised trunk gave Greenway the perfect target for a heart shot.

"For God's sake, man, shoot!" Charlie was in her path, struggling to get to his feet.

Greenway braced the stock of the rifle against his shoulder. Even at a distance, Sam could see that his aim was off. His finger squeezed the trigger. In the next instant, the deafening shot shattered the night.

As the confusion cleared, the bellowing elephant wheeled and bolted off, scattering the beaters in her path. The recoil had knocked Greenway onto his back. As Sam fought his way toward him, the aging hunter sat up, massaging his bruised shoulder and looking stunned. The gun lay where he'd dropped it.

Charlie lay face-up in the dust, his torso blasted by a shot that packed enough force to penetrate the armored hide of a rhino. He wasn't moving. Sam forced himself to look at him. Checking his vitals would be a waste of time. No human could survive that kind of damage.

Seeing Charlie's remains, and realizing what he'd done, Greenway curled into a shaking ball with his knees pulled against his chest. His shoulders heaved with silent sobs.

The hogs had scattered. The elephant, panicked but unhurt, was charging away through the thick scrub. Sam shouted at the workers to track her until she became calm and could be lured back to the compound with food.

He would make it his responsibility to see that she and the other animals went to safe places. Jasmine should know what to do. She would be happy to help him. If there was an inquest into Charlie's death, he would verify, as an eyewitness, that the shooting had been an accident and, except for incompetence and a bad case of nerves, Greenway was blameless.

Sam had just made the call to 911 when he heard a low groan from behind him. He turned. Charlie was looking at him with slitted eyes in a bloodless face. Incredibly, he was alive. But Sam's experience with severe injuries told him the man was on the verge of dying.

Crouching, Sam knelt over him. "Hang on, Charlie. The ambulance is on the way," he said.

"Too late . . ." Charlie's mouth twisted into a hideous grin. "You think you won, you sonofabitch . . ." Every syllable he spoke was bought with excruciating effort. "But you had questions . . . Did I kill my grandma? Did I murder Frank? . . . Now you'll never know. You'll go to your grave wondering." His laugh ended in a gurgle. "See you in hell, Agent . . ."

His expression froze in death.

The muffled ringing of a phone woke Jasmine in the night. She reached for her cell phone on the nightstand. Only then did she realize that the sound was coming from her dresser drawer, where she'd hidden the burner under a stack of underwear.

The phone was still ringing. Only Sam had the number. She vaulted out of bed and flung herself across the room to pull the phone out of the drawer.

"Sam?" She was muzzy-headed and out of breath.

"Yes, it's me. How are you?"

Jasmine hesitated. "I'm fine," she lied. "But you wouldn't be calling me just to ask. Is something wrong?"

"Charlie's dead." Sam gave her a few seconds for the news to sink in. "He was shot during a hunt. I saw it happen. It was an accident. Now I need your help."

"The animals!" She was already ahead of him. "Are they all right?"

"For now. I paid the workers to feed them. But they need places to go. Sanctuaries, rescues, anyone who can shelter them. There's the usual menagerie of hoof stock and cats. And there's an elephant, an old girl who's been through a rough time. I was hoping you'd have some idea who to call."

"An elephant? Good heavens! Yes, I know people with connections who can help. I'll make the calls for you first thing in the morning. I'm sorry I can't be there to take charge. I can't leave my mother."

"How is your mother?" he asked.

"I don't really know, Sam. Sometimes she seems fine. But then she has these headaches that are so bad she can't even get out of bed. She won't see a doctor. I can't make her go. But I can't leave. If she gets worse, or even dies, I'll need to be here for her."

"I understand, and I'm sorry." He paused. "I love you, Jasmine. I miss you like crazy."

"I love you, too," she said, knowing she couldn't tell him what was really going on or how scared she felt.

"We'll get through this," he said. "Just know that I'll be here for you."

"I know. I'll make those calls. It'll give me something positive to do."

"Thanks. Give the rescue people my number. I'll make sure they get to the right place."

Through the wall, Jasmine heard a stirring in the next room, where her mother slept. The ringing phone may have awakened her. "I've got to go," she said, forcing herself to end the call.

As she hid the burner phone again and closed the drawer, a wave of emotion crashed over her. She pressed her hands to her face, feeling the tears. Sam was the best thing ever to come into her crazy, messed-up life. She ached with love for him. But the hope of a future together was fading with every day she spent here—in a place that had become a prison.

"Jasmine!" Her mother was calling. Pulling on her robe, Jasmine hurried down the hall to the next room. The door was closed, as Madeleine preferred it, but the walls were thin. She had probably overheard much of her daughter's conversation.

A bedside lamp cast a glow over her mother's room. Madeleine sat propped against pillows that matched the mauve silk coverlet on the bed. Her abundant hair was tousled, her eyes smudged from the makeup she'd worn earlier to go out with Louis.

Jasmine hurried to mother's bedside. "What is it, Mama? Are you having one of your headaches?"

"No, dear." Madeleine raked her hair back from her face. With her chiseled, almost masculine features, she was a stunning woman. It was hard to believe she was so ill. "Your phone call woke me up, that's all. Who was it? Was it Sam?"

"Yes, it was Sam." Even a harmless lie could be a dangerous mistake.

"What did you tell him?"

"Nothing you'd be concerned about. He was calling because Charlie Grishman is dead. He needs my help finding rescuers for those poor animals. I said I'd make some calls."

"Anything else?"

"Yes. I told him I loved him."

"You're sure that was all?"

"I'm positive. You know that the last thing I want is for Sam—or the FBI—to show up here."

Madeleine nodded. "That's very wise. I'm fond of Sam. But if he gets involved with you here, I can't guarantee his safety—or yours. You know Louis. He isn't a trusting man. That's how he's managed to survive for so long."

"Yes, I know." How many people had Louis Divino killed—or arranged to have killed—just because he didn't trust them or because they knew too much and were no longer useful? A shudder passed through Jasmine's body.

She took a seat on the edge of the bed. "Why do you stay with him, Mother? He's not a good man."

"He's good to me. He treats me like he loves me, which is more than I can say for your father. We have fun together. And the sex . . . oh, my!"

"Mother!"

Madeleine chuckled. "Don't be such a prig, darling. You're over twenty-one. And since I don't know how much longer I'll be around, I plan to drain every drop of pleasure from the life I have left. Besides, Louis and I know we can trust each other. When I die, I'll carry his secrets to my grave—along with a few of my own."

In other words, he won't have to kill you to keep you quiet.

Jasmine knew better than to speak that thought aloud. She knew her mother was involved in at least some of Louis Divino's criminal enterprises. But aside from the overheard mention of drugs, she didn't know which ones or how deeply Madeleine was enmeshed. She only knew that getting caught with Louis's phone had signed her death warrant. If she were to leave and go on the run, she would be tracked down and killed. And if she stayed until her mother passed on, she would never leave the condo alive.

Madeline took a sip of mineral water from the bottle on her nightstand. "Go on back to bed, darling," she said. "I'm going to sleep now. I'll be fine."

Jasmine brushed a kiss on her mother's forehead. "All right. Call me if you need anything."

Wide awake now, she left her mother's room and wandered down the hall, through the parlor, and out onto the balcony. The night wind stirred her hair and raised glimmering ripples on the surface of the lake. She closed her eyes, savoring its coolness on her face. First thing tomorrow, she would call the animal rescue people she knew and give them Sam's phone number. But she would not call Sam again, not even on the burner. And she'd be wary of accepting any calls from him. The risk was too great. Even her own mother couldn't be trusted to keep their contact a secret.

She had to keep him safe, even if it meant that she'd never hear his voice again.

Chapter Sixteen

Sam got a call from the chairman of the animal rescue group the next day. They'd submitted the paperwork and were waiting for the death certificate that would permit them to move Charlie's menagerie to safety. Molly the elephant had been cleared for a Tennessee sanctuary before Charlie made Molly's owner a better offer. The sanctuary workers were on their way in a special truck, ready to take Molly to a new home where soft grasses, shady trees, and elephant friends would be waiting.

Jasmine had done her job well, but Sam resisted the urge to call and thank her. Last night, the caution in her voice had warned him against it. He'd sensed that something was wrong. But she'd told him nothing. Until he knew more, any interference on his part could be dangerous to them both.

For now, he owed Nick an update. He only wished he had better news. Nick deserved to hear that the case was about to be solved, not that it had become more complicated. Sitting in front of his computer, Sam made the call.

"Hi, Sam. Any news?" Nick's cheerful greeting sounded forced. Was he in pain? Was it time to give up the investigation and go back to Abilene?

"My news can wait," he said. "How are you?"

"Getting along. I heard about Charlie Grishman on the news."

"I was there, hoping to tie up some loose ends. Now that he's gone, it would be easy enough to name him as Frank's killer and close the case. I do believe he poisoned his grandmother to get her land. But killing Frank? The facts don't add up."

"I agree," Nick said. "The real killer is out there. I'm still betting on Roper McKenna. Motive, means, and opportunity, he had it all. And that syringe in the creek pretty much clinches it."

"But if we go to court on what we have, he'll walk," Sam said. "We need evidence. Has the lab determined how long that syringe was in the creek? It could've been dropped in the water any time after the murder."

"I'll mention that to the crime lab people. They're going over that syringe with a microscope, looking for anything we can use."

"Meanwhile, I'm trying to eliminate the other suspects," Sam said. "Like Miss Crystal Carter—and her ex-boyfriend, Judd, who just got out of jail. And I haven't forgotten Lila. She could still have done it. But we're running out of time, Nick. I know you need to get into treatment. Say the word, and I'll put this infernal case on hold and come back to Abilene. Finding Frank's killer is important, but it's not worth your life."

"Sam, I'm an old cop. Every time we step out the door, we put our lives on the line. I'll tell you when it's time to come back. Meanwhile, just do your job, and I'll do mine." Nick cleared his throat. "I haven't given up on nailing Louis Divino before I retire."

"Dare I ask how that's going? You've been after him since our Chicago days."

"It's come down to a paper chase. We've gotten our

hands on his taxes and some related business records—that's what finally got Capone, you know. The best account man in the Bureau is working on them. He's found evidence of money laundering and plain old-fashioned tax cheating. Divino's skated free before, but once we put the whole picture together, we should have enough on the bastard to pick him up."

"Is he still in Texas?" Sam asked.

"Austin. A team there is keeping track of him. One of his girlfriends has a condo on Lake Travis. And he's got a couple of other hangouts in the city. Once the evidence is rock solid, they'll pick him up and charge him. I've told the agents I want to be there when it happens.

"I wouldn't wait too long, if I were you," Sam said. "Divino's as slippery as a weasel and twice as mean."

"You're not telling me anything I don't know," Nick said. "Now it's back to work for both of us. Call me if anything breaks."

Sam ended the call, worry settling over him like a sodden weight. Nick, his old friend and mentor, hadn't sounded well. The sooner Sam returned to Abilene, the sooner Nick might be able to start cancer treatments. Nick had ordered him to stay on the case. But every week, even every day, without that treatment could mean the difference between life and death.

What if Nick already knew that? What if it was already too late?

Frustrated, Sam shut down his computer and walked outside. Standing on the porch, he surveyed the surrounding ranch through a yellow haze of heat waves and dust. In the paddocks, horses clustered in patches of shade and crowded around the water tanks, switching their tails to drive away the buzzing flies.

In the arena, Roper was working the horses. He'd been

there at all hours lately, pushing himself to exhaustion in his drive to be ready for the million-dollar competition. Sometimes he brought along his pretty younger sister, a horsewoman in her own right. Lila had stayed away, but Sam knew she watched him from the patio.

The money, the glory, and the beautiful wealthy widow. For Roper, everything was at stake here, including his freedom. Had ambition and desire driven Roper to murder his employer? The idea made sense, especially after the finding of the syringe. So, given the urgency of Nick's illness, why did Sam still hesitate to close the case?

It wasn't because he liked, even admired, Roper McKenna—although he did. That alone wouldn't have stopped him. No, it was something else—some deep instinct whispering that he already knew the truth. It was inside him, only waiting to be noticed.

Sam had seen Frank's killer face-to-face. He had talked with them. He had listened, but not carefully enough. Somewhere, buried in his memory, was the missed clue that would give him the answers.

Why couldn't he remember? What was he missing?

Perched on a rail of the arena, Cheyenne watched Roper finish the routine with Fire Dance. Roper was grateful to have her here. During these late training sessions, with the grooms and stable hands gone, his thoughts tended to wander dark paths, beset with the fear that he might lose his freedom soon and then all this work with the horses would have been a waste of time. Cheyenne was good company. Not only was she helpful with the horses but, more important, she helped keep him focused.

Roper had said nothing to her about his possible arrest. Until and unless it happened, he would spare his family the worry. Meanwhile, he would value his time with her.

She had a sharp eye for presentation, and she'd been giving him good pointers

"How did we do?" he asked, pulling the stallion to a halt in front of her.

"The stallion looked great," she said. "But you're leaning in hard on the turn. It looks off-balance. Try letting the horse do more of the work."

"Thanks. I never noticed that. I've been doing this a long time, but I've never had a coach. It's helping. Want to cool him down?"

"Sure." She hopped off the rail as he dismounted. Fire Dance was a lot bigger than her mare, but she swung into the saddle with ease. While Roper checked on the other horses in the stable, she walked the stallion around the arena. When he was ready, they rubbed him down and put him away.

"Fire Dance is magnificent," she said as they crossed the parking lot to the truck. "Just sitting on his back is a thrill."

"Does it make you wish you'd taken Frank's offer to teach you reining?" Roper asked.

Her only response was a stone-cold silence that lasted several seconds before she spoke. "I made the right decision then—just as I'm making the right decision now to get into cutting. I don't want to end up like Dad. If I keep doing rodeos, that could happen."

Cheyenne had deftly changed the subject. Roper sensed that he'd touched a nerve mentioning Frank. He'd be smart to back off. But given that he was a suspect in Frank's murder, he needed to know more.

"Frank was a fair boss," he said. "We always got along. Why do I get the impression you had a problem with him?"

She shrugged. "I was young. He thought he could control me. I could tell early on that it wasn't going to work, and I told him so."

"How did Frank take that?"

"How do you think? The man had an ego." She fell into silence for a few steps. "Hayden called me. He wants to take me to his family ranch and show me some cutting horses."

"He seems respectable enough. Did you say yes?"

She laughed. "Of course. And respectable has nothing to do with it. I'm a big girl, Roper. I've been fending off hot-handed cowboys for as long as I've been on the rodeo circuit. I can handle Hayden. It's the horses that I want to see."

"Well, go for it, then. But if he doesn't behave, remember your big brother's got your back."

"Sure, I will." She laughed as they reached the truck. "Let's head home and hope Mom's got supper warming for us."

Pleasantly exhausted, they drove up the road, crossed the bridge over the creek, and pulled in through the ranch gate. As they neared the house, they saw Rachel standing on the front porch.

"I know that look," Cheyenne said. "Something's wrong."

As they climbed out of the truck, Rachel came down the steps to meet them. In the glow of the porch light, Roper could see the hard set of her mouth, the sharp angle of her jaw, a sign of emotions too tightly reined.

"Rowdy's gone," she said. "He got in an awful fight with Stetson and Chance before they left for that rodeo in Waco. They wanted him to go along. But he blew up, said he was sick of this controlling family. Kirby got involved. When I tried to stop them, I got pulled into the fight, too. Rowdy said some awful things—curses so vile . . ." She shook her head, her voice breaking slightly. "I slapped his face so hard it hurt my hand. After that, he was quiet. He just packed his gear, loaded his truck, and drove away."

"When did all this happen?" Roper asked.

"After lunch, a few hours ago."

"Did he say where he was going?"

"No. But earlier, I heard him telling Chance about a new friend named Judd who'd promised to take him on a road trip." Her shoulders squared and tightened. "The last thing I said to him before he climbed into the truck was that he was going to hell! How could I say such a thing? I'm his mother! What if I never see him again?"

She seemed to notice Cheyenne for the first time. "Your father's alone in there," she said. "Go and see to him."

As Cheyenne hurried into the house, Roper made an effort to comfort his mother. He knew she was hurting. But it wouldn't be like her to show it. "You've been a good mother," he said. "After he cools down, Rowdy will remember that. Sooner or later he'll be back."

"Will he?" Her work-worn hands clenched at her side. "I've raised my children the best I know how. I'd have done anything for them, to keep them strong and keep the family together. Now it's as if everything is falling apart—as if I've been weighed in the balance and found wanting."

"You can't blame yourself," Roper said. "People are human. They don't always make the choices you'd want them to. It's called life. Rowdy has a good heart, but he's young and stubborn, and he's got some tough lessons to learn. Just give him time. Now let's go inside and have some supper. Things will look better in the morning."

But would they? Roper asked himself as he opened the screen door and held it for his mother. When she'd mentioned that Rowdy was in contact with Judd, his instincts had flashed a red alert. Judd Proctor was a hardened criminal and a possible suspect in Frank Culhane's murder. Rowdy wasn't just in bad company. He could be over his head in danger.

Despite what he'd told his mother, Roper couldn't let

Rowdy get involved with a man like Judd. He needed to go after the young fool and talk sense into him.

Without knowing Rowdy's plans, tracking him down would be a guessing game. Only one person might be able to help—the last man Roper wanted to trust.

Agent Sam Rafferty.

Darrin had checked with his stockbroker. The $100,000 cash that Crystal had demanded in return for her disappearance could be made available on two days' notice. Still, he hesitated. It was a lot of money to give an irresponsible young woman on a promise. Once she had the cash in her greedy little hands, Crystal could do anything she wanted to, and he'd be powerless to stop her.

Maybe he should demand an arrangement where he gave her a down payment to leave and wired the rest when she contacted him from another state. But why should she trust him to do that?

He needed to talk to her, at the very least. Maybe they could work something out. Maybe she would lower her price for cash up front. Or maybe . . .

The thought that had sprouted in his mind—a way to end his concerns once and for all without paying a cent—sent a chill up Darrin's spine. Earlier in the summer, he'd paid a stable hand to rig Lila's car for a freeway crash timed to make her death look like an accident. Only a stroke of fate had kept it from happening. This time, things would have to be different. He would need to do the job himself.

He had some hard thinking to do. Meanwhile, he needed to get in touch with the woman. Using the burner phone he kept hidden in a secret drawer, he found the card she'd given him and entered her number.

* * *

Lila had done more than her share of soul searching as she went about her days. She'd also spent time in private consultation with her lawyer. At last, after a long and painful deliberation, she had come to a decision.

She would adopt Crystal's baby and raise the child as her own.

The money would be paid in installments, but only if certain conditions were met. Crystal was to be examined and treated by a doctor of Lila's choosing. Lila was to be kept informed as the pregnancy progressed. She would have access to any and all medical reports. The young woman would follow the guidelines for a healthy pregnancy—good nutrition, exercise and rest, prenatal vitamins, monthly checkups, and no alcohol, illegal drugs, or unprotected sex—better yet, no sex at all.

Lila had shared the news with Roper during a break in his training. "I like to think I'm doing this for the right reasons," she'd said. "This can't be about keeping the ranch. It has to be about giving Frank's child a good home."

His right hand had stirred, as if to reach out and cup her face. But he resisted. They kept the distance between them. People could be watching.

"You'll be a good mother," he'd said.

She'd walked away, thinking of the years it would take to raise a child. Roper had mentioned nothing about being there for those years. With his future in peril, she knew better than to hope or to speak of how desperately she wanted him at her side. That would be asking too much of life.

Her lawyer was already preparing the contract for Crystal to sign. All that remained was to phone Crystal and invite her to a meeting in his office, where the offer would be presented. Of course Crystal could always refuse to sign. But if she wanted the money, this would be the only way for her to get it.

Lila had already tried to call Crystal once. There'd been no answer, not even a voice mail greeting. Maybe the battery had run down. Or maybe she'd lost it.

Lila tried again. Still no response. Impatient now, she sent a simple text.

Crystal, call me.

She wasn't really worried. Crystal would be anxious to hear from her. When she didn't, she was bound to call back.

But why now, of all times, had the troublesome young woman become so difficult to reach?

Without taking time for supper, Roper drove back to the Culhane Ranch. Earlier, when he'd left work, the lights had been on in Sam's bungalow. He could only hope that Sam would still be there, and that he'd be decent enough to help Roper track down his wayward brother

Roper had made several calls to his brother's phone. All of them had gone to voice mail. Rowdy was probably ignoring the calls. He didn't want to be scolded, lectured, or ordered home by his older half sibling. He was his own man now. He could be walking stupidly into danger. Maybe he was already with Judd Proctor.

As Roper pulled his truck up to the bungalow and parked, he saw Sam seated in a chair on the porch. The FBI agent was alone, sipping a beer, probably enjoying some peace and quiet. But that was about to end.

Sam stood as Roper climbed out of the truck. "You're the last person I expected to see tonight," he said. "I assume this isn't a social call."

"No. And before you say anything else, I need your help. I know what you think I did. I hope you can put that aside for now and listen to me."

"I'm listening. Have a seat if you like."

"I'll stand, thanks," Roper said. "Are you aware that Judd Proctor is out of jail?"

"I am now." Sam took the news without further comment. As Roper already knew, the agent was a man who kept his thoughts to himself. But anything involving Judd should be enough to catch his interest.

"Rowdy, my younger brother, has left home in his truck," Roper said. "He got to know Judd in jail, when he spent a night in the next cell. My family has reason to believe he's contacted Judd and they've gone off on a road trip together."

Roper waited for Sam's response, his fear deepening. If Judd, already a suspect in Frank's murder, was set on leaving the state, that could point to his guilt. And if Judd had mentioned the crime to Rowdy, the young man could be valuable as a witness—which would give Judd a reason to get rid of him or maybe hold him as a hostage.

After what seemed like an eternity of silence, Sam spoke. "Thank you for coming to me," he said. "Give me everything you've got, including your brother's description, a photo if you have one, and the license number of his vehicle. We'll need to move fast on this."

Wearing her robe, Crystal stood next to the bed, gazing down at the man she'd once loved—or thought she had. Judd lay sprawled on the sheets, buck naked and snoring like a bull, his hair leaving grease stains on her new pink pillowcases. A drizzle of saliva trailed from the corner of his mouth to lose itself in his tangled beard.

Until he showed up, she hadn't known he was out of jail. He would have showered for his trial, but it was as if the odors of bleach, open toilets, vomit, and sweaty underwear had seeped into his skin. While they were having sex—she couldn't call it making love—the smell of his body had almost made her gag.

For her own survival, she'd pretended to accept him.

Judd had a murderous, hair-trigger temper. If he'd known how she really felt about him, he would have punched her senseless—or maybe worse—to punish her for breaking up with him.

She had to get out of here.

Waiting for him to leave would be a mistake. He'd already talked about moving in with her, and that would just be for starters. Unless she wanted to become a prisoner, she would have to get away now, take what she could carry, and never look back.

Keeping her ears attuned to his snores, Crystal dressed quickly and began to gather the few things she really needed—her purse, a few clothes and toiletries, her cash, the keys to her car. Judd had already noticed the diamond ring on her finger. She'd managed to convince him that it was fake, like the rest of her jewelry.

Judd had taken her phone. When she'd tried to get it back, he'd thrown it on the floor and kicked it far back under the couch. Crystal could only hope the phone wasn't broken. Losing it would make things harder for her, but it was better than losing her life.

She froze, holding her breath as Judd snorted and rolled onto his side. As his snores resumed, she began to breathe again. But what would she do if he were to wake up?

She remembered the kitchen knife she'd bought and left on the counter of the kitchenette. Its blade was long and sharp enough to penetrate a man's body. For a moment, she imagined using it on him—plunging it into his chest or slicing his throat. But she dismissed the idea at once. She wasn't a murderer. And even if she were to try, Judd would be strong enough to take the knife away and use it on her. She should probably put it in the drawer, where he wouldn't see it.

But never mind the knife, or anything else. She just needed to get out of here.

She'd dreamed of the money she'd be getting from the Culhanes and how she would spend it. That dream had gone up in smoke when she'd opened her door to Judd. Now she could only save her freedom—and maybe her life.

With the keys in her pocket and her possessions stuffed into a black plastic trash bag, she crossed the small living room to the door. On the other side of that door, a flight of cement steps led from the basement to the driveway where her car was parked.

She had turned the doorknob to go out when she heard a voice from behind.

"Where do you think you're going, babe?"

Crystal's heart dropped. She spun around to find Judd standing in the bedroom doorway. The knowing grin on his face told Crystal she was in danger.

Gripping the bag, she scrambled for a reply. "I was just taking the trash out, honey. After that, I'll fix you some nice bacon and eggs, unless you'd rather go out."

"I'll have a look at that trash." With a lightning move, he lunged forward and ripped the bag out of her hands.

As he opened it to look inside, Crystal sprang for the knife on the nearby counter. Her fingers closed around the handle. But once again, Judd was too fast for her. Flinging down the plastic trash bag, he seized her wrist and twisted it until the knife fell from her hand.

"Bitch!" he muttered. "I should've known I couldn't trust you!"

His huge hammy fist slammed into the side of her face, triggering explosions of pain. Spinning off-balance, she went down hard. That was the last thing she remembered before her head struck a corner of the glass-topped coffee table and everything went black.

* * *

Breathing like a winded bull, Judd stood looking down at the woman who'd betrayed him. Her eyes were closed. Blood oozed from her scalp, staining her dark hair and slow-spreading in a crimson pool on the threadbare carpet.

She wasn't moving.

He thought he should at least check her pulse. But he wasn't sure how to do that. And she'd hit that table pretty damned hard. For all he knew, she could already be dead.

Only one thing was certain. He didn't want to go back to jail for what had just happened. He had to get dressed and get out of town.

Hands shaking, he pulled on his clothes and jammed his feet into his boots. He'd left his motorcycle in the driveway with enough gas in the tank to get him the first fifty miles. But he was going to need money. He'd left a stash hidden in his room above the garage. It should still be there, unless Crystal had helped herself. He'd stop by, get what he needed, and hit the back roads.

He took one last look around to make sure he hadn't left anything, then opened the door and started up the stairs. Remembering the trash bag he'd taken from Crystal, he was tempted to go back and check it for valuables. But he was running out of time. Besides, he didn't want to be caught with anything that could be traced to her.

His bike was waiting in the driveway. As he straddled the seat, he noticed the elderly couple on the porch of the house next door. They were staring at him, watching his every move. Bad luck. But he would soon be gone.

After starting up the bike, he roared off down the street.

So much for promises.

Rowdy sat in the sweltering cab of his truck, the windows down and the radio blaring. He'd been waiting for more than two hours at the address Judd had given him—

a run-down garage on the outskirts of Willow Bend. The place look deserted, as if it had recently gone out of business. On the second floor, he could see the windows of the upstairs room where Judd had said he'd be living when he got out of jail. There was no sign of life.

Once again, Rowdy gave himself a mental kick for not having memorized Judd's phone number. They'd spent only one night together in jail, but they'd talked for hours, mostly about what they wanted to do when they were released. That was when the idea of a road trip had come up—they'd take Rowdy's truck, with Judd's bike in the back, and go all the way to California, where they could hang out on the beach, pick up women, and get high.

The idea of adventure and freedom had set Rowdy's imagination on fire. No more building fences and shoveling shit. No more preaching from his mother. She'd told him he was going to hell. Maybe he would just prove the old lady right.

"We'll go as soon as we're both free," Judd had told him. "When you hear I'm out, just show up at my place with plenty of cash. I'll be waiting for you, and we'll take off from there."

Rowdy knew that Judd had been released. But where was he now? Had he forgotten his promise? He could always make the trip by himself, Rowdy supposed. But without Judd to show him the ropes, it wouldn't be as much fun.

He would give his friend another hour. If he didn't show up, he'd leave and maybe try again later. One thing was for sure, he couldn't go home. Not after the way he'd parted with his mother.

Rowdy slumped in the seat, angled his long legs, and put his boots on the dash. A fly, buzzing in through the open window, settled on his arm. He smashed it and brushed the carcass away. Closing his eyes, he drifted into a doze.

He was jarred awake by the roar of a motorcycle as Judd pulled up alongside his truck. “Hey, buddy,” he said with a grin. “Are you ready for our big adventure?”

Rowdy sat up and blinked himself awake. “You bet. I was afraid you’d stood me up.”

“Me? Never! Help me load this bike onto the bed of your truck. Then I’ll pick up a few things from upstairs and we’ll be off.”

Fifteen minutes later, with the bike loaded and Judd’s duffel tossed into the back of the club cab, they were on the back road out of town.

Giddy with anticipation, Rowdy drove. Judd reclined his seat and released an odoriferous cloud of gas. Rowdy lowered the window to let in some fresh air. The truck cab had already begun to smell like the jail. But never mind. Ahead lay a great adventure. He meant to enjoy every minute of it.

Chapter Seventeen

Groggy and disoriented, Crystal drifted into awareness. The first thing she felt was a throbbing on the left side of her head. Little by little, other sensations crept in—clean cotton sheets cradling her body. The faint beep and buzz of electronic monitors. The sting of an IV needle attached to the back of her left hand. Muffled voices. The click of cart wheels over a tile floor . . .

The memory stirred—Judd's fist slamming into her, the staggering fall, and the burst of empty blackness as her head struck something hard and sharp. Now, even before she opened her eyes, she could tell that she was in some kind of hospital. More surprising than that, she was alive.

She willed her eyes to open. The overhead light was blinding. She turned her head to one side. Even that slight movement brought a stab of pain. Her exploring right hand moved to feel the thick gauze wrapping. The flesh around her eye felt swollen, as well. She must look like hell.

The ring! Her heart slammed as she realized her finger was bare. Where was it? Could Judd have taken it?

"Hello, Crystal. Welcome back."

Startled by the masculine voice, she jerked her head to the right. The stab of pain made her gasp. She forced her gaze to focus.

Agent Sam Rafferty was seated in a visitor chair next to her bed. Crystal swore silently. Whatever the man was here for, it couldn't be good.

She found her voice. "Where am I? What happened?"

"You're in the emergency room at the Willow Bend Clinic. Blood loss and probable concussion. You were lucky. Your neighbors heard loud voices. They saw Judd leaving and got worried. If they hadn't found you and called for an ambulance, you might not be here now."

"Those nosy old farts. They're always watching me. I guess I owe them." She frowned. "What are *you* doing here?"

"Since you and Judd are both persons of interest in Frank's murder, the police called me. They found hair and blood on the sharp corner of that coffee table. Someone from the police might be here to question you later, but I need you to tell me what happened now."

"It was about the way you think. Judd wouldn't leave. When I tried to get away, he got rough and started hitting me. I must've fallen against the table. I don't remember anything else." Crystal tried to raise her head, but a wave of dizziness swept over her. She sank back onto the pillow. "Where's Judd? Did he get away?"

"The police have an APB out for his Harley. They promised to keep me informed." Rafferty's eyes narrowed. "There's something else you'll be questioned about. Because you were assaulted, the doctor checked you for possible rape. She found semen."

"Of course he did. That bastard Judd threw me on the bed and raped me. Didn't even bother with protection. In case you're wondering, it happened before he slammed me against the table. I was conscious. I remember it all, and I'm willing to testify."

"The police also found a knife on the floor and a bag with some things of yours in it."

"After the rape, I was trying to leave. I grabbed the knife when Judd tried to stop me, but he took it away. That was when he started punching me." Her pulse lurched as she realized that under the flannel sheet she was wearing nothing but a hospital gown. "My things—where are they?"

"Safe, in a locker here at the clinic. The police kept the knife for prints, but your clothes, your purse, your keys, and the things in the bag came with you in the ambulance. You'll get them back when you're checked out. The doctor talked about transporting you to the hospital in Abilene. But since you're awake and lucid, I'm guessing that won't be necessary."

"My ring—the engagement ring Frank gave me. It was on my finger. Now it's gone."

"I'm sorry, no one's mentioned it," Rafferty said. "Someone might have put it with your other belongings. I can ask about it."

"Oh please. It might not be worth much, but it's all I have left from Frank—except for the baby, of course."

"Oh course. But that brings me to another matter. When I asked the doctor whether your baby was all right, she gave me a surprised look. She told me she'd found no indication that you were pregnant. How would you explain that?"

Crystal felt something crumble inside her. Real or not, that baby had been her last hope for a future of comfort, abundance, and respect. Now there could be no more pretense. Tears of self-pity welled in her eyes. "I really was pregnant," she said. "The baby was Frank's. But I had a miscarriage. I couldn't help it. It just happened."

"So you decided to keep it a secret. You were going to

take what you could get from Lila and disappear before she learned the truth. Is that what you were thinking?"

Crystal let her silence answer the question. How could anyone blame her? That baby had been her ticket to a better life. Now she had nothing—not even a plausible lie.

"Does Lila know?" she asked.

"Not yet. But she will. I plan to tell her myself."

"I don't want to face her. Please don't make me."

"That isn't up to me." He moved the chair back and stood. "But I have a feeling that after what you've done to her, Lila will never want to set eyes on you again. You'll be lucky if she doesn't have you arrested."

"But I didn't mean any harm. I just—"

"We're finished here, Crystal." Rafferty turned to go.

As he reached the door, Crystal was seized by a sudden afterthought. "Wait!" she said. "I just remembered something important—something Judd said when we were fighting."

He turned back toward her. "I'm listening."

"Judd told me that he killed Frank—told me how he arranged to meet him in the stable and how he got the syringe and filled it with fentanyl. He said he did it for love. But if he loved me, why would he do this to me?" She gestured toward her swollen eye and bandaged head.

"Did he say what he did with the syringe?" Rafferty asked.

"No. But he was jealous of Frank. He hated him because of me. And he wanted me to know what he'd done. Find Judd, and you'll have your murderer."

"Would you be willing to sign a statement swearing to what you just told me?"

"Anything. Judd killed the man I loved, the father of my baby. I just want him punished." She strained to sit up, then fell back onto the pillow. "But right now, I'm not sure I can even hold a pen."

"That's fine. I have preparations to make. I'll be back

tomorrow with the document and a recorder. Meanwhile, think about the details—anything you remember."

After the FBI agent had left, Crystal lay with her eyes closed, struggling to collect her scattered thoughts. Had Sam Rafferty believed what she'd told him about Judd being the murderer? She'd made up the story on the spot, but it could well be true. Judd really had hated Frank. He had access to fentanyl, and he was capable of killing. He belonged in prison, maybe even on death row.

Judd would already have the FBI on his trail. But that wasn't going to help her now. After the lie about the baby, she could be in big trouble. If she wanted to remain free, she needed to get out of this clinic and out of Willow Bend. She could sell the ring if it wasn't gone. But the money wouldn't last. She needed as much cash as she could get her hands on.

Think, Crystal . . .

Then she remembered something. Darrin and Simone hadn't known about the baby or about her pending deal with Lila—not until she'd told them. And they wouldn't know about the miscarriage. If they thought she was pregnant, they might still be good for some traveling money.

It might be a long shot, but it was the best chance she had. She would check out of the clinic as soon she was able to stand, call someone from work for a ride home, find her phone, and make the call.

Rowdy and Judd had picked up Interstate 20 out of Abilene. By now, a few hours later, they were coming into Odessa and the truck was running low on gas.

Judd had swilled several beers and was in no condition to be trusted at the wheel, so Rowdy had done the driving. He was getting tired and hungry. It was time for a break.

At the next exit, Rowdy took the off-ramp and pulled up to the gas pumps at a 7-Eleven. As he stopped at the pump, Judd, who'd been dozing on and off, sat up with a yawn.

"What d'you say I fill the tank while you go inside and get some snacks?" Judd suggested. "I've got my Visa. I can pay at the pump."

"Thanks." Rowdy opened the door of the high cab and swung to the ground. "What would you like for snacks?"

Judd climbed out the passenger side. "Chips and a hot dog with relish. And a Bud Light. That should do it for me. After we're gassed up, I'll need to use the crapper. Give me your keys. I'll lock the truck and bring them inside to you."

Rowdy tossed him the truck keys. Judd caught them deftly with one hand, then turned his attention to opening the tank and working the gas pump. Leaving him, Rowdy went into the convenience store. After a visit to the restroom, he took a plastic basket from the stack near the door and began filling it with snack items—for Judd, a packet of barbecue-flavored chips and a hot dog from the cooker in the corner, set up with buns, garnishes, and paper bags. The beer probably wasn't a good idea. Judd had already downed several. But he wouldn't be driving. Maybe this one would put Judd to sleep.

For himself, Rowdy chose a granola bar, a pack of beef jerky, and a chilled Red Bull to keep him awake.

In line at the cash register, Rowdy took his credit card out of his wallet to have it ready. He had yet to see Judd come in. Pumping the gas shouldn't have taken this long. He'd probably gone straight to the restroom and would be showing up any minute.

By the time Rowdy had paid, there was still no sign of Judd. Maybe there'd been a problem with the pump or with his card. Or maybe he'd gotten into an argument with somebody. That would be like him.

Impatient but not really worried, Rowdy checked the

restroom. When he failed to see Judd, he went back through the store, opened the front door, and stepped outside.

Judd was gone.

So was the truck, with Rowdy's phone, his keys, and everything else he owned.

Lila got the call from Sam after supper. "I saw your light," he said. "There's been a development. We need to talk. Is this a good time?"

A development? A chill passed through Lila's body. What was he talking about? Had Roper been arrested? Heart pounding, she forced herself to reply. "Now's as good as any."

"I can come over, or we can sit here on the bungalow porch."

Lila thought of Mariah, whom she no longer trusted. Even now the cook could be eavesdropping. She didn't trust Sam, either. But she needed to hear what he had to say.

"Stay where you are," she told him. "I'll come out."

She left by the patio and cut around the house to the bungalow. The porch light was off, probably to discourage mosquitos, but she could see Sam sitting in the moonlight, an empty chair pulled up next to his.

She mounted the porch and took a seat. "No small talk," she said. "Just tell me. Is this about Roper?"

"No. It's about Crystal." His gaze followed the darting flight of a nighthawk chasing insects in the dark.

Crystal. Lila released a long breath. "What about her?"

"I saw her at the clinic. Her ex-boyfriend, Judd, got out of jail and beat her up pretty good. She'll be all right, but she fell and hit her head. Probably a concussion."

"What about the baby? Is the baby all right?"

He turned toward her, his gaze holding hers. "There is

no baby, Lila. Crystal miscarried. She chose not to tell you about it."

Stunned, Lila stared at him. "Why, that little . . ." She shook her head. Torrents of emotion washed over her—rage, pity, relief, disappointment, and finally, grief.

"I was actually going to do it, Sam," she said. "My lawyers were drawing up the contract. I was going to pay Crystal's price and adopt the little mite. I was ready to be a mother again. Now . . ." She sighed. "I don't know what to say. I don't even know what to feel."

"You could have her charged with fraud. She chose to go ahead with the scheme, even after she'd lost the baby. I'm sure you must've given her money."

"That's the least of it." Lila ran a hand through her hair, raking a stray lock back from her face. "But no, I can't change what's already happened. So why prolong this farce? Let her go. I've got other battles to fight. I'll call my lawyers in the morning."

Lila stood, still reeling with the impact of what Sam had told her. She'd pretended to dismiss the news, as if it didn't matter. But she'd already begun to imagine the baby—the tiny hands and feet, the hungry little mouth, the need for love. Frank's child, and Crystal's, would be innocent of everything its parents had done. She'd been prepared to love it. Now it was as if that small person had just died in her heart.

"Are we finished?" she asked Sam.

"Just one thing more." Sam stopped speaking and stood as a tall figure appeared in the moonlight, striding from the direction of the stables. It was Roper.

His surprised gaze met Lila's for an instant. Then he turned to Sam. "Any news?" he asked.

"Not about your brother," Sam said. "But pull up a chair. What I have to say concerns both of you."

Roper moved a chair to join the other two. In the fewest possible words, Sam recapped Crystal's miscarriage, Judd's attack, and the possibility that Roper's missing brother could have gone on the road with him.

"The troopers are looking for the truck and for Judd's Harley. So far there's been no word. We don't even know if they're together—all we have to go on is what young Rowdy told his family. With luck, he's just off somewhere having a good time. But I agree that Judd is bad news. I said I'd keep you informed, Roper, and I will."

"You mentioned there was something else," Roper said.

"Yes, I'm coming to that. When I spoke with Crystal, she told me something that—if it's true—changes the investigation into Frank's murder."

Lila could sense Roper's tension as he sat beside her. She checked the impulse to reach for his hand.

"Understand, Crystal had taken a beating. When I saw her, she had a black eye, and her head was wrapped in a bandage. She'd been brought into the clinic unconscious and bleeding from a head wound. I was there when she woke up. She was lucid, and she remembered the assault."

He glanced from Lila to Roper. "The last thing she told me, as I was leaving, was that Judd had confessed to murdering Frank. Her story is believable. Judd had a motive, and he gave her the details of the crime. Crystal has agreed to sign a sworn statement. I'll bring it by tomorrow, after she's had a chance to rest."

Lila and Roper exchanged startled looks. The news seemed almost too good to be true. "Are you saying that I'm no longer a suspect?" Roper asked Sam.

"I didn't say that. But if Crystal will give us a sworn statement, admissible in court, we'll have a presentable case—especially if we can find other evidence to support Judd's guilt. Of course if he comes up with an alibi, or something else goes against us, we'll be back to square one."

"Back to me, in other words." Roper spoke with a bitterness that Lila could feel. "I just want this over with."

"Believe me, so do I," Sam said. "My boss needs me back in Abilene. But it has to be done right, or the whole investigation will amount to nothing but wasted time."

"You know I didn't kill Frank," Roper said. "And I'll be damned if I take the blame just so you can earn your blasted gold star."

"I very much want to believe you, Roper," Sam said. "If I didn't, you'd be under arrest by now. Let's see how this plays out. If we can find enough evidence to support Judd's so-called confession . . ."

"Stop playing games with me, Sam," Roper snapped. "I've got a missing brother who may be on the road with a murderer. Right now that's the only thing on my mind." He stood. "I'm going home to my family now. You've got my phone number. Call me the minute you hear anything."

As he turned away, his gaze met Lila's. She glimpsed the frustration and worry in his face. But this was no time to reach out to him. There was nothing she could do.

As Roper strode away, headed back to the lot where he'd left his truck, Sam's phone rang. Sam took the call. As he listened to the voice on the other end, his expression went rigid.

"Wait—" He shielded the phone with his hand. "Lila, get Roper! Bring him back here!"

Lila sprang to her feet and raced down the path toward the parking lot. By now, Roper, walking fast, had almost reached the truck. "Wait!" she shouted at him. "Roper, wait!"

She reached him, out of breath. "Sam just got a call! He needs you to come! Go on, I'll catch up!"

Roper charged back up the path. Lila followed, nursing a painful stitch in her side. She had seen Sam's reaction to the phone call. Whatever news he'd been given, she knew it hadn't been good.

By the time she reached the bungalow, Sam had put down the phone and was talking to Roper. The look of utter shock on Roper's face warned her to expect the worst.

"The phone call was from the state troopers, Lila," Sam told her. "A red Ford pickup, with a license number that matches the missing vehicle, was involved in a collision with a tanker truck on I-20, twelve miles past Odessa. The truck driver made it out all right, but the pickup caught fire and exploded. Just one body was recovered, burned beyond identification."

Lila gazed at Roper, her heart breaking for him as he struggled to hold his emotions in check.

"Call them back, Sam," he said. "Give them my cell number and tell them I'm on my way."

"I'm coming with you, Roper," Lila said.

"No need for you to see this," he said. "Stay here. I'll call you."

"Don't be stubborn. You could use an extra pair of eyes and ears. And you might need somebody else who can drive. Don't do this alone. I'm going to get my purse. Wait for me."

She raced into the house. Minutes later, she returned with her purse and a light jacket to find him waiting at his truck. His stoic face masked the emotions that had to be raging inside him. "It's not too late to change your mind," he said.

"Don't worry about me. Just drive." She climbed into the truck, settled into the passenger seat, and buckled her seat belt. Roper started the engine. The truck roared out of the gate and headed up the road toward the freeway entrance. The three-hour drive would get them to the accident scene by midnight. By then, the highway crew would be clearing up the debris. The burned body would have been taken to the police morgue. Roper would likely be asked to confirm that the accident victim was his brother.

Lila studied his grim profile, the mouth set in a rigid line, the narrowed eyes watching the road in front of him. She had never met Roper's family, but she'd sensed how much he cared for them. Now he'd be facing an unthinkable ordeal. And there was nothing she could say to make it easier. Looking at him, she ached with love. But at times like this, even love wouldn't be enough.

In Big Spring, they stopped for gas. While Roper filled the tank, Lila bought coffee, which they drank on the road from Styrofoam cups. They hadn't spoken much, but Roper was grateful that she'd insisted on coming with him. This was a hell of a time to be alone.

They were more than halfway to Odessa and the site of the accident. Roper had yet to notify his family. He was struggling with what to say to them, when his phone rang. Once, twice, and then again as he fumbled it out of his pocket.

"Mr. McKenna?" The voice was a man's, crisp and official sounding. Roper muttered a response. "This is Sergeant Rasband of the Odessa City Police Department. I've got a young man here who asked me to call you. I'll put him on."

"Roper?" The familiar voice was a stab to his heart. For a split second he lost control of the wheel. The vehicle veered over the painted line before he wrenched it back.

"Rowdy? Where in hell's name are you?" Swept away by anger and relief, Roper was too shaken to drive safely. He pulled into the emergency lane and hit the flasher.

"I'm at the police station in Odessa. That sonofabitch,

Judd, stole my truck with my phone and everything. He drove off and left me at a gas station. I got a clerk to call the police. Then I had to wait for them, file a report, and finally got them to call you. Where are you?"

"On my way to where you are." Roper checked the traffic before pulling back onto the roadway. "Stay put, damn it. We'll talk when I get there."

Lila was staring at him, her expression incredulous and joyful. "Your brother's all right?"

"He's fine." Roper willed himself to keep a steady course in the outside lane. "Judd stole the truck. That burned body . . ." He swallowed hard. "It would be his."

"And Rowdy doesn't know about the accident?"

"Evidently not."

"Take the next exit," Lila said. "This calls for a break."

The exit was coming up. Roper swung the truck onto the off-ramp and pulled into the parking lot of a Kelly's Barbecue restaurant. Taking a long breath, he switched off the engine, unfastened his seat belt, turned, and pulled Lila close.

Lila wrapped him in her arms. His shoulders shook with dry sobs. As she felt his need, the love that flowed through her was bittersweet and so deep that it brought a surge of tears. But even then she understood that part of him belonged to his family. That part was what mattered now, more than her, more than their love.

After a few minutes, he released her and sank back into the seat. "Thanks. I'm all right now," he said. "Damn it, what a scare. When I see that rascal, I won't know whether to hug him or slap him silly."

"Do you want me to drive?"

"I'll be fine."

"I could call Sam. He'll need to hear the news."

"Go ahead."

While Lila made the call to Sam, he drove back onto the freeway, in control again but still silent. In an hour they reached Odessa and followed the GPS to the police station. A lanky young man with a brotherly resemblance to Roper sat on a bench outside. He looked as forlorn as a lost puppy.

"Stay here." Roper pulled into a nearby parking place and climbed out of the truck. Lila watched as he strode toward his brother. Rowdy stood, looking uncertain.

If she'd expected a heartfelt embrace, Lila would have been disappointed. She couldn't make out what was being said, but Roper was clearly taking a strip out of the young man's hide. Rowdy cringed under the impact of his brother's fury. When his expression changed to one of shocked horror, Lila knew that Roper must be telling him about Judd's accident.

Abruptly, the lecture ended. Trailed by Rowdy, Roper walked back to the truck and opened the back seat of the club cab. As Rowdy climbed inside, his startled gaze met Lila's.

"I believe you've met Mrs. Culhane, Rowdy," Roper said.

"Ma'am." Rowdy nodded. His face was pale and streaked with tears, but at least he remembered his manners. Roper started the engine and drove away from the police station, headed back to the freeway.

"Are we going home now?" Rowdy asked.

"Nope. We're going out to the accident scene so you can have a look at what happened. Then we'll pay a visit to the county morgue so you can help with a positive ID of your so-called friend. After that, you'll be going home to face your mother. If you'll apologize for what you said to her, she just might let you back into the house.

"Judd was drinking," Rowdy said. "Just beers, but a lot of them. I didn't let him drive, but then he stole the truck.

All my gear, my good saddle and everything I own, was in that truck."

"Whose responsibility was that?" Roper asked.

"It was Judd who took the truck and drove it drunk, not me."

"But who decided to leave his family and take off with a known drug dealer, jailbird, and murder suspect? Judd's ex-girlfriend told the FBI that Judd was the one who murdered Frank Culhane. He could've killed you, too. You're damned lucky he didn't. So stop whining and think about that for a while."

Rowdy settled into silence. Roper's dressing down had been harsh, but it had been delivered with love. Lila had seen Roper's despair when he'd believed his brother had died in the accident and his emotional response when he learned that Rowdy was alive. She understood.

Unbidden, her hand crept across the space between them and came to rest on his knee. He gave her a sidelong smile. Then his right hand left the wheel and came to rest on hers, large and warm and strong. His fingers tightened in a brief caress before his hand returned to the wheel, a subtle promise of what might come later, when the storm had passed.

At times like this, it was easy to dream of a future with this man—growing old together, maybe raising children if it wasn't too late for her. Roper would make a strict but loving father, that much she'd already witnessed. They could run the ranch, build the horse program toward a national reputation, make all their dreams come true.

But then, as always, reality came crashing in. Roper already had a family—one that depended on him for leadership, protection, and support. They wouldn't take kindly to his leaving their ranch to live with a rich widow who'd lost her husband that very summer. Lila had never met

Roper's mother, but it was a given that Rachel would dislike her, even hate her. The Culhanes were everything the McKennas resented—wealthy, privileged, condescending, and scandalous.

Roper's family would never accept her. And if she pressured him to leave them, he would never forgive her.

Maybe this was all they would ever have—a furtive handclasp in the dark, a rare tumble on a bed of straw, polite conversations in the arena with eyes and ears everywhere.

Would it be enough for her?

Would it be enough for him?

Chapter Eighteen

By the time Roper drove up to the Culhane house, the moon hung low in the west. As Rowdy lay snoring on the back seat, Lila leaned across the console to give Roper a light farewell kiss. They hadn't spoken much on the way home. But she was aware that the deepening love between them had raised the odds of looming heartbreak. Even though he might be cleared of Frank's murder, he could be forced to choose between her and his family—a choice she would never ask him to make.

From the front porch, she watched Roper's truck drive away. Turning to go inside, she could see the faint light from the kitchen. Mariah would be up early to start her weekly bread baking.

Exhausted, Lila crossed the dimly lit entry and made for the stairs. All she wanted was to shed her clothes and collapse into bed. With luck, she'd be able to get a couple hours of sleep before sunrise, when another busy day would begin.

But sleep, it appeared, would be delayed. Lila stifled a groan as she saw Mariah standing like a sentry at the foot of the stairs.

"You could have let me know you were going to be out all night," she said.

"This was an emergency."

"You could have called."

"I had more urgent things on my mind." Lila was too tired to remind the woman that keeping track of her employer wasn't part of her job. "Now if you'll excuse me, I just want to get some sleep."

"You were with *him*, weren't you?"

"Who I was with is none of your concern," Lila said. "This isn't like you, Mariah. What's going on?"

"There's something I need to say." Mariah stood with her arms akimbo, blocking Lila's path up the stairs. "I've been holding it back, but it's time I spoke my mind."

Lila sighed. "Go ahead. I'm listening."

Mariah took a deep breath. "I've worked for the Culhanes more than half my life. And I've taken pride in my work, knowing I served one of the finest old families in this part of Texas. Frank and Madeleine treated me like family. They even took care of me when I lost my husband and baby. I'd have done anything for them.

"When they divorced and Frank married you, it wasn't the same. But I stayed out of respect for Frank—and I tolerated you, even though I knew how you'd made your living before you stole a married man from his wife."

Lila refrained from speaking. She just wanted this lecture to end.

"After Frank died, I told myself that at least you were a Culhane by marriage, and Frank would want me to stay. But now things have gone too far."

"What are you implying?" Lila demanded. "Just tell me."

"It's the McKennas." Mariah's voice dripped contempt. "They've got no manners, no class. They're no better than hillbillies."

"They're good, honest people," Lila said. "And you're in no position to judge them."

"I know quality when I see it. And the McKennas aren't quality folk. They do rodeo. They dress cheap and talk like riffraff. And that house of theirs is no better than a cow shed. They probably sleep with animals and spit tobacco on the floor. And now, with your husband barely cold in the grave, you're carrying on with one of them. This house has been in the Culhane family for as long as it's stood. If you're fool enough to marry the man, he'll move in here with his whole family. The place will be overrun with McKennas. Even the Culhane name will be gone."

"That's enough." Lila reined in the urge to slap the woman. "My personal life is none of your business."

"Just let me finish," Mariah said. "The Culhanes were like family to me. I've been proud to serve them. But the first time a McKenna sets foot in this house, I'll be packed up and gone."

"That's your choice." Lila spoke with icy calm. "If you decide to quit, I'm sure Darrin and Simone would welcome your help, especially with a baby on the way. Or maybe Madeleine could use you in Austin. I won't force you to leave. But for as long as you stay here, we won't speak of this again. You're to perform your duties without question and be respectful to anyone who walks through that door. *Anyone*. Do you understand?"

Mariah's defiant gaze didn't waver. "Yes, ma'am. I've said my piece and given you fair warning. Now I'll get back to mixing my bread. Let me know when you want breakfast served."

As Mariah wheeled and vanished in the direction of the kitchen, Lila mounted the stairs, step by weary step. Every way she turned, she seemed to be fighting a new battle. And this one had the power to break her heart. She had never loved a man the way she loved Roper. But people, prejudices, and circumstances stood like a wall between them.

She wanted a life with Roper. But was she being selfish? Was she thinking of him or only of herself?

Lying in bed, with the moon shining through the west window, Lila forced herself to step back and view the situation with cold detachment.

With Judd's guilt unproven, Roper was still a murder suspect. That was mostly because of her. Darrin and Simone had accused them of having an affair while Frank was still alive. That wasn't true, but it was easy enough to believe. Even if he were to be cleared of the crime, as long as their relationship lasted, Roper's reputation would remain under a cloud.

Mariah's angry words had reminded Lila of another problem. Lila had told herself that she didn't care what the woman thought, or even that she'd threatened to quit. But Roper's family, especially his mother, would feel the same way about her—a former Las Vegas showgirl who'd gone after a rich man and broken up his faltering marriage, a woman who flaunted her wealth in front of her less fortunate neighbors and considered herself too fine to even pass the time of day with them.

In dreaming of a future with Roper, Lila had imagined them living in the Culhane mansion, even raising a family there. The reality was, if she lost the upcoming lawsuit with Darrin and Simone, she would lose the house and everything that went with it. Even if she were to win, how could she ask Roper to desert the family that was so dependent on him?

The idea of moving them into the mansion was hardly worth a thought. The McKennas were proud people. They would never consent to leave their ranch. More to the point, they would never live on the charity of the woman who had stolen their son.

Lila slipped out of bed and crossed the room to the French doors that opened onto the small balcony. With the breeze cooling her damp face, she watch the last pale edge of the moon sink behind the western horizon.

The answer she'd been looking for was right in front of her. It was time she faced it. If she truly loved Roper, she would do what was best for him. She would walk away.

Soon it would be morning. Roper would be here at first light to train with the horses. After the long night, he was bound to be tired; but with the Run for a Million a few days off, Lila knew he wouldn't spare himself for a rest. She would find him early, give him her decision, and leave. Putting off the pain would only make it worse.

By the time she'd splashed her face with cold water, brushed her teeth, and dressed in cotton slacks, a short-sleeved tee, and sandals, the sky was growing pale above the eastern hills. Roper should be here soon. If she met him in the stables, they could talk before he started with the horses. And she'd have the best chance of avoiding Mariah's prying gaze.

She slipped outside through the patio door. Roper's truck was already in the parking lot. He must have just arrived. She would look for him inside the stables.

The arena was empty. She could wait for him there, but he'd probably come in with a horse, ready to work. She'd be better off looking for him inside.

"Roper?" she called. There was no answer. As she walked down the first row of stalls and took a turn to the right, the nighttime security lights, which ran on a timer, switched off. Minutes from now, they might not be needed. But with her vision still adjusting to the change, Lila was plunged into sudden darkness.

As she groped forward along the row of stalls, she could hear the ventilation fans and the stirring, chuffing sounds of horses, but the way was still dark. Now, at the far end of the corridor, she could make out a dim light. She hurried toward it.

She was moving fast when her knees struck something in her path—a solid metal edge, hard enough to throw her off-balance. As she lost her footing and stumbled forward, she realized it was an oversized wheelbarrow, left outside the stalls. The rising fragrance told her that it was heaped with fresh hay.

She thrust out her arms to break her fall. As her hands sank into the hay, something moved—something alive. Lila heard an angry buzzing sound. She jerked away, but she wasn't fast enough. A sharp jab penetrated her arm, burning like fire as the venom invaded her flesh. She gasped, staggered backward, and sank to her knees.

"Roper!" she screamed. *"Roper!"*

Roper had stopped by his office to check for messages before saddling the first of his three horses. As he stepped out through the door, Lila's screams reached his ears.

Heart in his throat, he raced in the direction of the sound. Seconds later, in the dim morning light he found her. She was kneeling in the sawdust, cradling her arm. Her face was pasty white, her eyes wide with shock.

"There . . ." She gestured toward the wheelbarrow. Roper could see the rattlesnake. It was small enough to hide in the hay but big enough to deliver a deadly bite. Knowing he couldn't leave it alive to bite a worker, Roper dispatched it with a blow from a handy shovel. Then he swept Lila up in his arms and ran with her toward his truck.

Reclining the seat partway, he laid her on it and buckled

her in. The arm was already beginning to swell. He could only pray that the clinic in Willow Bend would have antivenin. There'd be no time to get her to Abilene before life-threatening damage to vessels and organs set in.

From the driver's seat, he gave her his clean, folded handkerchief to lay over the bite and soak up the blood. "Hold that in place," he said.

Her lips moved. "The horses, Roper . . . the training . . . You've got to be ready."

He started the engine. "Damn it, Boss, the horses don't matter. The Run for a Million doesn't matter. Whatever happens, I can't lose you."

It was midmorning when Sam made the drive to Willow Bend. His briefcase lay in the seat beside him, containing a prepared statement for Crystal to sign and a recorder to take her testimony. He would also be delivering the news that Judd Proctor was dead. Rowdy McKenna had identified the burned body from the custom belt buckle and the handmade gold earring in the shape of a devil's head. There were no usable fingerprints, but a dental match, if one could be found, would no doubt confirm that identity.

As Sam passed the seedy Blue Rose motel on the way into town, he remembered the partial night he'd spent in that place, with the noisy couple bumping the bed in the next room. When Jasmine had confessed that she'd been one of the pair, along with a cowboy she never wanted to see again, Sam had fallen in love with her honesty—swiftly followed by her playfulness, her warmth, her intelligence, and her stunning beauty.

Damn it, but he missed her!

Maybe now that Crystal had named Judd as Frank Culhane's killer, the case could be put to rest. Sam could return to Abilene, free Nick to start his cancer treatments, and reunite with Jasmine. Judd's death had removed the need for a trial. All Sam needed was Crystal's testimony, signed, witnessed, and recorded, for the inquest.

At the clinic, he noticed Roper's truck in the parking lot. But Sam had other things on his mind. He walked up to the front desk and asked for Miss Carter.

"She's not here," the young male receptionist told him. "She asked for her personal things, got dressed, and checked herself out. Somebody she'd called was there to drive her home."

"Nobody stopped her?" Sam displayed his badge.

"I'm sorry, sir, but she made the decision to go, even though the nurse on duty advised against it. We can't hold a patient against their will."

"Was she all right? Her head—"

"She was still wearing the bandage. But she was lucid and able to walk by herself."

"I'll need her address," Sam said.

"It's on her registration. But we're not supposed to—"

"I'm a federal officer. Miss Carter is a witness to a serious crime, committed by the man who attacked her. I need her address. Now."

"Yes, sir. I'll write it down for you."

Address in hand, Sam drove to a quiet street on the edge of town. The house that matched the number was a plain red-brick tract home with basement windows and an outside entrance down a flight of cement steps. There were no vehicles, either in the driveway or at the curb.

An elderly man and woman sat on the covered porch of the house next door. Sam assumed they were the neighbors who'd found Crystal unconscious and called for help.

"She lit out," the old man called to Sam as he approached the house. "Loaded up her car and drove off a couple of hours ago. She didn't tell us where she was headed. I think she was afraid that mean-lookin' hombre who beat her up might come back."

"Has anybody else been by looking for her?" Sam asked.

"Nope. A teenage kid in a Jeep brought her home, let her off, and drove away. She left in her own car about twenty minutes later. That's all we know."

"The apartment's unlocked," the woman said. "We went down and looked. She left the key on the table. The place is a mess. The landlord upstairs won't be too happy, but I guess that's the way of young people these days. Not like in our time."

Sam thanked the pair and went downstairs to the apartment. The place appeared to be much the way the crime scene team would have left it—the bloodstained carpet, the food left in the fridge, the open cupboards and empty drawers. Crystal's clothes were gone from the closet, her makeup and toiletries cleared from the bathroom. The key to the apartment lay on the kitchen table. There was no sign of her missing phone. The police may have collected it, or she may have found it and taken it with her.

After a careful inspection revealed nothing new, Sam left the apartment and drove back to the ranch. Rotten luck. He'd been counting on Crystal's sworn and signed testimony to close the murder case against Judd. Now, as things stood, the case would depend on circumstantial evidence and his own secondhand account.

She'd seemed so willing to cooperate. What had caused her to change her mind, load her car, and disappear without a trace? She wouldn't have known that Judd was dead. Maybe she was afraid that he would come back. Whatever her reason, unless she contacted Sam, he was out of luck. It was time to call Nick.

He made the call from the bungalow, sitting at the kitchen table with a tall glass of ice water. When Nick answered, Sam sensed the weariness in his voice. Guilt and urgency gnawed at Sam's conscience. He need to wrap up this case and get back to Abilene.

"How are you, Nick?" he asked, truly concerned.

"I'm hanging on. You know how it is. Tell me what's happening."

"I've got good news and bad news." Sam recounted Judd's story—his jealousy as a motive for killing Frank, his lack of an alibi and his easy access to the drug. "He could've called Frank, told him he wanted to talk about Crystal, and met him in the stables. Motive, means, and opportunity."

"Others had the same," Nick reminded him.

"But you haven't heard the rest. After he got out of jail on drug charges, Judd showed up at Crystal's place, raped her, and started punching on her. She fell and hit her head. Neighbors found her unconscious and called for an ambulance.

"I spoke to her at the clinic, where she'd just opened her eyes. She told me what had happened and claimed that Judd had confessed to killing Frank. When I asked, she agreed to sign a sworn statement and record her testimony as a witness."

"So you decided to wait?"

"She'd just regained consciousness. At the time, she could barely sit up. She was in no condition to sign anything. But the next day, when I went back with the document prepared, she'd checked herself out of the clinic, loaded up her car, and left town."

"What about Judd?"

"Dead." Sam gave Nick an account of Judd's fiery crash, which he'd learned about from Lila's phone call. "Driving drunk in a stolen vehicle. He zigzagged into the path of a tanker truck. The driver escaped the fire. Judd didn't."

Nick was silent for what seemed like a long time. "Let

me get this straight," he said at last. "In the absence of solid evidence and sworn testimony, are you suggesting that we pin Frank's murder on a conveniently dead man and declare the case closed?"

Sam bit back a curse. "Nick, we need to wrap this up, for you and for the Bureau. I have every reason to believe the bastard is guilty. He had motive, means, and opportunity. And he's dead. There'll be no need for a trial. I'll write my report, swearing to what Crystal told me, and you can start building strength for your cancer treatments. It's a win-win situation."

"What about that syringe?"

"Blast it, Nick, there could be a half-dozen explanations. Maybe it was planted. Maybe it was used to put an animal down. Maybe it washed downstream from somewhere else. Without prints and DNA, we can't claim it as solid evidence."

"And you still don't believe Roper McKenna's guilty?"

"I might have believed it once. But that was before I heard that Judd had confessed."

"You said Judd had motive, means, and opportunity. So did Roper."

"Roper swears he didn't kill Frank. So far, he's cooperated with the investigation in every way. This weekend he'll be competing in the Run for a Million. I trust him enough to allow him that."

"All right." Nick sighed. "We'll set a deadline. From now through the Run for a Million, you're to give this investigation everything you've got. At the end of that time, you'll make an honest assessment and name your killer—Judd, Roper, or whomever it may be. If you're still uncertain, we'll file the case as unsolved and bring you back to Abilene. Agreed?"

"Agreed. And I understand." The pressure was on, as it

should be. But Sam knew that it wasn't just from Nick. If he failed to solve this high-profile case, his career with the Bureau would be tarnished for years to come. Worse, somebody out there would be getting away with murder.

"How's your case against Louis Divino going?" he asked, changing the subject. "Any news?"

"He's still in Austin and still being watched. It's like he's thumbing his nose, daring us to catch him breaking the law. Our accountants are still going over his books, hoping to find something we can use. I'd give anything to nail the bastard before I leave the Bureau. But time's getting short. That challenge might fall to young pups such as you."

"Divino can't run forever," Sam said. "Sooner or later, he'll get too cocky for his own good and he'll slip. I'd just like it to be on your watch."

"So would I. But that's the way it goes. Keep me posted on your end. I'll do the same here. The lab's still got that syringe. If they find anything new, you'll be the first to know." Nick paused. "Someone's on the other line. Have to go. Keep in touch."

The call ended. Still holding his phone, Sam walked out onto the porch. The sun was climbing to the peak of the sky, its heat searing the landscape like a blowtorch. Heat waves swam like water above the asphalt of the employee parking lot. Roper's truck had been missing all morning. Strange that he wouldn't be here, with the Run for a Million days away. Sam hadn't seen Lila, either. Maybe Mariah would know what was going on. He would ask her at lunchtime.

Sam's thoughts returned to the conversation with Nick. Something tugged at the edges of his memory, something about Louis Divino. His pulse jumped as the thought struck him. Divino was a friend of Jasmine's mother. Earlier, Nick had mentioned that Divino had a girlfriend with a condo on Lake Travis. That was where Madeleine lived. Were the two of them together? Was Jasmine involved?

Maybe Jasmine knew enough about Divino's activities to be a threat to him. Or maybe Divino was interested in Jasmine and not in her mother.

But if that was the case, Sam asked himself, why hadn't she told him? Was she afraid? Was she protecting someone, like her mother? Like him?

Maybe she was unaware of the danger. Or maybe, he hoped, his hunch was wrong and Divino wasn't even in the picture.

Calling her would be risky. But not calling her could be even riskier. If Jasmine was in danger, he needed to know.

Decision made, Sam punched in the number of her burner phone and made the call.

Jasmine was in her room, working on an updated version of her résumé when her burner phone jangled. Caution warned her to let it ring. Madeleine was in bed with one of her headaches. Louis had come by with long-stemmed red roses and a carton of her favorite lobster bisque. Since it was Carmela's day off, he had taken it on himself to ladle the rich soup into bowls, ready to be heated and served with French bread when she felt like eating.

Jasmine had retreated to her room. The man repelled her. Worse, he frightened her.

The phone was still ringing. *Don't pick up*, Jasmine told herself. Her room was closed but the door was thin. Louis could easily hear the ring and the sound of her voice if she was to answer.

The phone had gone silent. Had it been Sam calling her? No one else had the number, but the call could have been misdialed. She would leave it for now and check later.

She tried to concentrate on the résumé, but her thoughts kept returning to the phone call. Sam wouldn't call except for an urgent reason. She could always call him back when she knew it was safe. But maybe he'd left a message.

Overcome by the need to know, she walked to the door, opened it, and looked up and down the hall. She could hear puttering sounds from the kitchen, the running faucet, the hum of the microwave. She would be all right for a few minutes.

Rummaging in her dresser drawer, she found the phone where she'd hidden it under layers of underwear. The battery was low. She would need to charge it tonight. But there was enough for now.

No text message. But there was a voice mail from Sam. Jasmine was tempted to play it. But that might not be safe. She would wait until Louis had left.

She had the drawer open and was about to turn off the phone and hide it again when the door swung behind her. Louis stood in the doorway, a suspicious expression on his swarthy face.

"What have you got there? Let me see it." He held out his hand.

"It's just a phone. I'm an adult. I'm entitled to my privacy."

"I said, let me see it!" He reached behind his back and drew a small, nasty-looking black pistol from a holster attached to his belt. If she refused, Jasmine knew that Louis was capable of shooting her. And then what? Would he shoot her mother as a witness? Jasmine couldn't take that chance. She handed him the phone.

He glanced at it, scowling. "Hmm. I see you have a voice mail. What do you say we play it on speaker?"

His finger stabbed at the phone. The voice on the speaker was Sam's.

"I'm worried about you, Jasmine. If your mother's keeping company with Divino, you're in danger. You need to get out of there while you still can. If you need help and can't reach me, Nick Bellingham at the Bureau has connections to agents in Austin. His number is—"

Divino slammed the phone onto the floor and crushed it under the elevated heel of his boot. His dark eyes had gone leaden. "You conniving little bitch!" he growled. "I should have guessed you were working with the feds."

The gun's muzzle came up to point at her heart.

"Please, Mr. Divino." Jasmine spoke through the knot of terror in her throat. "If you're going to kill me, don't do it here, where my mother can see. Take me away. I'll go with you, I promise."

"Shut up!" His expression was a predatory snarl. "I should have shoved you off that balcony when I caught you checking my phone." His finger tightened on the trigger.

The deafening gunshot rang out from directly behind him. Louis Divino pitched forward, his skull obliterated by the bullet that had entered from the back and exited at a steep angle.

As he crashed at Jasmine's feet, she saw her mother standing in the open doorway. Madeleine's lilac negligee was lightly spattered with blood. Her right hand clasped the grip of a snub-nosed Smith & Wesson .38 Special.

EPILOGUE

Shocked speechless, Jasmine stared at her mother. The gaze Madeleine returned was calm, almost cold.

"Gather your things, sweetheart," she said. "We've got to get you out of here."

Jasmine struggled for words. "But you just . . . What about the police? What about *him*?" She gestured helplessly toward the body of Louis Divino lying at her feet, his blood soaking into the white Flokati rug.

"It's all right, dear," Madeleine said. "I know people who'll come and clean up this mess. I'll call them. But you will need to be gone when they get here." She stripped off her blood-spattered negligee and laid it over the body. Underneath, her mauve silk nightgown was undamaged. "This isn't quite the way I planned it, but it's as good as anything, I suppose."

"What did you plan? Mother? You just killed a man!"

"A man who would have shot you. I believe that's justifiable homicide."

"But you said you planned something," Jasmine sputtered. "What's going on here? I don't understand!"

"Louis was getting soft," Madeleine said. "He'd been

making some bad decisions—bad for the organization. I'd been planning a way to take over, with plenty of support from his former friends. But I never expected I'd have to take him out myself."

"But—"

"That's enough, dear. The less you know, the safer you'll be. Now get your suitcase and start packing."

"But how can I leave you alone, Mother? You're sick! You're—"

"Dying?" Madeleine chuckled. "Honey, I'm not dying. I'm not even sick. It was all an act. As long as Louis believed I wouldn't be around much longer, he trusted me. He never imagined that I was working against him. Being terminal bought me some wiggle room with the law as well. And even with my children."

She stepped back from the doorway, leaving her stunned daughter to process what she'd just heard. "If you'll excuse me, dear, I've got some phone calls to make," she said, turning to go. "Now, be a good girl, pack your suitcase, go home, and marry that adorable FBI man. I can't wait to see photos of my blue-eyed grandbabies!"

Tucumcari, New Mexico, two days later

With the AC cranked high and the radio blasting an oldies country music station, Crystal sang along with Kenny Rogers as she drove west along Interstate 40. She wasn't sure where she was headed, but for now, that didn't matter. She was free.

Tucked into various parts of her underwear was the $30,000 in cash that Darrin Culhane had given her. In return for the money, she had sworn never to contact Lila and never to show her face in Willow Bend again. Crystal would have no trouble keeping her promise. She'd meant every word of it.

With a satisfied chuckle, she patted the wad of bills tucked into the left cup of her bra. The money was far less than the $100,000 she'd demanded from Darrin. But in her haste to get away before her lie was blown, she'd been willing to take what she could get. Until she found another source of income, she would watch every penny.

The diamond ring, which she'd found in her purse, was back on her finger. It could be pawned in an emergency. But she loved the look of it. She loved the way it made her feel. It was her good luck charm.

Behind her sunglasses, the black eye Judd had given her was fading. Her headaches were improving, too. A slight concussion, the doctor had called it. She would be fine. She still worried about Judd coming to find her. But every mile she drove widened the distance between them. She was beginning to feel safe.

Once her eye was healed, Crystal planned to get a beauty salon makeover, maybe change her hair, and buy some sexy new clothes. In the meantime, she would change her name—legally, if she could manage it. At the very least, she was going to need a fake driver's license. That shouldn't be a problem. She knew where to look, who to ask, and how much to pay. She'd done it before.

With her new identity in place, she would choose a location that possessed two vital elements—money and men. Crystal knew how to spot quality—an expensive haircut; a Rolex on the wrist; a tailored jacket; custom boots, exquisitely made but well worn; the right car in the parking lot.

She knew how to get attention. And she knew how to flatter a man, how to touch him, how to breathe in his ear and how to brush her hips subtly against his, just enough to tantalize.

It had worked with Frank Culhane. It would work again. All she needed was the right place, the right time, and the right, vulnerable man.

The Culhane Ranch, nightfall of the same day

Roper gave a final check of the horses that would be loaded at dawn for the drive to Las Vegas. The three-horse trailer, cleaned and prepared with hay and water, was already hitched to the heavy-duty Ram 1500 truck. At first light, he would load Fire Dance, Milly, and One in a Million into the trailer. Then, with Cheyenne and Stetson helping, he would be off to Vegas and the Run for a Million.

The two stallions had given him some concern. But Roper had stabled them next to each other, and they appeared to be getting along. One in a Million's aggression was down to an occasional snort. Fire Dance seemed no more high strung than was his usual nature. And Roper had made sure that Milly's progesterone shot, to keep her from coming into estrus, was up-to-date.

He was shortcutting through the arena, headed for his own truck in the parking lot, when he spotted a pale figure perched on the railing. His throat tightened. It was Lila, dressed in a gray sweatsuit with a bandage wrapping her left arm.

At the clinic, Roper hadn't left her side. He had held her hand while the antivenin was dripped into her veins, and he'd sat by her bed through the night. By the next morning, she was feeling better. The doctor had sent her home with pain medication and strict orders to rest over the next few weeks. Roper hadn't seen her since he'd delivered her to her front door. He'd turned her over to Mariah, who'd shot him a glare before helping Lila up the stairs to her room. Roper had hoped Lila would stay in bed. Yet, tonight, here she was.

Roper strode across the arena. Mindful of her arm, he lifted her off the rail and gathered her close. Warm and trembling, she nestled against him. She was so fragile, so precious, and he had come so close to losing her.

"Damn it, Boss," he muttered, "you're not supposed to be here."

"Then we won't tell anybody, will we?" she teased, stretching on tiptoe to offer him her lips. Their kiss was long and deep and tender, an affirmation of what they'd become to each other.

"I'm sorry you can't be in Las Vegas," he said. "You can watch the event on TV, but it won't be the same."

"I know." Roper sensed the mystery in her voice. What wasn't she telling him?

"If I win, it will be for both of us," he said. "It will be for our future, for everything we want to make of our lives together."

"Will we have a future, Roper?" she asked. "With so much hanging in the balance, I'm afraid to hope."

"Don't be afraid, Lila." His arms tightened around her. "Believe that everything will work out. We'll make it work out." He raised her chin and gazed into her face. "You're holding something back. What is it?"

"I was going to surprise you," she said. "But that's already spoiled, isn't it? Gemma is coming tomorrow to take care of me. If I'm strong enough we'll be taking a flight to Vegas in time for the big event. When you ride that beautiful red horse into the arena, I'll be in the stands, cheering you on."

Roper's pulse skipped. Until now, he hadn't realized how much he'd wanted her there. "That's crazy," he said. "You need to rest."

"I will rest—on the plane and in the hotel. Gemma will make sure of that. And if there's a problem, she'll know what to do. What can be safer than traveling with an almost-registered nurse who happens to be my daughter?"

"Give me your word that you won't go unless you're feeling up to it."

"I could give you my word," she said, "but you know that nothing is going to stop me."

"Yes, I know." He kissed her with tender restraint. "I love you. And when we get through this mess, I intend to give you everything that life has to offer. Trust me."

He looked into her eyes, saw the hope there, the fear and the love. She had her dreams. So did he. But making those dreams come true would take faith, hard work, and all the luck in the world.

Dear Reader:

Here's hoping you enjoyed this book. Our story will conclude in Book 3 of the Rivalries series. Watch for KILL FOR A MILLION in late 2025.